YOU WILL BE
SAFE HERE

YOU WILL BE
SAFE HERE

Damian Barr

B L O O M S B U R Y   P U B L I S H I N G
LONDON · OXFORD · NEW YORK · NEW DELHI · SYDNEY

BLOOMSBURY PUBLISHING
Bloomsbury Publishing Plc
50 Bedford Square, London, WC1B 3DP, UK

BLOOMSBURY, BLOOMSBURY PUBLISHING and the Diana logo are
trademarks of Bloomsbury Publishing Plc

First published in Great Britain 2019

Extract from J.M.Coetzee's *In the Heart of the Country* (Vintage) used with the kind
permission of David Higham Associates

Extract from Rian Malan's *The Lion Sleeps Tonight* (Grove Press) used with the
kind permission of the author

A catalogue record for this book is available from the British Library

ISBN: HB: 978-1-4088-8608-3, TPB: 978-1-4088-8609-0, EBOOK: 978-1-4088-8610-6

2 4 6 8 10 9 7 5 3 1

Typeset by Integra Software Services Pvt. Ltd.
Printed and bound in Great Britain by CPI Group (UK) Ltd, Croydon CR0 4YY

To find out more about our authors and books visit www.bloomsbury.com and
sign up for our newsletters

For Mike,
Bird by Bird

'Never, never and never again shall it be that this beautiful land will again experience the oppression of one by another'

Nelson Mandela, inauguration as President
10 May 1994, Pretoria

'Truly, events have a power to move unmatched by one's darkest imaginings'

J.M. Coetzee,
In the Heart of the Country (1977)

'There's no such thing as a true story here [in South Africa]. The facts may be correct but the truth they embody is always a lie to someone else. Every inch of our soil is contested, every word in our histories'

Rian Malan,
The Lion Sleeps Tonight (2012)

Prologue

1 October 2010, south of Johannesburg

Now the moment is here, Irma doesn't know quite what to do. She pushes the intercom again, careful of her new nails.

'They for sure know we're coming, *ja?*'

'Just leave it,' says Jan, fussing with his camera. 'Get in the picture, eh. Willem, shades off, arm round your ma.'

Willem's eyeroll is almost audible. No, he won't hold her. He feels her neediness and it grosses him out – if she really loved him as much as she's always saying, she wouldn't be leaving him here. For the whole three-hour drive he bored a deep hole in the back of Jan's thick bald head. Finally, Jan – who he'll never call Pa – leaned back and snapped *Answer your mother* but Willem just pushed his earbuds deeper, gloried as Harry was chosen for Gryffindor yet again. He didn't realise he was moving his lips to the words till he caught Jan smirking in the mirror and shuttered his face with his hoodie. Willem needs magic today, even if he is too old for it.

'Closer,' says Jan, edging them towards the white ex-demonstrator four-wheel-drive Ford with good fuel economy that his boss cut him a deal on. 'Let me get the truck in.'

Irma nudges Willem: 'Smile nice.'

Willem slides his Oakleys off and half opens his eyes – pilot-light blue, like his pa's. People are always telling him to smile. He's not been up this early for what, months, years? His ma swipes his hood off and curls the exact colour of Easter chicks spring away from his face. He's got a perfect library tan. He's hiding in his baggiest black hoodie and track pants and his feet flop in bright white Adidas Hi Tops, a puppy growing into his paws. The crappy Casio he got for his sixteenth is back home because who wears a watch now and he'd still be late anyway, Jan says. Willem braces for the flash.

'Smile,' sing-songs Jan, cutting the word in two: *SMY-ILL.* He holds the camera out, pushing Willem away. Irma turns her engagement ring, hopes it shows. Her eyes, smudges of no-run mascara, brim with her boy. *When did he get so big? Will this place fix him?* She tugs at the sleeveless white top that doesn't hug her where she doesn't want it to and loops her right arm through Willem's left. She pulls him closer. They've not quite finished arranging their faces when Jan clicks the button. The flash is lost in spring sunshine.

Willem bolts over to the gate. It's barbed wire, but barely man-high. Out here walls are lower – you can see gardens. Only the ground-floor windows have bars. There's no movement from the low redbrick homestead up ahead. A shady stoep wraps around it waiting for rocking chairs. A pocked satellite dish clings to the stone chimney. There must be security. Willem identifies some kind of *Prunus* guarding the gate, but the crows have had its fruit.

There are no other houses. No other people. A heavy-shouldered red barn squats on the horizon opposite. Behind it a vast dark steelworks blots out the sky. Clouds belch from giant cooling towers with the ghetto curves all the girls want. Lightsaber-green flames – bright even on a day like today – flicker from skinny sky-high pipes. The air tastes of old torch batteries licked on a dare.

While they stand around waiting for the buzz-click of electric locks Jan checks for cameras. Weekend by weekend he's filled their bungalow with them. He bribed Willem to put the feed on his phone and is gripped: watching empty rooms, waiting for people he knows to walk in and do what they always do. Jan dreams of a panic room. He gives Irma a look as she lights another menthol. She feels her boy moving further and further away. In her head, she goes over all the bits she's packed. The list from New Dawn was detailed, extensive and expensive: two pairs of trousers, two T-shirts, a cap and two dress shirts (all khaki), then boots, running tekkies, trunks, towels, sheets, sleeping bag, tin plate, mug and bowl and a Bible (travel size). No mobiles but she won't be the one to tell him. A hunting knife will be provided but used only under strict supervision. *Safety First At New Dawn!*

Willem's sick hearing about the camp. The badly photocopied leaflet slid from his Happy Sixteenth card which had boasted a red Ferrari (he has never expressed any interest in any car).

'You'll love it,' Irma tells him – tells herself – for the thousandth time.

Willem turns away and watches a column of dark brown ants besiege the gate: *Anoplolepis custodiens*, the Common Pugnacious. Nippy. He wills them towards Jan.

'It'll be *lekker*,' Irma chirps. 'Load of other boys and you'll all be proper rangers at the end!'

'He fuckin' better,' says Jan. 'I'm down 22,000 rand! He needs to man up, stand on his own two feet.'

The ants breach the gate and as Willem turns to answer back a battered red bakkie dust-clouds towards them from behind the house.

'Hush,' Irma begs, smoke-signalling distress with her menthol. 'For Chrissake, shut up.'

Big dogs tumble round the wheels. Willem makes out Boerboels. As the bakkie roll-stops they drop silently, stubby tails quivering, drool pooling round powerful jaws. They are as still as the stupid plastic giraffe his ma worries will wander from their garden. Like anybody would steal that.

The windows are security dark so the first Willem sees of anyone from New Dawn is a pair of dusty black boots with khakis tucked in. As he tries to imagine the rest a boy, barely taller than him, steps carefully from behind the door. His hair is black velvet buzzed to nothing. Willem spots a rusty cut on his head as he pulls on a camo cap. A short-sleeved khaki shirt flaps round pale arms. He holds on to the door.

Willem's shoulders drop. As the gate swings inwards he reaches for it, doesn't know why. Irma grabs him, nearly burns him with her menthol. She can't take any more of this – he doesn't listen, never thinks, stays up all night in his room instead of going out and being normal. She points to a yellow sign with a lightning bolt and skull.

Jan orders her back into the Ford so they can drop him off and get home before dark, they can't be driving then, not these days. The other boy shakes his head and steps forward, careful to stay behind the fan in the dust left by the gate.

'J-j-ust h-h-him.'

Willem raises a hand to his chest.

'But,' begins Irma. This is not how she thought it would go. 'His things.'

Jan pushes past and opens the boot, leans in and heaves out his old army duffel – Irma thinks he's sweet to let Willem have it. The tin mug clatters as it lands by the bakkie. 'He can get it. Good practice, eh?'

The boy glances back to the silent house then leans down as Willem steps forward. They almost bump heads. Willem feels the twinge of defeat as the other boy swings it onto the bakkie with surprising ease then gets in and throws open the door. 'Geldenhuys,' he says, pointing to his badge. He sounds like the boarding-school boys Willem avoided on the bus.

As Willem climbs in he realises he's not said good-bye. The door click-locks. The bakkie is already reversing so he waves to his ma who's waving back and getting smaller as Jan reverses onto the dirt road but she can't see him through treacherous mascara. Suddenly Willem doesn't want her to go. He feels the other boy glance and lays both hands flat then tries to spread on his seat Jan-style. Willem steals a look at this Geldenhuys who is spinning the wheel unworried by the chasing dogs. Up close the cut by his ear looks old but there are fresher ones. Willem wonders what his hair was like before. Passing the postcard old homestead they head straight for another bigger gate crowned with razor wire. A red, white and black flag snaps against the blue spring sky.

'H–h–howzit, b–b–bru?' laughs Willem, slipping his Oakleys back on. Geldenhuys can't even be bothered to be bothered, just brakes at the second gate and sounds the horn three times. A walkie-talkie crack-les from the floor: '*Veilig?*' Then, not a second later, in exasperated English: 'Safe?' Willem reaches for it but Geldenhuys grabs it, checks his mirrors, then hits reply: '*Veilig.*'

Willem tries another tack. 'So, bru, what's here then?'

'You'll s-s-see,' says Geldenhuys, as the gate slides back.

PART ONE

The Diary of Mrs Sarah van der Watt
Mulberry Farm, near Ventersburg
Orange Free State
1901

Tuesday 1 January, just after breakfast

We know they are coming. We've watched the smoke rise for two weeks now knowing they will soon be at our gates, the gates you promised to finish white-washing when you returned. All day, every day, tidy pillars billow straight up into the summer sky, no breeze dares bother them.

Day by day, farm by farm, the English draw closer. Even on Christmas morning we woke to smoke spooling across the sky like wool waiting to be wound. It cleared as you said prayers and we sat down to lunch – I still worry that pork was dry. The Kriels are only six miles east and when their big red barn goes up – the barn it took twenty men a winter to build – it'll be us next. The chair I'm sitting on, every berry ripening on the tree outside the window – every fruit, every tree. They will all go.

I still struggle to believe the news that reaches even our half-painted gates. Soon, everything we've built in our ten years here will be gone. I've taken to rising even earlier so I can wander our five rooms alone – remember when we had just one! I blink hard and press my eyelids together to engrave it all where I can always see it. I hope you remember it too, Samuel.

I've often embarked on a diary with the new year and found my thoughts ran out long before the pages, but I'm resolved to keep at this. I'm setting these words down for us and for Fred – he's outside bothering Lettie who is calling so I must go in a minute. I'm writing at our kitchen table where we sat and prayed and talked and laughed and worried all these married years. Every evening after dinner you tapped your pipe out and it left little scorches. Now I run my fingers over the marks regretting every tut. I'll read this to you when you return victorious. Our cause is just. God will preserve you, Samuel. Remember Psalm 110: *The Lord at thy right hand shall strike through kings in the day of his wrath.*

That day is coming.

Now I must go and see what Lettie wants.

She was only calling to say the chickens were fussing – Fred hadn't collected their eggs and you know they won't lay if they find another egg there, they're so particular. So we made a game of finding them all. Afterwards, Lettie helped me hide the tea service your family gave us for our wedding – twelve dainty cups and saucers, each wreathed in tiny pink roses. Still in the box it came in all the way from Pretoria. I only ever got it out once, that first time Mrs Kriel visited. You were at market, I think. She poked her plump little finger up in the air and lifted her saucer to peer below! She didn't stay for a second cup, but her eyes gulped down every little thing. Even she shunned my *koekies*. Samuel, it's a good job you didn't follow your own dear father because my baking alone would have made me a terrible pastor's wife.

Lettie and I wrapped each piece in rags and stuffed the box with straw then buried it under the mulberry — the first tree we planted. Now its branches hold our home and its big heart-shaped leaves give us shade. I know you find the berries too much. The market for them is not so big. Its roots are splattered with fallen fruit that Fred takes delight stomping on. Our apricots have never done better. Even when the sun scorches them or some small something gets in and twists them they still taste good. When we started putting them in you laughed at how familiar I was with the shovel — I don't think you really believed I'd grown up on a farm till then. It's a good job one of us did. Your hands were made for holding books. Each tree stubbornly marks all four seasons even though we really only get two. I think they remember Europe better than we who took root more recently. I wonder if they're used to summer in January? I buried Fred's silver christening spoons too, back in the ground they came from. Don't worry, we've not hidden everything — they need something to take. It's best that men with little to lose don't have to look too hard, you said. So, we bustle around preparing for our un-guests and now they're close I feel something like excitement. I've never met an Englishman, except in novels. There's strangely little to do now but wait.

I'm getting so carried away I nearly forgot dinner — we eat like kings now! The more we eat, the less we leave for the Khakis. Pork again!

Three entries in one day! I won't keep it up, I know. I can't sleep without you. Are you lying under the stars? Tucked up in a tent?

Since you rode out — was it really only a week ago? — we've been able to smell the smoke. We feed the strays that beg at our gates. Women and children and Kaffirs. More every day. We give what we can and listen to their tales — they can't all be true. The English are, after all, the same race as us. They share our faith if not our faithfulness. Our Father is their Father. They're losing everywhere but you are nowhere to be found which sends them mad. I knew you'd leave when Lord Roberts' order finally reached our gates: 'It is absolutely essential to force all the people to submit and it is now clear that this can only be done by severe measures. You must please have no mercy, and what you cannot bring away you must destroy … '

They're calling it Scorched Earth. I begged you to go and be a pastor instead – you carry your father's church calm. You said if Boer prayers could beat English bullets we'd have won already. Now you're not here. I understand, I do, and Fred does too, really. He's being very good, as grown-up as a six-year-old can be. My freckles speckle his face. I tell him they're like the stars that fill our sky at night which doesn't stop him trying to wipe them off. This morning Lettie caught him trying to ride one of the pigs and Jakob had to lift him out the sty. He was caked so we had to boil water for a bath. I told him he deserved it cold and I got tears instead of his usual giggle. I almost cried myself.

Fred is excited by the fires – I suppose all little boys must be. At night they're almost beautiful, which makes it hard for me to be stern with him when I catch him watching too. You need only raise your voice a little above your church tones – *FRED-ER-RICK*. He knows too well I can barely raise my voice, never mind my hand. Coming from a brood of girls such glee is strange to me but so little happens out here that any departure is exciting. Remember when the rains came a week early? It was all we talked about it till the next summer. The spruit behind the sties went from trickle to torrent and overnight the veldt frothed with flowers – yellows and purples tailor-made for town hats. The cracked red earth steamed like freshly baked bread. The three of us found a rock that had already dried and made a picnic and I complained that the sudden flowers didn't smell. You said they were doing quite enough already. You were right. All last week, thunder rumbled but it brought no lightning, no rain of relief followed by that sweetness rising almost visibly. It's charged with sparkling possibility, it's the smell of home, no – homeland. Is there a name for it? You'd know. You hoard words the way my father stored seeds. You have given me so many. Your father taught himself English, so he could pray with the Khakis dying in our first war with them, the war which pushed us out here where we might observe our own ways. A poor worldly tongue, my mother said: you only need the one book. But she'd never read *Wuthering Heights* or *The Woman in White*. Never read anything. My English is the English of the novels you and I squandered countless candles over. You always fell asleep first, so I admit now to reading on and pretending to be surprised the next night. It was easy to cry again for Little Nell. I loved the feel of your face next to mine as you turned teacher – words were not thought essential for one of six girls on a sheep farm a full day's wagon from the nearest town. Fathers taught sons anything that needed to be known and we all bowed our heads to the dominee when he rode up in his donkey cart once a month. I wasn't ashamed; just glad of another reason to be closer to you. I always had more questions but knew better than to ask. Never be cleverer than your man – my mother again. And now here I am filling these pages for you.

But this new thunder is the booming of the big guns brought over on great ships from England, more noise than has ever been heard in our young country. Thunder with deadly rain. At first the birds froze on their branches and even the crickets went quiet but now they barely budge. 'Maxim,' says Fred, with every boom. 'They've got Maxims and we've got Long Toms, but our Mausers shoot better than their Martinis.'

I let him sleep holding the Mauser you gave him on Christmas morning, just before you told him you were going. I thought he'd never stop crying and I loved you not stopping him. I've told him over and over how you carved it from the cherry tree you downed to make way for the new sty, how I helped you rope it to Oupa who dragged it over to the Kriels' barn where it dried for months – cherry is weak, a womanly wood, Mrs Kriel said. Certainly, it struggled, its leaves scorched before they were out. Sometimes I think nothing is supposed to live out here, not even us. My little vegetable garden can disappear in an hour if locusts get to it. The sheep endure but if the boys weren't there to burn the ticks off they'd soon stagger into the dust. Yet we're still here. I've told Fred how you sat by the fire every night for weeks whittling and polishing his Mauser so it looked like it could almost fire a bullet. Now he loves it even more. The more he takes aim, the redder it turns. For now, he's not much taller than it. He sleeps holding it. I sleep holding the key to his room. When I sleep. Most nights I pull my wrap round my shoulders and walk out onto the stoep and stare up at our stars. I can almost feel the world turn. Only after I've found the Southern Cross do I know I'll be able to close my eyes when I go back in.

Thursday 3 January

Already I've missed a day but it's only now, with night tucking in the corners of the sky, that I can sit down. If you were here, you'd read to me, but this is the next best thing.

While I was trying to make Fred eat his breakfast, another Kaffir stopped at the gate. The English really are freeing them all to roam wild with no thought for their welfare. After you gave ours the choice most went back to the bush to find their own. I can't think any of ours turned. Only Lettie and Jakob stayed. Even though it's just the two of them and they've been with us for ever I feel somehow outnumbered now. They sag at the end of every day. Lettie says she'll never leave – I know it's Fred that binds her here. And of course, Jakob would never abandon her – he's taken to sleeping across the doorway on our stoep instead of in his little lean-to by the pigs. He wouldn't dare if the *baas* was here but if you were he wouldn't need to. I used to let Lettie go out to him at night when you were at market, I'm ashamed to say. But maybe you already knew. It's hard to hide secrets out here with the bare soil and the bright skies and nothing but space stretching all around.

Anyway, this stranger was shouting at the gate so Fred stood up in his chair and I put my hands over his ears, pink as always, like he's been caught, which he usually has. I told Lettie to take something out. It was the Christian thing to do although the Lord is not much in evidence these days. The man was shoeless and shirtless but in khaki trousers and jacket, too big. He must have been one of theirs because anyone else would be shot on sight. He handed Lettie a crumpled blue envelope and she gave him a slice of thick-set pap from yesterday's breakfast, which he snatched before running towards the smoke. He didn't look back. It's addressed to you although they must know by now you're not here. A decisive signature marches across the page in dark blue ink. It's only the third piece of post we've had. It says:

To: Mr Samuel van der Watt, Mulberry Farm, near Ventersburg

By Order of Lieutenant-General Sir J. French

I beg to inform you that you and your wife and son are to be evacuated Sunday 6 January at 0600 hours. Refugees are being concentrated into regional camps. This is for your own safety. Take only what you can carry. No servants and no livestock.

I kept my hands over Fred's ears while he sat wriggling and read it to Lettie. She immediately fetched a sack and started filling it with bread and mealies and ham.

'But we've got three days,' I reminded her.

'Then we must work, *mevrou*,' she replied, stressing the 'we'.

Three days. Six months ago, you swore the Situation would be over any day – that's what it was then, the Situation. Our government would give the *Uitlander* gold miners the vote and let us stay independent and that would be that. When the Situation became the War, you swore we'd run them all into the sea by Christmas. Christmas has been and gone but they're still here and now you're gone too. We can't even go to the church at Ventersburg since they burned it to the ground we built it up from. Full of explosives, they said. Explosives they put there, you said, stuffing your pipe.

Writing is easier than talking, not that I've anyone to talk to now. So often I feel my words faltering, like parishioners waiting for a blessing. I wasn't always like this. I inherited it from my mother and sisters. Are they packing too? Even Lettie speaks without hesitation. Not once have I heard her raise her voice. I've told her she can't come, wherever we must go. She paused and filled her eyes with Fred – Fred who runs to her when he falls. 'Then we will wait, *mevrou,*' she said, picking up the milk bucket. 'Until you all come home.' I envy the animals – the days are no different for them. I sent Fred egg collecting after breakfast. Since you left we eat fresh eggs every day, even Lettie and Jakob. There's no reason to store anything now. Lettie milked both cows and Jakob loped off to deal with the pigs – I forgive them everything for bacon. I wonder if we'll ever eat this lot.

Oupa has been restless since you rode off on Gelda. He misses her. I know how he feels. I swear he's even older than Lettie – creaking when you brought him back from Ventersburg to do all the ploughing for the wheat that didn't take. Now he's practically Methuselah, grey streaking his chestnut. He's all but useless and happy enough plodding round with Fred on his back tugging at his twitching ears. Basuto ponies are patient, their big heads full of thoughts.

We're still picking the apricots which should have gone to market. The branches sag with fruits splitting in the heat. Word is out with the crows who chance our nets. I'd take a shot but you took the rifle. 'They can't shoot at you if you can't shoot at them,' you said. I'd shoot them all if I could. Last harvest we had the Kriels and their five children and a dozen field Kaffirs besides. What was I doing? Something indoors, more mending for Fred. My mother never let any of the indoor women touch her needle and thread. Somehow it was forbidden. Lettie never even tries though I admire the pretty white curtains she made for Jakob's lean-to. Fred is hard on his clothes for a boy who doesn't like to get dirty. He's inherited your fastidiousness. Now, mulberry juice stains my hands and won't shift, no matter how I scrub. Even Lettie's palms are whiter than mine.

Tonight, we had mutton shoulder roasted with mulberries (an experiment I won't repeat) then apricot pie. Jakob even took some mulberries to the animals and said he'd never seen a pig smile. My skirts feel tight when I smooth my apron down. Fred is bewildered at being told to eat all the fruit he can. 'What about my belly?' he laughs, pulling up his shirt and pushing it out. He was such a fat little baby, thighs you could bite. Now he's shooting up faster than mealie corn. He will be even taller than both of us, Samuel. He will see further.

That last harvest was so good we saved nearly five pounds in our little chocolate tin. They were to replace the thatch – I recall the rain pattering prosperously on Mrs Kriel's new tin roof as she smiled directly to heaven while we sat socially upright in her *voorkamer* dripping with lace doilies. She has run to fat but then so has President Kruger's wife. It's hard to find such ankles patriotic. I begged you to take all that money and finally you nodded. Tonight, I found the tin still there under our bed and it's still full. You lied, Samuel. Never lie to me again.

It's late and I've been decadent with the candles. My eyes are tired – I've never written so much, never had so much to say. Lord knows what I'll spend it on but it's gold the English have come for and they won't have ours. I've sewn every shilling into the hem of my strong black work-dress. I think I'll sleep now.

Friday 4 January

Fred was shouting for you in his sleep so I went in, which I wouldn't have done if you had been here. Lettie was sitting at the foot of his bed and he'd kicked off the quilt your mother made. I realise I've only seen Lettie past dinner once before, when Fred had that fever and she brought those wet roots to boil. I gave them to the pigs who were violently sick, which only proves I was right to stick with the goat dung tea. How many nights has she been in here instead of the kitchen? I was the same with our Anna. When my sisters teased me out of bed I'd go into the kitchen and fit myself in next to her on the floor by the stove bathing in the warm of both. My mother was not a woman to go to in the night.

Lettie hushed me while she hummed a long low lullaby. It wasn't happy or sad yet somehow both – like the wind rippling over the love-grass and bending the seed heads in prayer. It's not a hymn. I don't know what it is. But it reached Fred and soothed him. He lay there, his chest heaving, cheeks red, and eventually his little fists let go. I love watching him dream. When he arrived early there was no woman to help and you wouldn't let Lettie in until I was past screaming. At the end I even wished for my mother. Though I was sure by then I'd never get to meet him I gave him his name. It was Lettie who knew what to do. She told you – *told you* – to leave, then knelt over me and reached up under the sheets. She turned Fred inside me. It was Lettie who saved us all. After that I sometimes wonder what she sees when she looks at me.

She kept humming as I got up to leave and her strange song followed me but she didn't. I pushed my face into your pillow and wept until I heard the dawn. I woke after what felt like minutes and reached for you. Bed without you is not just empty. It's a particular emptiness the way that silence after a hymn is not the same as the simple quiet before. I can't get used to it; I'd even welcome my sisters back. The longest you left before was market day when you hitched up Oupa and Gelda. That was almost a holiday because I knew you'd return next day with town news and a new book and something for Fred. Now, even in summer, our bed feels cold. This morning I rinsed my face in the plain enamel basin Lettie leaves then considered myself in the mirror – did I tell you Mrs Kriel took to calling hers 'a looking glass' after she got that new roof? She dreams of fish knives.

I've never been vain, my mother saw to that. I've little to be vain about. I keep expecting to wake white with worry, but my hair remains stubbornly red like the soil when it's been turned. Thankfully I'm not curly. Barring my freckles, I'm still paler than I should be for all those years following my father round the farm. My eyes are puffy, but it may be all this writing. A complaining face, my mother chided. You never seemed to mind me being as tall as you. *My Rossetti*, you called me when you came courting. I didn't know who you meant until you showed me in one of your father's books. I couldn't believe his library. A whole room filled with stories. The air rich with leather and paper and waiting words. Does that smell have a name? Your people, ministers to a man, came in from the coast during the Great Trek. My lot have never looked beyond the fences of their kraals. Less adventurous than their sheep. I wept when no one from my side came to our wedding but I was also glad, I'm ashamed to admit. I remember the softness of your mother's hands as she welcomed me and the passing look as she tried to pretend they were as smooth as her own.

We were nearly twenty then and thirty now. The last to get married. I was terrified of becoming *Tante Sarah*, everybody's nursemaid: an old widow trapped in black, mourning a marriage that never happened. You saved me from all that. It's not the same for men. What did I save you from? We hoped to copy our parents and have six of our own but it was not to be, despite our prayers, my mother's cures – she even threatened to get some magic from a sangoma. For so long I carried only shame. You never reproached me, Samuel. After a while I thought maybe you didn't care or didn't want me that way. Then, after we'd given up, Fred arrived. He has your quiet and my freckles and he is enough.

I hear Lettie starting breakfast and can smell the coffee. It won't do to set a bad example now.

Saturday 5 January

They are here. We're safe, God help us. We are safe. Fred is finally sleeping and I've left Lettie with him. This is the first I've sat down all day. Let me tell it to you and see if it makes sense.

The first arrived this morning. I made sure to greet Lettie politely when I got up though, Lord help me,

I didn't want to, which seems petty now. I still can't get her strange song out of my head. I hummed it as I stirred my coffee. Instead of breakfasting on the stoep, as she has done for ten years, Lettie ate standing in the corner with her back to me. Silence cooled the morning air, already stifling.

'Where is Jakob?' I asked her broad back, which promptly straightened, brown hemp flexing across her shoulders.

'With the pigs,' she replied, turning and smoothing the apron she keeps so white. 'I thought I will milk the cows, Fred can see the chickens and *mevrou* might – '

'*Mevrou* might what?' I snapped, slamming down my knife and fork.

Lettie stood silently but did not bow her head. I raised myself slowly, placing both hands on the deal table I scrubbed every morning, noon and night before we got her.

'I might what?' I repeated quietly, so Fred didn't hear.

Then the door burst open. 'They're here,' Jakob panted, careful not to come in, worrying your old felt hat in his hands. '*Mevrou*, Khakis!'

Lettie rushed forward and I snatched up the knife I'd just cut my bacon with and slipped it in my apron, instantly worrying about stains. I pushed past Lettie and Jakob and stepped onto our stoep expecting an army.

A single soldier stood by our gates. A full head shorter than you, Samuel, but still a soldier. He leaned a bicycle against our fence, which explains how we'd not heard him. I'd not seen one before, except in Fred's drawings.

'Good morning,' he called brightly, like Mrs Kriel dropping by with mildly interesting news. Something about the weather or a worry about rinderpest. Here he is, the enemy, as young as my youngest sister. The undisturbed morning air elongated his vowels, making a mockery of them by the time they reached me.

'Good morning,' he tried again, taking off his white helmet, pushing our gate open and walking down our path – the path you carried me down when it wasn't even a path, when our house was just one room. 'Mrs van der Watt?'

'*Ja,*' was all I could say. I thought of all the other words I might use: Tommy, Khaki, *rooinek*. '*Ja,*' I repeated then forced out the first English word you taught me: 'Yes.'

'Good, you speak some English. That will make things much easier. Mrs van der Watt, I am Corporal Johnson of the Cheshire Regiment. I believe you've been expecting me. I am here to take the inventory.'

'In-ven-tory?' I sounded it out idiotically, a Scrooge-like word. I grasped its meaning as he gestured around with both arms. 'The letter said Sunday.'

'Yes,' he said. 'Early bird and all that.' As he talked he strolled towards me, trailing his left hand through the gerbera which have done so well this year. They bowed their scarlet heads and I hated them for surrendering so easily. I noted his scalp pinking beneath thinning blond hair and imagined his young wife disguising her disappointment at the bald red man who would come home. Immediately I wished I'd not allowed myself a thought in which this Khaki returned alive because surely it would mean one of ours taking his place in the grave. Up close, this corporal looked older. I wondered why he was alone. I was planning what to say next when Lettie stepped in front of me.

'Tell your Native to move,' he sighed, picking the nearest flower without breaking his stride. He stuck it in his lapel and put his helmet back on. His right hand twitched towards the mortal weight by his side. Then Jakob stood in front of Lettie, arms stretched wide. Corporal Johnson unclipped his holster. He spoke slowly as if to a child: 'I will count to five – they can count, can't they? If, on five, they have not stood aside I will be forced to fire. Do you un-der-stand?'

I slipped a hand into my apron pocket and felt for the knife, wished I'd grabbed something bigger. 'They speak no English,' I apologised, tightening my secret grip. I stepped out from behind them and as I did Fred leapt off the stoep waving his gun shouting, 'Tommy, Tommy, Tommy!'

A single shot.

He landed in a heap by the soldier's feet. Screaming, Lettie and I rushed as one gathering him up and passing him between us turning him over and over looking for blood shouting, 'Fred, Fred, Fred!' Was he breathing? His eyes fluttered open and I remembered the very first time they did and how all the pain left me in that moment. 'Lettie? Ma?' He looked past us to the bicycle. 'Is that for me?'

'Quite enough fuss for one morning,' said Corporal Johnson, stepping around us, his revolver trailing smoke. With his gun he gestured past Jakob who stood slack-mouthed. We all turned and only then did we see Oupa, his legs crumpled beneath him, his great head lolling, his ears no longer twitching. I pulled Fred to my bosom but he saw, he saw.

I can't sleep knowing they're coming back.

Jakob dug a pit in the orchard before the sun got too much. It took him three hours and looked like a great red wound but at least the soil is summer dry. Lettie brought him a tin cup of water then they took a leg each and started dragging Oupa over. After half an hour, he'd barely budged and his eyes were skating with flies. I couldn't stand it so I grabbed the lace pillowcase my sisters made that we never use and ran out and pulled it over his head. Lettie shifted to his fetlock and I took his hoof. I thought of all the work he'd done for us, the rest we promised him. Eventually we got him to the edge of the pit but by then his legs were stiff and sticking straight up. Jakob swung his shovel but Lettie stayed his hand. I hurried away with my hands over my ears but still heard the first leg snap. Even Lettie cried out.

While we buried Oupa, Corporal Johnson walked around with a clipboard counting: twenty chickens, four pigs and two milking cows. I explained that all our sheep were out on the veldt with the herd-boys enjoying summer pastures. You instructed them not to come back until you returned, and somehow they keep watch and know to stay away.

'Your apricots are delicious,' the corporal remarked, his tongue flicking between red yet bloodless lips. 'Is that your only water?' he asked pointing towards the well you spent that whole first month digging. I nodded. Every night you clumped muddily into the kitchen. Every night I'd ask about buried treasure and you'd promise 'tomorrow'.

The Khaki took all morning counting. I was relieved to see he'd brought his own lunch. 'Wouldn't want anything upsetting my stomach, would we?' he said, unpacking bread and a canteen from a box on the back of his bicycle. I thought of the dark green bottle we keep locked in the barn where Fred can't find it and wondered if, instead of putting it on the pigs, I made coffee for our guest … he must have read my face: 'If I'm not back for Lights Out they'll send some chaps and they won't be half as nice as me.'

He spent the afternoon double-checking this and that. I put Fred to bed and left Lettie with him. Swallows scythed through sky catching their last before the bats took their place. Finally, he pedalled away. Lettie rushed out to close the gate and I only relaxed when I heard the bolt drawn, not that it will make any difference. She swept the path too. He says he'll be back tomorrow to take in-ven-tory indoors.

I can hear Fred asking Lettie about the bicycle and the soldier. I think I'll join them tonight. We'll sleep with our clothes and shoes on as you said we should now. I'll put on my black work-dress with the coins in the hem.

Monday 7 January

We're on a train going north, I think. They won't say where. There are no windows so we can't see out to tell. Afternoon light seeps in between the planks. Just enough to write but I doubt you'll make this bit out. They came at dawn. I managed to save this diary and my little church Bible but not your family Bible, Lord forgive me. It was your father's, I know, and his before. Now I fear it's ash with everything else. Or worse, a souvenir, because they take the things they want.

We've been in this box for a day and night with no stop or food or water. Fred presses his face to the gaps in the floor and makes a game of counting the rails. His little fingers itch to reach out. It's his first time on a train so he's excited. I tell him I am too; this is a holiday. The sack Lettie packed is already half-empty. We sweat by day and shiver all night but must be thankful we're still alive. I don't know where Lettie is – she was screaming for Fred. They bundled her and Jakob on wagons with everything else. I didn't think we had so much until I saw it all stacked up.

Counting the voices in the dark, I think there are twenty women and three times as many children and some old men. We're all pressed together on plank benches. Mrs Kriel is here with her twins, Cornelius and Isaac, and her daughters, Johanna and Olive, and a little Kaffir girl. Her big boy Jan, who is thirteen, ran away to find his father and fight. I said I pray the Khakis don't find him first. All our servants have been taken. The girl is the only Kaffir.

There's much retching from the jolting and the smoke. The wooden buckets in each corner are busy with flies. Where do they come from? We shunned them to start with but after a day we had no choice, even Mrs Kriel. Darkness doesn't hide sounds. When a bucket overflows Mrs Kriel's girl lifts a plank and slops it on the moving rails.

Where are they taking us, Samuel? Where are you?

There's nothing to do but sit and worry or join the gossip so I'm writing this for you. My only other train trip was to Johannesburg to see a famous pastor preach. So many flocked to hear this great Elder, who had been to Utrecht, that the service was moved to the railway station – great green pillars of iron holding up vaults of glass, the biggest in all Africa, a temple to transport. We never actually got into the city, which Mother said was just as well. As our train arrived, there was a great rush of Indians. They're not allowed to sleep in the city, Father explained, so must travel in and out every day. Mother pulled us close and glowered but they ignored us. On a raised stand in the centre of the station, across thousands of hatted heads – glossy top hats, plain lace kappies, dirty felt doppers and feathered city fancies – a stooped white-haired man shuffled to a lectern helped by his younger, black-haired self: you.

On the train home everyone pretended to be used to all the stopping and starting and the smoke and sparks flying past the windows and the world seen at speed. They all spoke loudly and approvingly of the sermon, of the sullying powers of the gold below the city, of the need to preserve our ways. *The just shall live by faith!* Your father had quoted Romans 1: 16–17. My sisters went on about city fashions and the Indian women in bright silks. Soon the up-and-down city gave way to the wideness of the veldt and finally we arrived back at Ventersburg where a wagon jolted us the two hours back to our farm. All I could think of was you, Samuel.

We're stopping.

There was talk of a blockade. Fred shouted that you'd cut the tracks! We didn't hear guns or anything and just sat there until the train jerked forward. Fred is trying to make friends with Mrs Kriel's boys who should know better than to tease him. All he wants is to be big like them. He seems happy being rebuffed so I'll finish telling you what happened.

Jakob woke us shouting, 'Khakis!' before somebody struck him dumb. Lettie hushed Fred. I went out.

They met me in the kitchen, six of them, looking round as if a band of commandos might jump out of a cupboard. I wished they would. Corporal Johnson spoke: 'Before we get started, perhaps you'd like to use the er... ?' He gestured vaguely behind me. 'I know we've arrived rather early.' His eyes wandered down my body stopping at my waist. I suppose this was a kindness but I refused to leave them alone in my kitchen.

'In that case, please sit. Mrs van der Watt, this is Brigadier Durham,' he said, as if introducing us after church. So I sat. At my own table. Through the door I saw Jakob laid out on the stoep, his hands bound behind his back, rolled to one side so they wouldn't have to step over him.

Brigadier Durham took off his helmet, which sported a dusty ostrich feather, and placed it in the crook of his left arm. The others promptly followed. His grey moustache twitched into a taut smile. From a scarlet leather folder embossed with gold, the corporal passed the brigadier a crisp sheet of cream paper which he slid over to me. It was neatly typed in our language and theirs.

'This is the Oath of Neutrality,' he explained at a schoolroom pace. 'You speak English, yes, Corporal Johnson said?'

I nodded almost imperceptibly, not wanting to give them anything, even the smallest gesture.

'This oath says you will cease to offer support to the Republican rebels, that you will surrender any and all possessions which can offer material aid to said rebels, and it proclaims you as a subject of Her Majesty Victoria, by the Grace of God, of the United Kingdom of Great Britain and Ireland Queen, Defender of the Faith, Empress of India.'

I pushed it away.

The corporal lifted the lid off last night's mutton still warm on the stove and took a deep sniff. 'As I said, sir,' he chimed, 'these Boer women, out here for far too long, quite uncivilised.'

The brigadier stood and put his helmet back on and his men followed as one. He sighed. 'Mrs van der Watt, nothing you say or do can stop what is about to happen but if you sign the oath I promise you it will go easier on you after.'

I had not thought there would be an after.

'We are not here to harm you,' the brigadier insisted. He leaned over me, so close his moustache almost brushed my cheeks, his breath rich with an officer's diet. 'We are here to stop this war, to bring peace. And to do that we need you to stop giving support to your men out there on commando, the ones cutting our train lines and shooting at us from farms where the white flag flies. These same rebels are even burning the homes of your fellow country-men who see the sense of what we're doing.'

'Hands-uppers! They're not my countrymen, they're cowards!'

'They are sensible, Mrs van der Watt. Resistance only prolongs matters, stops us protecting Her Majesty's loyal subjects here and securing what is rightly ours. There is no *Volkstaat*. We are simply here to make sure all men enjoy equal rights under British Law. All Christian men. Sign the oath and we'll take very good care of you and little, is it, Frederick?'

'You will not touch him,' I said, pushing myself up. The corporal placed his hands on my shoulders from behind and shoved me down so hard I bit my tongue. I thought again about the dark green bottle in the barn.

'Madam,' said the brigadier picking up the paper and handing it back to the corporal who placed it carefully in his folder. 'There's no need for a scene. Corporal Johnson, have your men begin.'

One of them kicked Fred's bedroom door open and Lettie rushed at him screaming, wielding the hairbrush with mother-of-pearl inlay you gave me when Fred was born. He stepped aside as if making way for a lady at a ball and she slammed into the wall so hard our pictures trembled. Another moved forward and trussed her like Jakob tying a pig and dragged her onto the stoep. Fred ran to me and I carried him out. We sat under the mulberry on the very spot where I'd buried our few precious things.

All morning Brigadier Durham sat at our table signing paper after paper issuing orders to the corporal who relayed them to the men who worked around us like we weren't there. They were so orderly, one holding a ladder while the other climbed, whistling and singing all the while. They filled basket after basket, not missing a single apricot until half a waggon was filled. Their song stuck in my head:

> I have come to say goodbye, Dolly Gray,
> It's no use to ask me why, Dolly Gray,
> There's a murmur in the air, you can hear it everywhere,
> It's the time to do and dare, Dolly Gray.

The chickens were kekkeling for Fred to fetch their eggs. The corporal strode towards their coop and I shouted stop but his hand was already on the bolt. Out they streaked between his boots, little white comets. Fred broke from my arms and dashed after them and the men watched laughing before taking over. Methodically, they rounded the birds up – moving low and slow, cornering them against the wire, the cockerel turning left and right for a last dash, but most knew what was coming and just stood panting. This is a farm, Fred knows what happens, but I told him not to look. Still, he saw the first one done, heard her startled squawk and the high blue laughter. I wished for Lettie and her kind blade. Squadrons of wasps, drawn by the blood, buzzed over the small white cairn of heads.

'Mrs van der Watt,' shouted the brigadier, stepping out from the quiet of our kitchen.

Instantly the laughter stopped. 'We are about to begin indoors. You may have five minutes to remove anything you can carry. I see your husband has quite the library. Dickens, eh? Can't be all bad.'

'They're my books,' I said skirting past him.

I grabbed my church Bible, Fred's christening cup, my needlework case, this diary and pencils and the sack of food and clothes Lettie fixed. Everything else they carried out and stacked neatly on the second wagon, Corporal Johnson merrily ticking his inventory. Ten years of our life gone in a single morning while I sat and watched: the bowl and mirror from our bedroom, the bedstead you carved for our first anniversary, our little wicker chair, Fred's bed, our table and chairs, my pots and pans, the armchair, the pictures of our parents, Fred's christening robe and my wedding gown, such as it is. I'm surprised they didn't take the very air.

'Material aid,' said Corporal Johnson, who made me sign it all away before handing over a receipt, 'is anything that can offer comfort to the enemy.'

In that moment I imagined him in my wedding gown and snorted. He tilted his head at me and turned as another whistle blew. They all stopped for lunch. The cows were crying for not being milked and the pigs were chuntering. Lettie and Jakob lay tied up on the stoep. At least they were in shade, though they don't suffer the sun like us. A soldier, not one of the ones who killed the chickens, laid a bowl of water by them. Jakob lapped from it but Lettie turned away. Then he brought me and Fred some of our own bread. 'Done soon, love,' he said. 'Don't worry.' I made Fred eat mine.

After lunch, the brigadier came out again wiping his lips with a linen napkin monogrammed with somebody else's initials. 'Last chance, Mrs van der Watt. Sign!'

'No,' shouted Fred, in English, which showed he has been eavesdropping. 'No, No, No!'

'Takes after his father, I see,' the brigadier said. 'Where is his father? Is he perhaps watching right now, training field glasses on us from that kopje?' He pointed across the veldt to the only hill for miles, its flat summit crowned with thorns.

'He's away,' I repeated, as calmly as I could. 'Visiting family.'

'Family? Really? Let us hope they all have a good view.'

The brigadier nodded at the corporal who took out a box of matches, struck one and tossed it on our roof. Lettie began wailing, kicking over the water. Jakob bellowed, 'Mercy!' I sprang up cursing him. Two men hauled Jakob and Lettie onto the wagon where they nodded dazed as they were tied to it. The corporal struck another match and held it to the thatch, whisper-dry midsummer. It took three more matches to smoke properly. I felt proud of every straw for holding out.

'The remaining animals,' said the brigadier, strolling over to a waiting horse as the flames crackled. From nowhere the corporal produced the blade Lettie uses for the chickens and handed it to a man with arms like thighs who lumbered towards the sties. I didn't know whether to cover Fred's eyes or ears. 'Let him watch, Mrs van der Watt,' said the corporal. 'Let him see what happens when you don't do as you're told.'

And so I watched Fred watch as our cows and pigs were slit nose to tail, mulberries still in their stomachs, screams still in their throats. The big man with butcher's arms worked fast, hacking and sawing and swatting away the flies. Soon our animals were no more than cuts of meat arranged with surprising delicacy in wooden crates. They shovelled the innards down our well. 'That'll keep any who come after thirsty,' winked the corporal. Then they kicked sacks of bright white salt over our now empty vegetable garden, scuffing it in with their boots. Nothing will grow there. The skin on my face drew tight as the flames danced across our roof. The brigadier pulled Fred from me kicking and screaming and shoved him next to the bloody meat on the back of the wagon as it began rolling away. Fred reached for me as I ran to him, pulling myself up.

As we looked back the roof sighed and after just a few more yards it fell in, blowing the door and windows open. For a moment, the gingham curtains I made billowed as if to wave us off. Our books flew up into the air, stories taking wing. Despite all this and the smoke in my eyes I didn't cry. Really, not one tear. I wasn't sad. I was terrified. And furious – angrier than I thought possible. They rode in columns alongside. A hundred yards away our wagon left the track joining us distantly to the Kriels' and turned east, the love-grass rising high around the wheels and the horses' haunches. Dozens more wagons were heading the same way. Then we were called to a halt. The men put their hands over their ears and some looked back at the farm. The soldier who'd given us food made a show of sticking his fingers in his ears then pointing at Fred who copied. I followed his gaze and saw a thin black cable snaking from the first wagon all the way back to our house. I noticed, proudly, that the chimney you built was still standing. No sooner had I followed the cable than I understood.

'Remember, remember,' chanted the corporal, bringing together two silver wires.

I will never forget. I only pray Fred will. He's sleeping now, the rocking of the train comforts him. I need to use the bucket but can't move with him in my lap so I'll rest while I can. Genesis 28:15. *I am with thee, and will keep thee in all places whither thou goest.*

Where are you, Samuel? Where are we? How will you find us now?

Thursday 10 January, Bloemfontein Camp

There are seven in our tent, not counting flies or ants: Fred and me and Mrs Kriel and her lot. Her little Kaffir girl sleeps right outside. I expect another family soon because we're far from crowded judging by the noise either side.

We were on that train for ever. The first night was the longest of my life, apart from when Fred was born. He kept asking for Lettie, shouted for her as we were all herded on, and every time we stopped because the tracks had been cut or I don't know – none of us knows anything for sure. Rumours buzz like the flies that cover everything here. Somebody said they've been tying our women and children to the trains to stop the shelling. I don't believe it.

The midsummer sun is barely down before it's back up and the nights are as cold as the days hot. I barely slept. The thin itchy blankets we've been issued offer little comfort. I can hear my mother telling me I've grown grand before blaming you, Samuel, with your books and manners. In the night our breath condenses on the insides of the tent making a kind of dew which covers everything, bejewelling Fred's eyelashes as he sleeps. I've made it sound pretty when it's not, whatever touches it comes away damp. Everything here is tear-stained. We're all hungry. 'I've got four mouths to feed,' moaned Mrs Kriel this morning, straightening her white lace kappie. 'I suppose you're lucky to have just the one.' I smiled as best I could.

Our tent could claim to have been cream once. It's round and high – even I can stand up in it. A bell tent, they call it. It's just about held aloft by ropes pegged all round. Our floor is the bare earth which offends me as it never did when I was growing up. Already ants are finding their way in but I fear they'll leave empty-handed. The sack Lettie filled is long empty. One thing is certain: the English can't bake, their bread is even worse than mine. We were each thrown an iron wedge as we left the train. As soon as he woke, Fred got to work plugging the gaps with the small stones that pushed into my back all night. A rain-spider or worse won't be deterred but it'll keep him busy till kingdom comes. It seems he's

already forgotten about Oupa and the chickens and
the farm. He has, after all, been on a train and there
are soldiers with real guns and lots of other boys to
play with – more children than he's ever seen. I wish
I could forget. At least they didn't find the things we
buried. Fred keeps asking what I'm writing in my
little blue book. I tell him I'm writing to you so he
asks have you shot any lions or Khakis and when will
you come back? Hurry.

'When are we going home?' was his first question
this morning. Then: 'Where's Lettie?'

'We're on a holiday,' I repeated, gesturing round
our tent. 'And Lettie is too. Camping!' I looked to
Mrs Kriel to back me up but she continued furiously
brushing Johanna's hair, each stroke a vicious tug
from scalp to shoulder daring a louse to settle. The
girl's head tilted back so her throat pulsed tenderly.
I thought again about our pigs, wondered who got
our bacon. 'Indeed, we are lucky to be here,' said
Mrs Kriel, as she huffed up and left, trailing Olive
and Johanna, who patted her hair as if to make
sure it was still there. Her boys were already out on
'reconnaissance'.

No sooner had Mrs Kriel sailed out than a greasy
bonneted head poked through the tent flap like a
chicken pecking for corn.

'Morning.' She raised a busy city voice above the
dawn chorus of hundreds – thousands? – outside.
'I'm two to the right, Helen Grobler, here a month,

transferred from Vereeniging with my Liese. You're Sarah.'

'Yes,' I said, marvelling that this woman I'd never seen before in her grease-stiff kappje knew my Christian name and was so easy with it. I suppose nothing now is as it was.

'How did you know?'

'No secrets here,' she said, her words rushing into one another. 'No walls!' She laughed and tugged at the ropes and the whole tent wobbled, spattering us all with the night water. Fred giggled and it was good to hear.

'You wait till it rains!' As she spoke her small dark eyes roved over our pathetic belongings. In-ven-tory. Under all that dirt was she twenty-five or forty-five? There was no wedding ring. I turned mine conspic-uously. I saw our visitor as Mrs Kriel would but nevertheless stood up and put out my hand. I've felt more strength in Fred's fingers and only just resisted the urge to wipe my hands on my apron.

'Say good morning, Fred.'

Fred did a little bow and she curtsied.

'Just you two?' she asked, looking around.

I thought again about my mother and sisters and their families up near Mafeking where they moved after Father died and our son-less farm was finished. You're the closest I had to a boy, Mother said when she wrote telling me he'd passed away. Where are they now? I should think of them more. In the ordinary way of things, I barely think of them at all. And what of your lot, Samuel? Have you found your brothers? I'm only glad your parents are not alive to see two Christian countries at war again.

'Less to worry about,' said Helen. 'You'll want breakfast. I'll get your rations.'

Rations? Hungry as I was, I craved quiet. In the past week I've seen more people than I have in my whole life except when I first saw you at the station that day. Perhaps sensing this Helen smiled. 'Fine, you stay here, settle in, and I'll get your bits. And some extra coffee, maybe. Private Gladstone lays it on for the new girls.'

Before I could reply, she winked and was off. I flopped back on the nest of blankets with Fred. 'I'm hungry,' he said. 'Mama, when's breakfast?' You can imagine how that made me feel. I told him the funny lady would be back soon with food and he got on with building his ant barricade.

Let me finish telling you how we got here. We pulled in to Bloemfontein as the sun disappeared. One day I would like to see it set as it does in Europe, at least in novels about Europe. Here it just disappears like a coin rolling off a table: it's light or dark, one or the other, no in between. The railway station frothed red, white and blue and a military band played 'God Save the Queen' over and over to cheer them or depress us, I don't know. They wouldn't be welcome in our poorest church. I searched for your face as I look for it everywhere now. There were a surprising number of men your age, hard to tell if they were hands-uppers or prisoners or what. We blinked onto the platform then were herded onto another open wagon and bumped along for hours. At least the sun was down. All around were wagons stacked with stunned-looking folk carrying whatever they could: pots, chairs, shovels. One *vrou* cradled a goat. Two little girls dragged a brass bedstead. I half expected a piano. The soldiers piled everything bonfire-high then set us on top. Most folk fell straight asleep, as if it was just another trip to market. There was one man your age on our wagon but we all ignored him except Fred who asked, 'Where's your Mauser?' At this there was kekkeling and the man jumped down to help the little girls with the bedstead. Every fit man should be fighting. I didn't think us particularly prosperous until I examined the women round me: hems worn, aprons smeared, kappies askew and all in a manner that suggested they were before. Not all wore wedding rings. Many were scratching. I held Fred tight till he fell asleep.

Gradually in the darkness ahead I began to pick out hundreds of dim lights. As we got closer they formed neat rows which seemed to slope down and away. Fireflies, I madly wondered, but no empire can organise nature. Do you remember once Fred and I spelled out *WELCOME HOME* in glow worms in front of the house but you were late back from market and the worms wandered off mocking my spelling? As our wagon halted a young soldier, barely twenty, loomed up lit by a paraffin lamp held by a Khaki Kaffir.

'Welcome,' he smiled, trying his best in our tongue, his teeth white and even as the sugar cubes we saved for Oupa. I could tell he was proud of his wispy moustache from the way he tilted his head. He offered his hand and I remembered you asking to walk with me around the square at Ventersburg – it was two years after I first saw you that your father's tour reached our little town. He spoke on the exact spot where our new church was to be built and everybody turned out to see who was prospering and who wasn't, to read too much into the smallest thing. Again, you helped your father to the stage but he took longer and as he preached you listened as if for the first time while standing ready to catch him. Afterwards, you cut straight through the crowd to where I was standing right at the back. Your first words to me were: 'You again!' Mother didn't know where to look. Which might be why Father actually smiled.

I refused the soldier's hand and climbed down. His face crumpled. I didn't think manners mattered in war. Is this war? I suppose it is. I'm determined to refuse all help from the English. If you are without aid – and you must be, wherever you are – then I will be too. Mrs Kriel was helped down like a duchess, complaining of her ankles, oh her ankles. Fred leapt off, gun in hand. He aimed at the soldier who fell back laughing. 'Bloody Mausers!' I gathered up our few bits and noted Mrs Kriel's luggage – four big bags. Her Kaffir girl heaved them down. 'Careful!' snapped Mrs Kriel, cuffing her.

'This is Bloemfontein Refugee Camp,' said another soldier in English. 'I am Captain Cooper of the Devonshire Regiment. Please follow me.' He turned to leave. Sensing only stillness behind him he turned round and tried a mangled Dutch. Some folk sniggered.

Mrs Kriel bustled past and leaned in to this captain the way I've seen her commandeer Reverend Frankl after church, her charm worn smooth as the pebbles in the bottom of the spruit running behind our sties. Another wagon pulled up right behind and a tide of bodies surged into us. I gripped Fred's hand and there was a moment of confusion while each group struggled to stay together. Fred was lifted off his toes but didn't let go as we all coursed towards a high barbed-wire fence. Just as we were being forced onto it Captain Cooper shouted in English and it turned into two gates which swung inwards, swallowing all.

Maybe fifty of us stood on a dirt square lit by lamps strung on ropes. Posted around were half a dozen or so bored-looking Khakis with rifles slumped over their shoulders. It was getting cold so I put my hands in my apron and felt with a shock the knife I snatched off our table when the corporal arrived. A hundred years ago now. I gripped the handle, calculating odds I knew I couldn't win, then let it go. Older folk slumped on the ground. I offered the woman nearest our sack as a cushion and she took it, laying an ebony cane by her side. 'Thank you, daughter,' she said, extending a ringed hand which I could only half shake without letting go of Fred. She patted my knee. 'I'm Mrs Botha.'

'Welcome, again, to Bloemfontein,' said Captain Cooper, reading in English from a creased blue card. 'This is the Assembly Ground where you will collect rations, attend church etc … Please forget what you might have heard about British hospitality. You are not prisoners here. You are refugees. We are concentrating you all in camps like this for your own safety and at great expense.'

Mutterings all round. Mrs Botha tutted and shook her head.

'You and your children will be well fed and adequately clothed. Camp rules will be explained in detail tomorrow. For now, you will be shown to your accommodation. Lights Out in fifteen minutes, after which there is a curfew so do not greet your neighbours just yet. Please be assured, you will be safe here.'

He repeated the last words.

Led by the young soldier, we trailed into the camp itself. Mrs Kriel introduced herself to Mrs Botha, who nodded politely. I held Fred closer, feeling his familiar weight, his breath hot against my neck. In every direction tidy rows of tents glowed in the dark. There were hundreds of them stretching as far as I could see. The occupants were brazenly silhouetted like the shadow plays you put on for Fred when he couldn't (or wouldn't) sleep.

Every sound imaginable spilled out: clattering pots; tired lullabies; mothers pleading *Please, please, my darling*; simple prayers; coughs of every texture and cries of every colour and even possibly bedroom laughter. And from the tents in darkness, only low animal weeping.

A dog barked, then another, then from out on the veldt the high, clever howl that makes us worry for our sheep. Up ahead a young woman from our cart tripped and the young soldier dashed forward to help. Each tent was numbered and each row marked out by whitewashed rocks. Other than this, they all looked identical. How will we find our way around? I wondered. Will we be here long enough?

'You get used to the noise,' said the young soldier in English.

'*Dankie.*' I bobbed my head and pretended not to understand. *I will be the stupid Boer huisvrou.*

'*Jy is welkom,*' he said. 'Private Gladstone.'

'*Jou taal is goed,*' I told him.

'Intelligence.' He tapped his cap, flashing the smile his mother missed. 'I want to get into Intelligence. You see at least ninety per cent of Intelligence is

44

listening. Information is ammunition.' He glanced down at a list, snapping his fingers at his boy to hold the light closer. 'Now, you two are on Row 6 in Tent 125.' He reached for Fred whose head was lolling. 'Can I help?'

I turned away, holding Fred so tight I'm surprised he didn't cry out.

'Or your bag maybe?'

I felt it ease from my shoulder and cursed myself for accepting his help. Private Gladstone did a little bow as well as he could carrying my bag and his rifle.

Our tent was at the very end of a very long row at the very edge of the camp. It took an hour to find. Beyond there was only the darkness of the veldt where you were, somewhere. Mrs Botha was across the way. Of all the tents we passed only these were empty. 'You're lucky,' said Private Gladstone. 'Typhoid.' Mrs Kriel pushed in with her brood spreading their belongings everywhere. Soon everyone but me was sleeping.

Now, even over all our new neighbours, I can hear Mrs Kriel clomping back complaining. I hope Helen is not far behind. The ants are already testing Fred's defences. He is as hungry and persistent as them.

Helen did bring food, a slice of pap and some gritty coffee. Then she took us to the Assembly Ground for our official 'welcome'. I've never seen so many people. Or so few servants. I trailed Fred by the hand

and he kept turning this way and that, distracted by all the dogs and children and noise.

At the Assembly Ground I recognised a few women from our train and nodded, pleased none of them looked any fresher. I was flanked by Mrs Kriel, who tutted at Helen, and Mrs Botha, the end of her cane red with dust. It was already hot and we sagged as Captain Cooper relayed all the rules – so many, we were each given a blue booklet, which I've saved for you.

We're banned from talking about the war. What else is there to say? All the talk is of spies, victory, defeat. Also: no swearing; nothing to be said against the British sovereign; no slops to be thrown out in camp (where else to throw them?); no visitors (who would choose to come here?); no papers to be passed out – letters must be sent via their censor (if we write something they disapprove of we're made to read it aloud at Assembly). Diaries are also forbidden so I'm writing this in the tent when it's just Fred and me and I'm keeping it tucked away. I've already caught Mrs Kriel's Kaffir snooping. Fortunately my writing is all but illegible even to me. I don't have much space so the pages are turning black with thoughts. You'll have to bear with me when I read them to you. We're allowed Bibles but no other books. Our tents must be kept scrupulously clean and the lower part rolled up every morning; Reveille at 5 a.m. with trumpets; Lights Out at 9 p.m., no matter what.

Official welcome over, Helen started our tour. I couldn't see the half of it when we arrived – was it really only last night? How many nights without you now? How many more?

'Keep up,' she said, darting ahead avoiding the main paths and shouting to me over her shoulder while I skipped the tent ropes. 'This place gets bigger every day.' Fred hurdled after her and I shouted him back. It would be so easy to lose him here.

'Can't we walk on the path?' I nodded to the invitingly empty official lanes. Just then, an arm reached out of a tent and emptied a night bucket. Nobody objected.

Helen laughed. 'Anyway, don't need anybody knowing your business more than they already do.'

Above us all stands a guard tower topped with a wire nest where a pair of soldiers sit smoking. They strike matches off what must be a machine gun. Doubtless Fred will know the exact model.

'Where are you taking us?' I asked Helen.

She stopped. 'I'm not *taking* you nowhere.' She gestured all around. 'Find your own way if you like – '

'I didn't mean … ' I said. 'I'm sorry.'

''S'all right,' she smiled. 'Now, ovens. Most important. Then latrine then school then shops.'

'School? Shops? What shops? Miss – '

'Helen, I told you.'

'Helen, who's looking after your little girl? Have you other children?'

47

Helen stopped again, looked down then turned to face me. 'Liese's all I've got, God help her, the others I lost before. Liese's in their hospital, I see her at 4 p.m. Five minutes, we get, five minutes once a week.' Her voice rose as she stepped closer. Whatever meat she'd had was rotting between surprisingly even teeth. I pretended to cough so I could cover my mouth. 'They tie the little ones to their beds, stops them falling out, they say. And they're not allowed to talk case they get tired and we're to be quiet case we *upset the patient*. Five minutes!' Fred began to shuffle away from her and she ruffled his hair. 'But you'll be at school!' Her hands were filthy. He dodged away but she didn't seem offended. He's never been touched by any woman but me or Lettie. 'School, 6 a.m. to 1 p.m. every day.' Fred looked unsure. 'Extra bread in class!'

Helen resumed her hectic pace with Fred bobbing more cautiously alongside and me loping after. This place is so crowded, so dirty, I might take a cord from my dress and bind his hand to mine. Let me try to describe it properly for you. It's hard to know where to begin.

Our camp – there are others – has 250 tents. The official limit is supposedly fifteen per tent. So, there are at least 3,000 of us. A week ago, we were all farmers. Now there are no farms. We are 'refugees'. The ratio of prisoners – that's what Helen says we are – to soldiers is a hundred to one. But they've got guns.

The only gate is the one out front. There are no fences or walls to keep us in. Where would we run to? Bloemfontein is two miles away. The camp sits on a slope and, just as at home, we can see for miles but there's nothing out there – no houses, no farms, no grass even. It's all been burned, even the Native huts. The few little kopjes breaking the horizon have been stripped for firewood. There's not even a cloud in the sky. We all worked so hard to tame the land. Perhaps none of us are meant to be here.

Because there are no trees there are no birds. There's nowhere for the weavers to hang their nests, no cover for the guinea fowl. When I mentioned this to Mrs Kriel she just pointed to the vultures circling.

'There were some bushes,' Helen says.

Firewood is kept in stores guarded by hands-uppers – yes, they're in here too. They have whistles to summon a proper soldier if they catch us breaking rules. I swear I'll break more than rules if one of them comes near me. It's not enough the Khakis have burnt our farms but now they keep us in here with traitors. Helen says they live in luxury in a special section. The final indignity is the Khaki Kaffirs set to spy on us. I grieve to see them turn against the people who gave them shelter and work. We are all sons and daughters of the same soil. It's a sin that will not quickly be forgiven.

We're permitted to forage for fuel on the veldt but Helen says everything worth burning went months ago. Even the wild mules have been conscripted into pulling the big guns. One or two rebels still roam about leaving dung that burns all right when it's dry. We can buy wood from the shops – yes, shops. More than in Ventersburg! A dozen or so all staffed by the good burghers of Bloemfontein who come and go with carts they set up by the gate. Helen says you can get fresh enough meat and milk, and candles, cloth and soap. We can even order sewing machines! Make some new dresses for a ball, maybe. But it's not charity. The prices! This morning I felt for the coins in the hem of my dress, worked out how far they'd go. Enough to feed me and Fred for four months even at these prices but you'll be back by then.

Helen says you can even apply for a pass to go shopping in town but you must leave your children behind and your rations are halved if you're not back in four hours. It's two miles each way in this sun and we're not permitted to hitch a ride even if a cart stops in case we pass on letters or information.

The men in here are truly sad, mostly cripples from the last war. They busy themselves with the hardest labour – rolling barrels of water from the Modder which flows past us to the town. We need to boil it clean but with what? We're each given one pint of good water per day but spillages are likely if you don't smile at the hands-upper ladling it out. Just one pint, in this heat, for drinking and cooking and washing (no longer a priority, from the state of Helen). It quickly scums with the dust that blows everywhere so Lyle's Golden Syrup tins, with their tight lids, are much prized. Then there are the very old men, the age your father was when he passed away, who seem content enough to sit outside and mind the flocks of children.

More wagons arrive hourly with their cargo of misery. Some of us sit by the gate hoping for news. There are reunions sometimes but mostly it's just waiting. Although our tent is furthest from the gate (where everything useful is) we are also, mercifully, furthest from the latrines: two long grave-deep trenches. I retch describing them and wish for our polite bucket in the bush back home. A wire runs between them which you have to hold so you don't fall in backwards. The stench reaches up to pull you down. There's nowhere safe to look and closing your eyes makes no difference. The buzz of exultant blowflies is so great it actually drowns some of the awfulness out. 'Grim, eh?' said Helen as she squatted next to me. I think I managed to nod. 'Blushes'll go,' she said, hoisting herself up and extending her hand. I couldn't take it. The worst of it is that there's only *one*. The men are very good and try to wait but often rush in unhitching breeches and apologising. Modesty, it seems, is the first casualty of war. The ground around the latrines is almost grimmer than the place itself. 'They don't all make it,' said Helen, holding her tiny waist. 'Typhoid.'

Right by the latrines is a wire enclosure topped with thorns and in the middle of it sits a windowless cube of corrugated iron. 'The Bird Cage,' said Helen. 'Break their rules and they shove you in there singing on your own day and night. Best avoided, take it from me.'

And there are tents right up to the very edge of all this! Helen says the people in them are quite happy. Apparently, they're paid to be there – tents are allocated randomly so if a woman with means ends up by the latrines she can pay a poorer family in a better spot to swap. There are all sort of schemes on the go, Helen says. The Khakis don't notice or are happy not to. The garrison isn't far but there are very few soldiers. Most of the work, if you can call it that, is done by Khaki Kaffirs. I suppose they've nowhere else to work, now all the farms are gone. I keep looking for Lettie and Jakob.

I've got to go – I promised Fred proper bread. We bake three loaves at once in ovens improvised from hollowed-out anthills – the ants don't take too kindly to being evicted from their domed clay palaces so it's best to find one they've abandoned.

Friday 11 January

Not so windy last night but just as cold. Our tent is full of holes. Fred was so tired he fell asleep on me – thin as I am, I'm more comfortable than the ground. My back complains but that's all right. We never got him down so easily at home. Mrs Kriel snores which is one of the many things I wouldn't have learned if she still lived six miles rather than six feet away.

I wonder if you even have the luxury of a tent? You have constant variety, I imagine, a different camp every night, the day's adventures to share. We are doomed to sit here day after day waiting and waiting, staring up at the same patch of sky for some kind of sign. Before I met you, I measured time from waking to milking in the half-dark to prayers before bed, from Sunday to Sunday, from sowing to harvest. Since you and your clock I now have the agony of endless hours without you. Every second stretches.

Saturday 12 January

My bread was a success if you had a loose tooth to budge. But it still beat the English. 'Lettie's is best,' Fred said. He's right. He cries for her at bedtime, which Mrs Kriel remarks on. It was already dark by the time I found my way back and I can't afford to waste our one candle and anyway Lights Out is at 9 p.m. I write during the day when nobody else is about, which seems to be almost never. In some ways, I've never been busier. Everything takes so long in this heat and there's no shade although some women carry silk parasols, their brightness blooming in the dirt. You always complained about my cooking so imagine what I have to make of this. Twice a week each woman receives:

½ lb meat
1½ lb meal or rice
1½ oz coffee
3 oz sugar
1 oz salt

It's so long since I've had to worry about ounces of anything. You've spoiled me, Samuel. The coffee tastes like the acorns on Corporal Johnson's buttons. The 'meat' I was handed this morning was wrapped in a sheet of their *Times* which I saved to dry for kindling after reading the headlines through the blood. Madly, I hoped for news of you – a story of a daring raid led by Samuel van der Watt! But of course, the newspaper was months old – the Court Circular, all princesses visiting the poor then running away. Apparently, their Queen remains at 'Osborne House' marooned in grief. This so-called meat came from something equally old. They say cow but I say goat, maybe even mule. It rotted in my hands and where you hope for fat there were these bright blue specks.

'What's this?' I asked Helen – she skewers meat thinly on knitting needles so it cooks faster and uses less wood. 'What are these blue bits?'

'Poison,' she said. 'Slow poison but it's that or starve.'

Mrs Kriel, who was supervising the roasting of a whole leg of mutton, chimed in, 'Nonsense, it's simply a preservative.' Helen asked her where she got her meat from but she just turned away. Some say the English put fish-hooks in too.

Children over twelve get adult rations. Because Fred's only six he gets a whole one sixteenth of a can of condensed milk each day. That's it. How do they even measure a sixteenth? Consequently, you see few fat mothers. Thank God for our coins. Samuel, the children here are scraps, sleeves flapping round their wrists. It's agony. I won't let Fred get like them, I won't. They remind me of Ignorance and Want – from *A Christmas Carol,* do you remember? The apparitions revealed by the Ghost of Christmas Present: 'They were a boy and a girl. Yellow, meagre, ragged, scowling, wolfish.' These ancient children make Mrs Botha seem youthful. I fear no victory will restore them.

They don't give us any soap, then call us vermin. I check Fred every morning for lice and so far we've escaped their attentions. It's only a matter of time. Perhaps you've got it even worse and I shouldn't complain. None of this is necessary, the Khakis don't look like they're starving and smell like soldiers probably should.

'Is this right?' I asked the corporal in English when he handed me my ration ticket.

'Ah, Mrs van der Watt,' he drawled. 'Our favourite guest. Settling in?'

'The rations are not,' I said, reaching for the right word, 'adequate.'

'Certainly, they are not,' he said. 'But they are sufficient and far better than those enjoyed by our boys being kept busy by your husband and his friends. You can always write to the Camp Superintendent if you feel at all unfairly treated.'

Johnson pushed a wad of his notepaper across the table. It's thick like the hotel stationery you wrote to me on, from that last tour with your father. For months, I dreamed of the Grand Station Hotel in Johannesburg. If you had time, you'd do me a sketch and I'd imagine the rest: brass door handles hot in the sun, dust not daring to spin through the revolving doors which Fred would love playing in, vast staircases stretching up to carpeted rooms with electric lights and a four-poster bed with a feather mattress and blazing fires. I don't know why the fires were always blazing but in my head they were.

I snatched the paper up and the corporal slid another bundle over. 'Take as much as you like, Mrs Gaskell,' he said, already looking over my shoulder to the queue behind me. 'We are all very keen for a glimpse into the mind of the white savage woman. Next!'

Fred is at least still sleeping well but is listless. Last night he wouldn't say his prayers and I had to make him. There's so little shade outside and it's so clammy inside – our tent is like the lung of an ailing sheep.

Sunday 13 January

Church. The English started it in the little school used by the various societies set up by the various Mrs Kriels – this war has given her more good to do than ever. There's so much to wring her hands over, so many mouths to feed (always her own first). She juggles a full calendar and trails her brood everywhere as evidence of her great patriotism. The Bloemfontein Women's Choir. Can you imagine? At least it drowns out the constant roar. Then there's the Welfare Committee, the Spiritualists' Society (which I was surprised to find Mrs Botha attends) and even a Gardening Club. What bitterness grows here.

The English underestimated our faith, so church was moved to the Assembly Ground. Church is where you make it, your father said at the railway station that day. It is wherever we gather, one *volk*.

I've nothing decent to wear, only the dress I was carted off in, but I spared some water to splash my face and clean Fred up. As much as he hates me dabbing at him he hates being dirty more. Finally, the smell of the farm burning is leaving my clothes. It's the nature of smoke to drift but memories only become more fixed. I've never had such nightmares and they don't always stop when I wake.

As always, the cheerless trumpet sounded from the guard tower at 5 a.m. Something like a Sabbath silence settled over the camp. At home, we'd spend the afternoon reading verse and praying and singing, our little church of three. You'd preach as if to thousands and later read aloud whichever novel you found in town, your cadence carrying us all to an early bed for the week ahead. *It was the best of times, it was the worst of times.* Fred didn't understand but the rhythm kept him from running out to find Lettie. I still don't know where she went on Sundays.

Our pastor here is the Reverend Charles Fernie, a Baptist – we're forbidden the comfort of our own 'seditious' church. Even in this heat he wears black robes over black shirt and trousers so he looks like a skinny sweaty crow, more likely to have a mother than a wife. He's from a place called Liverpool and speaks only apologetic English in an accent much like our own. His every utterance is accompanied by chatter as we all half translate.

There were no Khakis at church but there's always the guard tower with its great glinting gun. Mrs Botha joined the older women up front shoulder-to-shoulder on the rough benches. I stood at the back and tried to forget where I was. I wished I wasn't tall enough to see over everyone, that I only had to see what was right in front of me. Reverend

Fernie chalked *Job 6:11* on the blackboard: *What is my strength, that I should hope? And what is mine end, that I should prolong my life?* Faintly below it I traced the words of yesterday's lesson – they are teaching our children English, preparing them for the world to come.

We are all Job's wife here but I must say I felt my heart lift when Mrs Kriel led her choir, even though we're not allowed to sing Republican hymns. Just being together, I swear we all looked cleaner though we didn't smell it – I nearly wished for a Catholic just for the incense. In silent prayer, no one can hear me, not the Khaki Kaffirs, not the hands-uppers, not the English. So, I closed my eyes and summoned a vision of the whole camp swept away in a flood and every last Khaki tossed in the latrines and drowned. Except the Reverend. I'm sure I wasn't alone. But I shouldn't think of vengeance, for that assumes victory. First, we must survive. I will get through this for Fred and you. Just weeks ago, I was waiting for the apricots, looking forward to our tin roof, working up to asking you to trim your moustache because it tickles. They chopped our trees down, you know, every last one, even the mulberry.

It was a comfort to see Fred looking bored at church. Helen arrived late and stood by me at the back, not bothered by looks. Her singing voice is sweeter than you might imagine, much finer than mine. I saw her again as Mrs Kriel does. Who is she really? What was she before? How much lower has all this brought her? She smiled up at me, took my hand and squeezed it. My hands are nearly as dirty as hers now.

At the close of service Reverend Fernie read aloud the names and ages of those who passed away this week and with each name a sob erupted. Soon almost the whole congregation was weeping. Even the Reverend struggled. So many children – cheeks rosy with fever, eyes glassy, hacking like hags. Fred doesn't understand why I won't let him go out and play. Death is our constant companion here. Typhoid and malaria are the official causes. Starving and poisoning really. As we filed out we met a flock of men and women in perfect Sunday dress with plump-cheeked offspring. Precious few of them had the decency to look away as we shuffled past in our rags. I hate the Khakis but hands-uppers disgust me because they surrendered, they gave up the land we fought the Zulu for at Blood River. God cannot grant their prayers.

Monday 14 January

I let Fred run a little bit ahead when I went to fetch our rations – we spend our lives queuing.

Some ladies pay Kaffirs to do their waiting. I was confronted by the corporal when I got to the front.

'Administrative error, should have noticed. Your husband is, of course, still on commando … ' He thrust a pink ticket at me.

'What's this?'

'Your new card.'

'I don't need one,' I said, holding mine out, checking the name, the date. Everybody listened behind me as the corporal snatched it.

'Rules are rules. Here is the ration ticket for Undesirables.'

'Undesirables?'

He raised his voice over the muttering, addressing us all. 'Women like you – with husbands who insist on fighting. Undesirables. Your husbands have abandoned you and your children, forcing us to feed and house you and provide you with the modern medicine and schooling you so obviously lack. All at the expense of the generous British taxpayer. We don't want to keep you here any more than you wish to be kept and yet you all refuse the oath.'

Booing erupted and beads of sweat gathered in the corporal's hairline, which was beating a retreat from his increasingly ruddy face.

'You choose filth and hunger because it is what you are used to. If you sign now, Mrs van der Watt, you can have your old card back. Little boys cannot grow big and strong on pride alone.'

Fred tugged at my hand. I said nothing but not fast enough and immediately came the hiss of

'Hands-upper'. I thought of you, Samuel, and took the new ticket without looking at it – I wouldn't give him the satisfaction.

But how are we to live on this?

½ lb meal
½ oz coffee
1 oz sugar
1 oz salt
One eighteenth of a tin of condensed milk (for children)

No meat, Samuel, no meat! Maybe I can make pap and let it dry into cakes, if I can get enough water, if there's any meal left. Back home I could almost see Fred growing but he felt lighter when I picked him up this morning. It's not even been a week. Rotten meat was better than nothing. I suppose you eat whatever you can shoot. Vultures and rats are all we see here.

I'm hoarding the paper Corporal Johnson gave me – I never expected to have so much to say. Mrs Kriel walked back in just now licking what cannot possibly be jam from her lips. 'Shopping list, dear?' she asked, peering down at my diary. I'd better stop for now.

I've still got about four pounds so I went to the shops but nobody would sell me anything I needed.

Undesirables are forbidden to buy extra rations and the burghers lose their pitch if they bend the rules. We're not allowed soap which will be hell if we get the typhoid – I've seen sorry cases wearing flour sacks. No candles either. Or wood. But I can order a gramophone. Maybe I should buy one and chop it up.

I met Helen coming from the hospital. She looks dirtier and thinner by the day. 'That lot are only selling back what the English stole,' she spat. 'Their best customers all live up there, top of the camp, fenced off. They get the good meat and candles after dark and servants and all.'

'Who?'

'The hands-uppers.'

'How do you know?'

'Know what?'

'That they have candles at night. The curfew, we're – '

'Curfew!' Helen cackled. 'The curfew, well, yes, we're not s'posed to be out after 9 p.m., are we? But we don't all do as we're told, do we?'

'Don't we?' I looked down at Fred who was chasing one of the little dogs that run around. I can't leave him alone here even for a second. I think of all the rules and even the rational ones, like no fires in tents, make me bridle. I see myself setting our tent alight and dancing round it, flames flashing in my eyes.

'Oh, it's a busy old place at night,' said Helen, laying her palm flat in front of me. A sore oozed weakly on her thumb; she didn't flick the flies away. 'Sarah, just give it here.'

'What?'

'Your money.'

'I don't have any.'

'Sarah, your dress has been sweeping the ground since you got here and if you're not careful the fortune in that hem will get banked in the latrine.'

I reached down pretending to pick something up.

'Subtle,' Helen sighed, rolling her eyes.

Indeed, the hem was frayed. It was all too easy to pop out a shilling – the cleanest thing I'd seen for days. I rubbed it, hoping for some of its smooth glimmer, before dropping it into Helen's open palm. She closed her fingers over it then stroked my cheek lightly before turning to the shops. I watched her beetle from stall to stall scooping up meat, wood, even milk. Fred jumped up and down as her arms filled. Nobody questioned her. She could buy whatever she liked. As she carried it all back smiling I finally realised what she really was.

'Come on,' she said, walking past holding up some meagre ribs. 'Dinner.'

Tuesday 15 January

Mrs Kriel is out at her afternoon choir meeting. You laughed at my singing but now I'm glad I can't hold a note. 'There are other social groups for women of standing,' Kriel said, adjusting her kappie in a mirror propped by a trunk. I don't remember her arriving with a mirror. Or a trunk. 'Of course, the Spiritualists shouldn't be allowed, but I suppose it gives comfort to the lower sorts.'

I agreed absent-mindedly, still feeling warm from Helen's feast last night. I'd forgotten what real hunger was like. You come from a house with napkins. I remember being reluctant to wipe my fingers on such a pretty thing. At last a daughter, your mother said. Fred has never wanted – he's only ever known the pleasant rumble of anticipation. He's got some colour back this morning. I sat watching him rebuild his little ant blockade. He's still not bored of it.

Because the English are obsessed with 'fresh air' we're forced to open our tents every day and sweep the bare soil. Corporal Johnson and his Kaffirs go round with clipboards cutting rations for any infraction. For some reason we're forbidden to air our blankets on the tent ropes which means we must beat them together, which means more dust. So, every morning Fred's little walls – which do actually work – are destroyed. Daily rebuilding keeps him busy. The Kriel boys still won't let him join their commando games but they always ask for his gun (and he refuses). We don't often see them: they're part of a boy's army. There are no official orphan tents, only sad little packs that sleep in the same tents.

Waiting for their Fagin. All they talk about is running away to fight. To distract them, Private Gladstone stages sports. Cricket is proving popular and I take Fred to watch. Mrs Kriel said Corporal Johnson told the Welfare Committee there are no orphans here: 'They all have fathers who can lay down their arms and fetch them home should they wish to.' Two boys, barely ten, got caught taking bread from a hands-upper girl and were made to dig out the latrines. Mrs Botha donated her water ration so they could wash but they went down with typhoid and weren't seen again.

'The Spiritualists,' Mrs Kriel went on, 'claim this place is buzzing with psychic energy. I expect it is. The whistles never stop.'

The noise here is so constant I barely notice the whistles: three sharp bursts easily lost among all the shouting and coughing and beating of blankets and fretting over fires and children somehow managing to play. I'd sooner notice silence. By night, the whistles are all too loud. Folk from even deeper in the country than me believe a child can't die in the presence of light, even the faintest tallow candle. So, to them, Lights Out is a death sentence. The English know this but still enforce darkness. These poor mothers tend whatever feeble glow they can. Consequently, there are fires – a tent of five perished last night. A braai smell hangs over all, appetising until you know what it is.

'Every whistle is an angel getting its wings,' said Mrs Kriel, towing her daughters, as always. 'I expect your good friend Helen is one of those who attends the deaths.'

She does not. Helen hates the grief hags, the wailing women who crowd the tents of the sick, swaying and praying, feasting on sadness. As soon as the whistle goes up they drift off to the next. We passed their coven the other day and Helen cursed them. They call themselves the Sick Comforters. Their leader carries a child's doll clad in black because she says it comforts the little ones: 'Who could afford to miss the prayers, the counsel, the consolation of the dying which are never so effectual as when they are breathed in pain and never so wise and gentle as when they are spoken by one half over the border, almost in sight of the Far Land?' It must be said the English have no truck with these orgies of sorrow.

I cover my mouth now because of all the coughing. Everybody is scratching away. Measles, typhoid, even suicide, some say: the Reverend can't keep up. He looks fit for the grave himself, flapping from dying here to dead there.

Just now I caught Fred crushing an ant between thumb and finger. 'It got in,' he said blankly. 'It got in.' Fred who used to cry for every crow you shot. I've never seen him hurt another living thing intentionally. It grieved me more than I can say.

Wednesday 16 January

Last night a whistle close by. Fred slept on but I sat up straight. The moon was nearly full and milked through the canvas. I dread the end–of–summer rains but surely they'll have to give us beds then. I heard a woman crying but she was drowned out by a weird prayer-song. The grief hags. I pressed my face so close to the canvas my breath sucked it towards me. I daren't peek out. They hurried closer as some lanterns approached and paused outside before passing over. Then the whistle went up and more crying and somebody shouted, 'Shut up, shut up, for the love of God, shut up!'

Fred's stomach gnaws itself in his sleep and I stroke it gently.

Thursday 17 January

His first words this morning were: 'I'm hungry.' It's the same every day. As always, Mrs Kriel pretended not to hear. Helen says they get extra bread at the school so I'm going to have to send him. He's excited but I can't bear the thought of letting him out of my sight. I've told him to pretend he doesn't know any English and to do as he's told. I've said you'll test him when you get back.

'It's lessons or labour,' said the corporal at ration time. 'He can fetch water from the river, build him up a bit.'

'He's only six! He can hardly carry himself two miles.'

'Or he can dig out the latrines, we're having to make them deeper.'

'No!'

'Do you like digging?' he asked Fred, who nodded then darted behind me. 'I've seen the little walls you make in your tent. Do they work? This country is full of pests. We're building walls too and fences.'

They're trying to defeat the land itself, dividing it into neat squares to stop you from moving around, to corner you. They call them 'drives' and head out of camp in the morning whistling. They return reeking of smoke with carts piled high and brag of the size of their 'bag'. Yesterday they 'donated' a piano to Mrs Kriel's choir but I admit it's a pleasure to hear.

'He'll go to the school then,' I told the corporal.

'Will he? He likes digging so much we could probably use him out at the cemetery. It'll be measles season soon, when some rain finally arrives and we've an end to this heat … and there's always the typhoid you people bring in; he'll be kept busy.'

'My son is not one of the Kaffirs you set over us.' I stepped back, took a deep breath. 'And he's only six, he's no good to you. He'll go to the school, school will be fine.'

'And what about you, Mrs van der Watt? What skills do you have?' He paused and appraised me as you consider ewes at market. 'Perhaps in the officers' laundry? We pay one shilling per a hundred items. I'm told the wash-house air is a good deal more fragrant.'

'Perhaps,' I said, not knowing if I meant it or not. 'Perhaps while Fred is at school but I have so much to do with sweeping the tent and fetching wood and water and the queues are so long. But perhaps.'

'Perhaps,' he said and I gripped Fred's hand as we left.

I dropped him off this morning – Reverend Fernie doubles up as the teacher. The Kriel children were already there sitting in pairs. I tarried by the door, watching Fred sit down at the back, and smiled at the pastor who nodded without stopping his lesson on Noah and the Ark. I stood listening to the animals go in two by two until he laid down his chalk and turned to me. I ran off to find Helen who I've not seen since our feast.

Helen is a hands-upper. I know. Don't be angry. I wanted to walk away when I realised but I couldn't, not when she had all our food.

'It's not what you think,' Helen said, stringing the meat on her knitting needles. 'I had to.'

'Nobody has to, Helen.'

'Liese was sick, the coughing, there was blood. Hands-uppers get to see the doctor first so I signed. And now I get the good card so I can buy extra for you and Fred.'

'But you're not in with the rest of them.'

'I paid to get moved.'

'How? You've no money.'

I wish I hadn't asked. 'All women have currency,' said Helen, in horribly coy English, not caring about those who paused to watch what passes for excitement here. 'We sit on it.' She let that sink in. 'The English are very happy to cash it in. And the Welsh. And the Scottish. And the ones from Australia and New Zealand. The Indians are especially grateful.'

I was disgusted. I wanted to go, but where? She was cooking our meat and Fred would be hungry after school and I was too. You can't escape an argument here – we wander round and round all day dragging our stories in the dust. There's never a private moment. Sometimes on the farm I craved company but now all I want is to sit quietly under the mulberry with you and Fred. Was Helen one of the perfumed women at the railway station that day I first saw you? I pitied them jostling on the platform, gazing up at approaching trains to welcome back the miners, gaudy hot-house flowers turning towards indifferent suns. Or did this place turn her?

'My man's out there as well, you know,' Helen went on, holding our meat over the feeble flames. 'They came to our place. Didn't take them long. They burnt the rest then sent me and Liese to Vereeniging by the Val, full of mosquitoes and God knows what. Write and complain, they said, but I can't, then Liese got worse and nothing worked, not the tea, the bleeding, nothing. So, I paid the only way I could and got us here but she was so weak and hot and … '

Helen looked down. Her tears seasoned the meat. 'The smoke,' she said, smearing her face with her apron.

We ate in silence, leaving most for Fred and Liese. Helen took her tiny parcel off to the hospital and I took mine to the school. You can't leave anything out here. Monday was our last full meal. Today is Thursday.

Friday 18 January

I keep reaching for Fred and panicking but he's at the school, he's at the school. There are lots of Freds here so whenever I hear his name my heart drops.

I tried to rest but Mrs Kriel wasn't getting the hint and suddenly seemed to have lots to do. Even she appears a little slimmer or at least less glutted. She smoothed what she calls her waist and asked to borrow my sewing kit to take her dress in. I looked in her mirror and my cheeks are hollowing. Her little Kaffir does all her chores and only sweeps out her half of the tent.

'Have you tried the black camp?' Mrs Kriel asked.

'The what?'

'The black camp, dear, on the other side of Bloemfontein. I'm fortunate to have my girl but the Superintendent understands a woman of my stature can't be without help. The delicate families of white refugees must be housed before anything is done for the Kaffirs. In any case, they're used to living outside so it's perfectly possible for them to erect their own shelters and find food as they did before we arrived.'

I thought of Lettie and Jakob and the cosy lean-to by the sties with the bright white curtains that stopped me peeking in. What would they make of such a place?

'I don't imagine it's so bad,' said Mrs Kriel. 'It's not as if they burn in the sun and camps will stop them running wild. A wife arrived yesterday and her daughter had been ... attacked. The Kaffirs are rising up all over, like they always wanted to, now we're not around to keep them civilised. We're safer here. When this is all over our husbands will come for us and things will go back to normal. You'll see.'

It seemed for ever till school finished, so I stood around while the Reverend ended his lesson. Fred was embarrassed and I had to prise him from some other boys. The Reverend says he's doing very well but seems to be getting a bit of a cough. All the way back to our tent he recited the alphabet in English faster and faster until one letter leap-frogged the other and on the Z he started coughing and couldn't stop. He seemed fine when he left this morning. 'It's

73

just the dust, Mama,' he said. Everybody here coughs all the time and not daintily into handkerchiefs. He let me carry him back the rest of the way.

Saturday 19 January

Five whistles last night. They're getting closer. The nearest woke Fred – I told him it was the soldiers in the guard tower spotting a lion on the veldt. He coughed all night, a dry sawing. Mrs Kriel tutted before rolling back to her snoring.

He seemed a bit better this morning so I let him scamper ahead – they do a half-day on Saturday. I fetched my broom. Lettie would make short work of this place. Hot winds whip across the veldt and stir the red dust into little devils which sweep through camp like rumours. Whisk one out then in whirls another. Some women have stopped bothering altogether. There's a great deal of sitting about, especially in this heat. We wait and wait and while we wait we are eaten alive by flies and boredom and memories. You didn't like Mr Micawber but I admired his hopefulness: something will turn up. What? Victory? What is victory now? A clean, well-fed child. We all just want to go home. Except Fred who actually wants to go to school! I wasn't back an hour when he drifted in alone, I don't know how he found me. He said he'd been sent home. I can't believe they let him wander on his own. He fell asleep right away and I'm watching him as I write. His forehead is hot. When he wakes up I'll ask Helen to fetch whatever she can to build him up.

My own hunger is a sort of anxious emptiness. I feel like I might float up to the top of the tent. It's worse knowing there's plenty to be had – decent food is only a simple signature away. If I sign the oath I can get Fred whatever he needs.

The women who've stopped cleaning, who give in to the waiting, get their rations cut. So, they just end up hungrier and dirtier. Then the Welfare Committee intervenes and a cadre of volunteers arrives with brooms. Mrs Kriel gives this work her blessing but can't help, not with her ankles. If one woman surrenders her neighbour often gives in too. Low morale spreads like the cough. I sweep for Mrs Botha who just can't manage. Fred asked her how old she was and she laughed and told him her story. She came inland as a baby on a cart with her family on the Great Trek after the English stole their slaves. They didn't want to be taxed or troubled again. Somehow, they survived the massacre at Weenen when the Zulu smashed babies against the wheels of their wagons. She lost her husband in the last war and now her people are scattered. She can't shift for herself but is mortified to be anything less than immaculate. She wears several loops of beautiful jet beads 'in mourning for our brave Republic'.

'They're eating our country up. Since Old Testament days when was a whole nation held captive?' I couldn't answer her. Fred submits to her attentions, he's never had a grandmother. She's teaching him chess, of all things – we're white and the English are black. It's strange the things you see in here – tin baths with no water to fill them and rocking chairs and elaborate bedsteads. Reminders of how near, and far, we are from home. I've saved a tiny amethyst of lavender soap which I cup in my hands until it warms. It's the only thing in here that still smells of itself but it shrinks every day. That first night at your parents', I found a linen square of dried lavender under my pillow. It was so luxurious. I kept meaning to plant some and make my own but we were always so busy. The stench of this place permeates everything and everyone. I smelled something like it once before – I pressed my bridal flowers in a book and opened it on our first anniversary and sweet rotten flakes fell out. I burned them in the stove and didn't tell you then worried about what it all might mean. Not everything has to mean something, my mother said.

I'd not seen Helen for a day and a night and found myself missing her. I asked after her at the shops which only fuelled more gossip – the one commodity they always trade. I even looked for her at the latrines. When she stumbled into our tent she was in a state – her face half-clean from weeping. Fred woke up and started coughing and crying all at once.

'She's worse,' Helen sobbed. 'They say it's the malaria, we just have to wait. She needs dung tea, not this quinine they go on about, but –'

'Helen, please,' I said, pointing to the high-backed chair Mrs Kriel had acquired. 'For Fred.' Slowly she eased herself down. The sore on her thumb now covers half her hand and she worried at it idly, barely bothering the brazen green flies beading it. I longed to wash it but looked away.

'Quinine costs too much, they say. I told them if they fed her proper she could fight it but they say she can't even keep milk down. They open all the doors and windows all day, all night, fresh air, fresh air, fresh air. I gave her my blanket but I bet the doctor took it, that bastard. They won't let us keep them with us, won't let us wrap them up to sweat the fever out. Five minutes we get! Fresh air!'

I felt my hem for the remaining coins and thought about what they could do. Without Helen we'd have no meat or soap. If she didn't shop for us we'd have only what they expect us to be so grateful for.

'I can't take your money,' said Helen, as if I'd offered. 'I couldn't.'

I didn't argue and as I burned with relief she toppled forwards. Fred yelped and rolled aside as I braced myself too late. Her dress weighed more than she did. Her face was meat hot and dry as Bible paper, her cheeks rouged with fever. I rolled her off, worrying briefly about lice. Fred shook her arm.

She didn't move – it took barely an hour for poor Oupa to go stiff. But for Fred I would've screamed though nobody would have come. If we ran to every cry we'd never sit still. I pressed my cheek to Helen's lips. I could feel her breath on my face so I ran out for water. When I got back she was sitting up with Fred in her lap, looking round like nothing had happened.

'Liese,' she said. 'Got to go.' And she was gone. Fred drank her water but his cough didn't ease.

Sunday 20 January

A letter! Private Gladstone brought it this morning on his bicycle. Fred begged him for a go and he said yes but I refused. This place is dangerous enough.

'Delivery for "Mrs Sarah van der Watt and Fred," said Private Gladstone. 'Someone's popular!'

The folded note was on rough paper and had no envelope. 'Didn't have one,' said Private Gladstone, mounting his bicycle. 'Saved me opening it. Intelligence, remember? Church in fifteen minutes!'

I assumed it was from you – if it was then you must still be alive. Then I imagined you lying injured as you wrote it. Fred was jumping round shouting, 'Pa, Pa, Pa!' I snapped at him to sit.

No, not your handwriting. Nevertheless, my eyes rushed to find comfort in the contours of your name.

Mevrou

Jakob is with God now, Nkosi. His heart gave on the train. We buried him by the tracks to Bethulie. I am in the camp here. We have no food or water but what we beg. They say we must work in their camps but no. Not all here are Christian. What of home? Bloemfontein is nearest so I send there. I thank the priest who wrote this. I pray for you and the baas. I know Fred is living, Nkosi. Sing him my lullaby, you know it.

Lettie

Lettie's faith in us does much to restore me. I can't bear to think of her in a place even worse than this and all alone. I will pray for her.

Mrs Kriel says somebody stole the Union Jack from the Assembly Ground last night so all tents are to be searched after church. I'm going to bury my diary in the patch worn smooth where I sleep.

Oh God, Samuel. They took him. Two hands-upper women carried him off to the hospital. Two of them for one of him. I tried to stop them, I did everything I could. Private Gladstone pinned my hands behind my back then threw me in our tent – said if I came back out I wouldn't get visits. Where were you? Fred's in there for his own good, they say. I'm pressing his blanket to my face and breathing him in now. I don't know where Kriel is and

I don't care. It's nearly Lights Out so I must be quick.

It started after church.

'I didn't see your good friend just now,' Kriel said.

'Her daughter is in the hospital, so she'll be trying to see her and she's not my good friend, she's –'

'She's … ?'

'She's helpful, she's kind … '

'To some, perhaps, at night.'

'Helen is a good Christian mother!'

'Well, if her child is in their hospital that's even more reason for her to keep in God's good graces. A coffin is the only way out of there.'

To see her sing in the choir, her bosom heaving like bellows, you'd think Kriel was actually holy. I walked ahead to the latrines. We wordlessly went to opposite ends. I grabbed the wire trying not to think about all the hands that held it or what was below. Kriel shrieked and pointed. We all looked down then there was hooting and some women spat where she was pointing. Mired in the bottom of the trench was a mess of red, white and blue. A pair of hands-uppers bustled in blowing whistles then Khakis came running excited for something to do – their faces fell when they saw their flag. We were all sent to our tents.

Arriving back, I found Corporal Johnson and Private Gladstone, who did a little bow to Kriel which anyone but her could see was facetious. All my things were laid out neatly –blankets, sewing kit, cooking things, my church Bible and Fred's gun. His christening cup wasn't there. How long had it been missing?

I reached down to pick my Bible up but the corporal blocked my way. As I dodged round him I felt something behind me, a dim animal sensation. Then I was choking. Private Gladstone held me in the crook of his arm.

'It is an offence for a prisoner to lay a hand on a soldier,' he hissed, spit speckling my face, voice unrecognisable. Blood pounded in my ears. I focused on the texture of his khaki sleeve unfolding in front of me like a vast muddy landscape pitted with craters and just as everything blurred I fell to my knees. He unfolded a handkerchief from his pocket and cleaned his hands – I marvelled at its brightness, its neat edges and wondered who ironed it for him. 'You don't get to touch us,' he said. 'Not that way.'

We were all in a tableau. The corporal's eyes widened. Mrs Kriel gawped. Fred, thankfully, was still walking Mrs Botha back from church.

'At least you're calling us what we really are,' said Helen, appearing from behind our tent. 'Prisoners.' Her English, learned on her back, is not perfect. But the Khakis got it.

'And what exactly are you?' asked the corporal. 'A thief? A spy? A whore? You're all the same: scratch the thin white veneer and we find the savage below.'

Just then Mrs Botha arrived with Fred. She held his hand and spat at the Khakis, cursing richly.

'Bit too old for the Bird Cage, that one,' laughed Private Gladstone.

'But she's not,' said Corporal Johnson, pointing at Helen who turned to run. 'Search her, Private, her hidey-holes aren't hard to find.'

Gladstone grabbed Helen and she bucked and kicked as he rifled through her dress, pulling out a fork, a pink ribbon and a scrap of red, white and blue.

'Souvenir, eh?' said the corporal blanching beneath his red. He took the scrap and folded it as I had folded letters from you. Helen kept kicking and tried to bite Gladstone. What had she left to hide?

'My cup!' shouted Fred, pointing as it fell. Helen looked down and went limp.

Mrs Kriel swelled and bellowed, 'Thief!'

I couldn't believe it.

'The quinine, I needed,' Helen gasped, her head drooping as Gladstone cuffed her hands behind her back. 'Liese.'

All the while Kriel's little Kaffir stood smiling. Gladstone went over to her, bent down and handed her a bread roll and a couple of shillings. 'Good girl,' he said and she skipped off leaving Kriel slack-mouthed.

'Intelligence,' he said. 'Where did you think all them rations was coming from? Eh? And proper meat. That mirror, your chair, all them blankets? Eh?'

Kriel shook her head. 'I just thought … She told me she was doing extra work in the laundry. I didn't know.'

'Didn't want to know,' hissed Mrs Botha.

'A week in the Bird Cage,' said Corporal Johnson pointing at Helen. 'And a stay in the hospital for that boy of yours, Mrs van der Watt. Nasty cough.'

Fred darted into our tent but the corporal pulled him out by one arm and dangled him as he shouted, 'Pa!' Gladstone held me so I couldn't even move my arms. All I could do was shout, 'I love you,' and, 'It will be all right, I promise.' Mrs Botha cried, 'Devils, devils, taking our children!' Women ran from all around. Kriel just flopped in the dust, mumbling and demanding to speak to the Superintendent.

Lights Out so I'm finishing this by the moon, which is going too. Knowing you will someday read this, believe this, is all that's keeping me sane. I don't think I could tell you face to face. I talk to you in these pages and in my dreams. Can you hear me, Samuel? Come for us. We need you.

Wednesday 23 January

The sun has never taken so long to rise. Whistles all night and each one was *Fred-Fred-Fred*. I wanted to go to him but can't risk losing visits. I'll run to the hospital as soon as the trumpet goes. I can't find his gun, I'll get it back, I'll get him back.

No trumpets today but lots of shouting so I peeked out. 'She's dead,' cheered Mrs Botha, buoyed by distant catastrophe. 'Look!' She stabbed her cane at the Union Jack sagging to half-mast. Gladstone cycled by sporting a black sash shouting, 'Assembly now, Assembly now!'

Off in the distance from the kopje above Bloemfontein came gunfire like bursts of fat in a frying pan. Was that you celebrating? Are you really watching us? A crowd pulled me along to the Assembly Ground all rigged in red, white and blue bunting threaded with black crêpe. A Khaki was shouting, 'God save the King!' Their band was playing a slowed-down version of their national anthem.

All I could think was Fred, I've got to get to Fred. Now they've got him I see there's nothing I wouldn't do to get him back. I looked round for Helen but she was still in the Bird Cage. Did she even know? Would somebody take her water?

'Ladies,' said Reverend Fernie, adjusting his robes as he ascended the low wooden platform. 'Ladies, please!'

His words settled like dust before blowing away again with all the excitement. Kriel, trying to gather her choir, looked like she might actually cry. 'Witch,' cackled the woman next to me. 'Queen of hell!' Hell, hell, hell.

We closed round one another like boks at a watering hole. I felt even hotter and lighter and swayed but was held up by the press of bodies. My eyelids drooped as the corporal walked on.

'Respect!' he bellowed as Khakis lined up behind him, bayonets glinting. 'Respect for the Reverend!'

'Last night we lost our Queen,' stumbled Reverend Fernie. 'And our Royal Family – our Empire – lost a mother and grandmother.' Some current thrilled through us all. He pushed his half-moon glasses up and glanced back at the soldiers, their expressions stuck between church boredom and parade-ground pride. Nobody seemed quite sure what to do or how to be.

He went on. 'We can be sure Her Majesty departed this life for the next as certain of her place there as here. Finally, she is joined again with her beloved and faithful husband, Albert, their daughter, Princess Alice, and their son, Prince Leopold. Her passing serves to remind us all of our own mortality. Compared to the glories of the everlasting the sufferings of this life are mere moments. Exodus 15:18. *The Lord shall reign for ever and ever.* Indeed, he does even, and especially, when he is not to be seen moving among us. In times of grief, of war. Her Majesty's faith sustained her through her long and eventful reign as your own does now.'

'Deuteronomy!' came a voice from behind me.

'Yes!' came another. 'Do not quote our book at us!'

'Silence!' demanded the corporal, stepping forward. The Reverend flapped him back with his robes as the first voice went on, 'Deuteronomy: When you enter the land the Lord your God is giving you and have taken possession of it and settled in it, and you say, "Let us set a king over us like all the nations around us," be sure to appoint over you a king the Lord your God chooses. Do not place a *foreigner* over you!'

The corporal couldn't comprehend her but understood the cheers as the crowd surged forward carrying me with it. He put his hand on his holster and bellowed, 'Today is a day of mourning across the Empire. As such, everyone is excused labour except those digging graves. And now, the National Anthem.'

Mrs Kriel turned to face her choir and raised her arms. 'The Anthem!' The band struck the first chords and she windmilled to silent singers. Then the Deuteronomy woman started singing our anthem, the end to every church service, the tune you hummed when happiest: 'With songs of freedom, citizens, we'll sing of this dear land so bright.' From somewhere else came the next line: 'It's freedom from foreign chains.' Corporal Johnston snapped his fingers at Private Gladstone who hesitated on the edge of the boiling crowd. The corporal shouted, 'Louder!' at the band then to Kriel, 'The words!'

'The words,' she stuttered in English. 'They cannot all sing English.'

'Just the chorus,' said the corporal, miming conducting. '"God save our gracious … " Then everyone will join in.' He pointed out at all of us, squinted into the sun and shouted, 'Or there will be no water!'

The band drowned out our brave few as Mrs Kriel leaned pleadingly towards her choir who half chewed a chorus.

'Amen,' said Reverend Fernie. Then we scattered.

I headed for the hospital and found a mob at the gates, some waving visiting orders, others trying not to slosh cans of water. The gates stayed shut. After some minutes a grimy little face with blond hair was held up at the window by a nurse. We turned as one and cried, for he, she, could have been any of ours. After a second a doctor pulled them both back.

'Fred!' I shouted, not caring any more. 'Fred!' And with that a chorus went up. 'Anna!' 'Dede!' 'Jan!' We shook the gates till the wire rattled but still no one came out: 'It's visiting day! We've waited! We demand our five minutes!'

Then from all around the camp rose a *clang-clang-clank* as pots and pans were taken up and struck with spoons, shoes, hands. With no Khakis to keep order we ran amok.

'They do what they want,' shouted the woman next to me who looked half Kaffir. 'Starve us, keep us like animals! You cannot keep us from our children!'

Fred was in there. I shouted his name until my throat was raw. A gang led by the Kriel boys headed for the shops. 'We're going for the hands-uppers,' one stout lady cried, shaking a broom, and everybody followed.

So, I was the only one left when the hospital doors opened as if exhaling for the final time. A young nurse came out shuffling carefully in men's boots, carrying a limp bundle wrapped in a sheet. It was only ten paces but each step took for ever. I was glad, didn't want her to reach me, didn't want to know who she was carrying – the floppy limbs a cruel parody of sleep. I noted how horribly light her burden was. As she reached the gates a Khaki stepped out and opened them gently. Up close I could see the nurse was younger than me, Helen's age. I reached towards her bundle but couldn't touch it. Tenderly, she lifted the cowl.

Smaller – so much smaller – and thinner – so much thinner – and younger – so much younger – yet so much older, Helen's face looked back. Liese.

I must have screamed because the soldier stepped forward. Helen needed to know, she had to say goodbye, I had to tell her. I fled into the crowd pulling me this way and that. I tripped on my hem and it ripped – our coins, our chance. I stopped to look but was getting trampled so had to go on.

There were no guards at the Bird Cage. Nothing of value here.

'Helen,' I panted. 'Helen!'

Silence. Could she hear in there?

Rifles cracked from the Assembly Ground and shouts turned to screams. Flinty smoke drifted over, a cold relief from the usual stench.

'Sarah?' Her voice sounded like bandages ripping.

'It's me,' I gasped between gunshots. 'Helen, I –'

'Go away!' Her voice stronger now. 'You let them take me, I only took your cup because Liese –'

'I know, it's all right, you –'

'You'd do the same.'

'Yes,' I said. It's true. I'd do anything for Fred. You would too. Maybe after all this Helen can come home with us and we can plant new trees and get new horses and chickens and forget. I don't care whose anthem we sing. I fell against the fence wailing, trembling against the tense web of wires scratching my face and pulling my hair. I couldn't tell her, I couldn't.

'Sarah,' she croaked. 'Water.' A pause. 'You crying? Is that guns? Are they here? What's going on? Sarah?'

The walls wobbled feebly.

'I … ' My voice was barely a whisper. 'I'm sorry.'

'Sarah? I can't hear. It's all right, I'm sorry, I should've asked, I'm sorry –'

I forced myself to shout, 'It's Liese.'

At this the machine gun in the guard tower rattled to life and two Khaki Kaffirs appeared, their paws everywhere, their triumph total as they dragged me away. I bit the hand over my mouth. They dropped me. I looked back at the Bird Cage. If I could hear anything above the chaos it would be silence, not just the absence of sound but the total impossibility of articulation, a throat stopped for ever with grief.

Monday 28 January

All visits stopped. We're confined to our tents. A doctor at the hospital gate said their patients are getting better all the sooner for it. I listen for whistles day and night turning this way and that like a frantic bird.

I think they surprised themselves with the machine guns. Our 'uprising' stopped right after. Ten killed ('trampled') and dozens hurt. Afterwards the hands-uppers searched every tent and the Khakis let them take anything 'suspicious' – rings and nice things mostly. I wonder if anybody found our coins. Kriel has never been back and all her things are gone. Good.

I woke to find Fred's gun. Somebody laid it in our tent in the night. It disturbs me that I didn't hear. He'll be so happy. I picked it up, took aim, then held it to my face, summoning him from the grain. I pulled the tent closed and dug for my diary with my hands. I dreaded Mrs Kriel's Kaffir had spied me writing but no, there it was. Not many pages left. I didn't expect so much to happen.

The whole camp is being punished. We're watched even more closely. Helen is still in the Bird Cage and I can't get to her, they say she's mad. Crates came from England marked *South African Women and Children's Distress Fund* – we've not seen their contents. Every morning we're dragged from our beds by hands-uppers and marched to the latrines then the Assembly Ground where we're made to sit in tent-neat rows. We're forbidden to speak in case we try to spread some message. We eat on the ground like Kaffirs: bread as dry and hard as the anthills it's baked in and maybe a slice of mouldy pap. Only half a cup of water now. I pray for rain so I can put a pot out. We're only allowed up to use the latrines but our chaperones don't always look away. Some ladies simply go where they sit. I remember over and over our picnic among the flowers and Fred trying to catch the bees and how we stayed out till the fireflies lit our way home. They can't stop me thinking.

And every day the sun rises just the same.

Mrs Botha died last night. She didn't have the cough or the spots but she wasn't as strong as she liked folk to believe. I think it was a broken heart. Her whistle went up just before dawn. I thought I'd cried all my tears but this brave old soul was so kind to Fred. She flew for them when they took him. I try to imagine my own mother fighting for me and all I can see is Anna gently brushing the farm tangles from my hair. She's part of the farm not the family, said my mother when she sold it all off after Father died. Maybe right now she's pulling herself up to her full five feet and facing down the Khakis. Is she in Brandfort or Volksrust? Vryburg or Ladybrand? We're constantly told that this is one of the best – those who pay to escape Bethulie say bodies lie unburied where they fall. They say the Khakis take whatever they want at night, that their doctors try new medicines on our children,

I've seen countless animals killed on the farm, plucked a thousand chickens but until Mrs Botha I'd only ever seen one dead person up close – your father, God rest his soul, laid out in the cathedral while mourners filed by for days, longer in winter than they could in summer. My father was buried before the letter arrived saying he'd passed away. There's no wood for coffins now, the living need it more than the dead. The last one I saw was made from old crates stencilled with *MILKMAID*. It had a picture of a smiling rosy-cheeked girl with brimming pails and was carried by two boys barely ten. It scarcely bothered even their shoulders. They walked it to the cart where the Reverend hurried a prayer as a hands-upper stacked it on. Ten minutes is the time allowed for funerals now. After, the Reverend handed the slightly taller boy some kind of receipt, which he screwed up and dropped. Nobody knows exactly where their loved ones end up because we're not allowed to go to the cemetery. Escape risk, they say. Where would we run to? The whole country is a prison.

We made a shroud for Mrs Botha. Her neighbour helped stitch her blankets, hurriedly fixing her hair and arranging her dress. She's with her husband now.

I'm glad she'll see no more of this. The neighbour nudged me. My eyes followed hers to the loops of jet round Mrs Botha's neck. I felt their dark glimmer. 'No good in the ground,' the women whispered, reaching forward. 'She won't mind.' I slapped her hand and she backed off. I pricked my finger looking away as I put the last stitches over Mrs Botha's face. As I finished two Khakis arrived, one fresh off the boat, part of the great reinforcement we hear about. His boots and eyes still shone. I couldn't lift Mrs Botha alone so he stepped forward. I sucked the blood from my finger as the cart rolled off. 'Waste of blankets,' said the older soldier.

Fred, Fred, Fred. All I want to do is write his name over and over and over. There's a rumour visiting is back on tomorrow so I must look well and strong. I've got a plan, Samuel. I will get our boy back but you must come for us. And Helen. We need you.

Tuesday 29 January

It's true. We're to be admitted in groups of five for five minutes. 'You are not to touch patients or staff,' said the corporal. 'Do not tire patients by speaking to them. Do not bring food. Any displays designed to cause upset will be stopped immediately and all visiting orders rescinded.'

We nodded as one. I would crawl on broken glass for just the chance to see Fred. I get in at 4 p.m.

He's alive! Fred is alive! Our boy. He was awake and his cheeks burned bright but he didn't have the spots. He asked for his gun and I said it was safe. I wanted to touch him and reached out but stopped – the mother next to me kissed her daughter's forehead and a Khaki just lifted her up from behind and carried her out kicking and yelling. The rest of us just sat there and bade our babies do the same with long-practised looks.

Fred was bound with linen strips to a big iron bed. Nurse Kennedy said he'd been getting up to find his mummy. She had a sing-song accent, said she was Scottish. It was she who looked after Liese and carried her out. I was glad Helen's daughter got to see at least one kind face. I asked to sit on Fred's bed and she nodded but the doctor said no. Fred felt smaller, barely bothered the blankets tucked round him. He was lucky to have his own bed. There were some adults too but nobody visited them. All the windows were open and flies hurried in and out settling where they liked. Fred's nose twitched as they danced round his nostrils. I daren't even brush them away.

He didn't cry, you'll be proud to hear. At least not when I was there. His face and hands were spotless and not one louse on his blankets. He did smell of brandy. From the doctor's breath, it's not just the patients who take it. There was a blackboard for lessons.

'Malaria,' Nurse Kennedy whispered. 'We think. He can't seem to put on weight but we are feeding him, I promise.' I nodded. I believed her, I think. He needs what Helen was talking about. The quinine.

The bell rang and I mouthed 'Thank you' to Nurse Kennedy as we were all pulled away.

Quinine. I must get the quinine.

Wednesday 30 January

Captain Hume, the Camp Superintendent, has offered to meet some of us to 'clear the air'. Reverend Fernie got me five minutes with him. I hear he's Scottish, like Nurse Kennedy. I'm going to ask him for the quinine and see about getting Helen out. She's my only friend here, the only friend I've ever had, apart from you, Samuel. I need her help.

I want to sleep but can't and feel sick constantly. My belly is a parody of pregnancy. I know you wanted more children. We imagined them all playing together and helping on the farm as we grew old. You can never be as disappointed in me as I am. Until I get Fred back I've got our whole ration. It all tastes rotten. I started writing back to Lettie but couldn't tell her about Fred and refuse to lie so just left it. I will spend the rest of the day praying. I'm not sure God can hear me here.

Thursday 31 January

Rain in the night. No thunder, no lightning, just a deluge so momentous the parched earth couldn't drink it all. I couldn't tell if it was falling or rising. Water bled through the canvas. Fred's little ant barrier washed away. He's dry in the hospital, that's all that matters. I ran around piling our things up then put a pot outside which filled in minutes. Then it was over. I doubt anybody slept except the hands-uppers in their cosy feather beds. When it rained at home I'd roll over to your side of the bed and find the place where you let me nestle, stroking my hair until it was time to get up for the animals. Memory makes a mockery.

At Reveille I splashed outside. The dust is now mud with children jumping in it, their mothers grabbing them back and slapping their legs. Let them play. The air is clear for the first time in weeks. Oh, and the smell, that wonderful clean charge rising from the soil tugging my spirits with it.

The wagons keep arriving. It's the feeding of the five thousand without the miracle. Today I queued for three hours, shuffling in mud, my skirts getting heavier, hoping to get rations before my appointment with Captain Hume.

'Ladies, a problem,' announced the corporal. He raised both hands to quiet the immediate groans. 'Your rations are coming but the weather means they'll be late. You'll just have to wait.'

'All we do is wait!' came a shout. 'Wait for you lot to go back!'

The corporal got the message and sat down quickly. I ran to the front ignoring the shouts.

'Corporal, I've got an appointment with Captain Hume at 9 a.m.'

'And?'

'If I have to wait here I'll miss it.'

'And you won't get another, Captain Hume doesn't take kindly to waiting. So, which is it?'

I'd been hungry since we got here. One more day wouldn't matter. I need to get Fred's medicine and I need Helen's help.

A Khaki Kaffir marched me to Captain Hume's tent. It was four times the size of any other. A sodden Union Jack twisted round the flagpole. Several women waited, some holding papers, one pinched her cheeks to pink them. Two Khakis stood extra tall outside, rifles crossed. The Kaffir gave my name and I was waved right in to shouts of 'Not fair!'.

Captain Hume was pinned behind a vast mahogany desk snowed with paper. 'Ah, Mrs ... ' He fished a sheet from the nearest drift without looking up from what he was writing. Behind him hulked a heavy carved bookcase with every shelf packed.

Queen Victoria glowered toad-eyed from a gilt frame shrouded with black crêpe. A brass chandelier hung from the central pole and animal skins covered the ground, some digging their way out. I coughed.

'Van der Watt, Mrs Sarah van der Watt, sir.'

I extended my hand. He half stood leaning forward and patted his pockets like he was looking for something.

'Pardon me,' he said, replacing the lid on his blue glass fountain pen. 'You speak English?'

I nodded.

'Good.' He gestured to a cushioned dining chair. 'War manners. Please, sit down.'

I sank onto it feeling my bones settle through my skirt. So, this was Captain Hume, the face of Empire barely visible over teetering folders. At least twenty years older than you with thick silver hair tamed into a side-parting and a boot-black moustache clipped over resolute lips. His eyes danced behind me to dismiss the waiting soldier then wandered over his paperwork again before finally settling where my face should be. I was pleased to see flies buzzing even in here.

'Now, what can I do for you Mrs … van der … ?'

'Watt. My son is in the hospital, he – '

'He's getting the best of modern medicine, let me assure you, Mrs van der Watt. I hear all the rumours – the fish-hooks and poison, but none saddens me more than those regarding our brave doctors who come all the way out here at great personal risk.'

'He has malaria, they say.'

'Yes,' he said. 'A little early for measles though the rain is finally here.' He paused and picked up a sheet of paper blue as a baby's veins. 'Maybe we'll have an end to these flies! Last month we had twenty-five malaria fatalities, sixty-two from typhoid as well as 152 scurvy cases and that's just your lot. I myself have terrible toothache.'

He patted his jaw. I wondered which of the orderlies who let me in shaved his face this morning. My gaze shifted to the bookcase and I tilted my head. All in order: Balzac, Burns … my eyes ran along to Dickens and all the ones we longed for: *Bleak House, Great Expectations!* His library beat your father's. Sitting right by *Hard Times*, filled with freshly sharpened pencils, was Fred's christening cup. I had to laugh.

He swatted the air pointlessly. 'Mrs van der Watt, are you quite well?'

'Yes, I, I'm sorry.' The word choked me. 'Nurse Kennedy says my son needs quinine.'

'Nurse who? Well, yes, if he does have malaria and he's not too far gone he could be in with a chance but, you see, there's a queue.'

'A queue?'

'Yes, perhaps your admirable English doesn't stretch that far.'

'I understand. But my son has no part in any of this. He's just a boy, he's six —'

'All soldiers were just boys once upon a time, madam. I am reliably told I was one myself. But you must understand we have limited supplies. A queue is a queue.'

'I can pay.'

'Pay?'

'Yes.' I pointed over his shoulder to Fred's cup. 'With that.'

Captain Hume glanced back at his shelf filled with other people's things then leaned forward and squinted at me as if I was very far away.

'I am not quite sure what it is you're alleging but whatever it is, you cannot pay –'

'I can –'

'And there simply isn't enough quinine. Did they not tell you at the hospital? As you can see, I have a great deal of work, reports to Pretoria, telegrams to London. Next week we are being treated to a delegation of lady inspectors from London, Miss Hobhouse and her Liberal friends come to see how well we keep you all. Suddenly everyone wants to know what's going on out here. I simply don't have time '

'Please … ' I slid to my knees. 'Fred is only six and if he doesn't get this medicine he –'

'He may very well die, yes, I understand, and I am not unmoved but you cannot ask me to put one of my boys in his grave instead.'

'Captain Hume, you are a Christian man, I beg of you, please have mercy.'

'Mrs van der Watt, a queue is a queue and I cannot break with procedure –'

'You will not.'

'Get up!'

I stayed kneeling, hands knitted in prayer, and closed my eyes.

'You're making a scene, woman. That's it! Private!'

'Please!' I wailed. The Khakis picked me up and carried me out dropping me in the mud where I knelt weeping. The next woman stepped round me hoping for better luck.

Friday 1 February

More rain. Down it comes and in pour the spiders. They never bothered me at the farm, Lettie got rid. These are bigger: plate wide and whip fast. One scuttled over my face as I tried to sleep and I pulled the place apart looking for it. I will kill it. Each leg lifts with independent purpose and is covered with tiny hairs that hold droplets of water. They rear up flashing black and yellow undersides. As a child, it was the chameleons I hated, stone-still, unnoticed, watching. Now the spiders horrify me.

Every tent is moated by pots and pans filling musically drop by drop with pure, delicious water. We're all drunk on rain. Finally, we can see our neighbours' faces. We tell one another how well we look, ignoring the rashes and scabs, the spreading sores, the fever kohl ringing our eyes. Faces painted with disease. I'm saving some water to wash the hospital off Fred.

Helen got out, I don't know how. I was waiting for firewood wondering why you'd bother to put up a silk parasol when I felt a tug at my sleeve.

She was a sight. Nearly Kaffir black, despite the rain. Her lips were split and her gums were bleeding. I embraced her like a sister or as sisters should. She was just bones. We stood holding one another till the queue moved.

She was oddly calm, the usual crackle gone. 'Liese' was her first word. I bobbed my head hoping a small gesture would be less painful. I told her how Nurse Kennedy had carried her out and how I'd prayed for her in the minutes allowed before they carted her off.

'Where?'

I pointed in the direction of the cemetery, an hour's walk.

'Where exactly?'

'Her marker is a Bovril jar filled with white pebbles. I scratched her name on with my darning needle.'

'And Fred?'

I shook my head. 'Hospital.'

She strode away shouting back, 'Courage, courage!'

It's nearly Lights Out and she's still not back. Some say the rain is uncovering the dead; that the Reverend is out there praying over a vast pit of bodies.

Saturday 2 February

We're confined to our tents. They say it's too slippery out, the hospital is inundated with broken limbs. Another day with no rations. I feel so light. I might blow away in the winds that have come with the rain. It's so much effort just to lift my head. Writing is exhausting but it's all that keeps me going. I'm sorry it's so messy now. I have to pray standing up because of the mud and turn Psalm 34:17 over and over: *The righteous cry, and the Lord heareth, and delivereth them out of all their troubles.* Am I not righteous? Has He forsaken us? What did we do, Samuel?

Somewhere in the middle of the day hope visited. Mrs Botha's tent was filled by a new family – a mother and four children. Not yet cowed, they sang: 'With songs of freedom, citizens, we'll sing of this dear land so bright.' Then free voices from all around: 'It's freedom from foreign chains, May our Republic ever live.' The Khakis couldn't rush around in the rain silencing us all so I let my voice soar. I was joined in the last line by Helen! She burst in soaking singing, 'Protect our home with vigilance, because liberty's our lord!'

After a great burst of clapping and cheering Helen sobbed, 'I found her, I found her, and we can save Fred, I know.'

We spent the rest of the day planning and praying. I can't believe she's willing to do this for me, for Fred, for you – who she's never even met. She says there's no other way. She's not seen me writing in my diary before now and asked if she was in it and beamed when I said of course. She says it's not very neat and you don't have to be able to read to tell that. I promised to teach her after all this. It felt good to make a promise again.

Samuel, I begin to think you might never read this, which is perhaps for the best. I couldn't bear for you to witness my shame. Perhaps after I bury it tonight they will bury me and it will never be discovered. Perhaps you are already dead. I don't know. But I must keep writing, if only for myself.

Monday 4 February

The rain stopped and we queued for rations under a rainbow. God's Covenant, said everyone I waded past, smiling in the mire. Their joy irritated me. This mud contains a thousand chamber pots. I try not to think about it. The Welfare Committee is paying some Kaffirs to lay eucalyptus on the paths. I almost miss the dust.

Helen and I waited together. Everybody saw her leave my tent this morning. Far from raising her up to respectability our friendship seems to have dragged me down. Such teacup fripperies seem mad now. Visiting is tomorrow so we must act quickly. As we reached the front I tasted fear or maybe just a new flavour of hunger.

'Mrs van der Watt,' said the corporal, snatching my ration card. 'I see you've gone down in the world since Mrs Kriel.'

Helen did her best impression of demure.

'Tamed, are we?' She nodded vigorously. 'Then perhaps we'll have order at last.'

'I was hoping to see my son again, Corporal,' I said, knowing the answer already.

The corporal shook his head.

'But he needs medicine.'

The corporal shrugged.

'Maybe … ' Helen leaned in on cue. 'Maybe I could pay for a visiting order, help with the medicine too?'

'Your currency is devalued, *mevrou*. Next, next in line!'

Helen blushed even under the dirt. The corporal laid down his pen.

'Unless Mrs van der Watt has something to spend?'

Helen shook her head and tugged my sleeve. I looked down at him and thought of Fred.

We're to meet in the Bird Cage at midnight. He promises to bring the quinine. Helen and I had a horrible fight – I should never have let her volunteer herself. We didn't even have the luxury of shouting. Round and round the tent we went, unable to sit in the mud, unable to stand still, until I stopped and she ran into me. Her whole body pressed into mine, a benediction of bones. For the first time since you left, I felt seen. Even in the dark. For a moment the whole camp was quiet. We stood like this until I had to go. As the tent flap fell behind me Helen whispered, 'God help us.' Forgive me, Samuel, I beg you.

The sun is up and looks no different. I didn't sleep, I'll never sleep again. Helen did. Every time I close my eyes I see his face.

We got the quinine. Visiting is at 4 p.m. I'll take it to Nurse Kennedy and pray it works.

I did what I had to, Samuel. I imagine you've done things. Will you ever read this? I don't think I could bear you to. But here is what happened.

As I slipped through camp three more whistles went up, three more funerals. Not Fred, not Fred, not Fred. The Bird Cage gates were open. Corporal Johnson sat in the cell, his cigarette blinking red in the dark.

'I don't have much time,' he said, patting the plank bench. 'Her Majesty's funeral tomorrow, lots to do.'

I sat arm's length away. He spread his coat with obscene courtesy.

'Now, now,' he said, shuffling along. 'We won't get anywhere fast like that.'

As I leaned away he swung me round onto his lap and started pulling at my skirts.

'Let the dog see the rabbit, Mrs van der Watt.'

I slapped his hands away.

'That's more like it, eh, still got a bit of fight?'

He held my face in his hands then leaned in and spluttered, 'No tooth powder in those rations. Never mind, the old chap is less particular.' In one familiar movement, he dropped me to the ground then clamped my head between his knees. I felt a scream form but he tilted my chin up and slapped me hard then shushed me as he unbuckled. As his belt clanked I closed my eyes, pressed my lips together and thought about the apricot blossom pinking on the breeze and the gingham curtains I made and anywhere but here and anything but this as he curled my hair in his fists and pulled my head forward then leaned back, tilting his hips, damp heat rising and then …

His knees fell apart. Blood pounded back into my ears. I opened my eyes.

He slumped drunkenly, his features frozen between pleasure and surprise. His left eye stared unseeing. The handle of my breakfast knife stuck out of his right eye. I patted my apron pocket. Empty.

Familiar arms lifted me up from behind.

'Hurry,' whispered Helen, stepping past and rifling through his pockets. 'Help me! Be quiet!'

I stood staring then retched until my empty stomach held less than nothing.

'Yes!' she hissed pulling something from his jacket pocket. She handed me a phial. I ran out and read the label in the moonlight. It said *Quinine*. It said hope. Helen tossed the corporal's coat on the ground then straightened it out as he had moments before. 'Help,' she asked. I took his shoulder. He landed face down, head propped at a hideous angle. 'For God's sake grab the hem.'

'What? What are you doing? They'll –'

'They'll what? What'll they do? Grab his coat and they won't know anything!'

As we slid him across the floor slick with blood and mud he rolled onto his back. It was raining hard again, there would be no patrols. Drops bounced off his unblinking eyes.

'Come on, you bastard.' Helen kicked him.

'Where?' I croaked, slipping, looking all around, anywhere to avoid his stare.

Helen took a deep breath, renewed her grip and pulled hard towards the latrines.

As we splashed back, the Southern Cross rose above us in the midnight dark. Did you see it too? Where are you, Samuel? Where are you?

PART TWO

I

March 1976, Johannesburg

Rayna's Monday was a day to cut out and keep. Due to a quaint outbreak of measles half her class was off so she got quality time – that's what it's called now – with her favourites. You're not supposed to have favourites. Why can't all children stay five for ever, she wondered, as she read aloud the Simplified Scripture of Daniel in the Lion's Den. Afterwards they made collages of lions and she let them squander paper on extravagant manes. She told them how her parents had taken her to Kruger when she was little and she'd seen real lions and how in her grandparents' time lions were everywhere but now they were penned in big reserves safe from poachers.

Rayna loved the school's smells: powdery palettes of paint, tiny perfect suns of colour; the secret papery darkness of the stationery cupboard where hyacinths were forced; even the boy's-toilet tang of the glue pots – the smell familiar if not pleasant. Chalk dust floated for ever in shafts of sunlight. She enjoyed cutting out sugar paper, turning it in her hand to make complex shapes. If a child was very good she snipped out a special zigzag-edged star then wrote their name on it and tacked it high on the wall. After her probationary month she was presented with her own pinking scissors with a neat typed label on the handle: *MRS BRANDT – TEACHING ASSISTANT*. Today she cut out whole skies of stars. She remembered herself as a little girl, rushing home waving a glowing report card. Her parents used to be so proud.

Rayna had always been good – an only child, everything she did somehow meant more. Every success a triumph, every failure a tragedy. She wished for brothers and sisters if only to share the attention. You must always set an example, said her mother and father, both teachers in and out of the classroom. Then it happened. On the way home from her last day at school. She was freshly sixteen. She never told them, never told anyone. She still got her matric but told her parents she didn't want to be a teacher any more. While they were still open-mouthed she got engaged to the most serious of the young vergers from their church, the one who always looked genuinely pleased to hand out hymn books. Pieter was equally surprised by Rayna's hasty interest but she knew she didn't have much time – always slender, she'd be showing in weeks not months.

Pieter's hair was the colour of cornflakes. He was big and broad as the church doors – a classic *boerseun* who'd completed his National Service in the South African National Defence Force with honour. He was gentle to the point of barely there on their wedding night so she wondered if he wanted her at all. That night and every night after, and most days too, she tried not to think about what had happened. The tall thin man with the straight red hair that caught in his constantly blinking invisible eyelashes who said he'd been sent by her father to collect her, who just had to stop on the way, who invited her in for a Kool-Aid, who dropped her home after. *Now I know where you live.*

After the wedding, her parents rented them an identical four-bedroom house two streets over and even though it wasn't far she felt a bit safer. Little Piet arrived long before their first anniversary. He had none of Pieter's colouring or quiet but nobody mentioned this. Her son seemed to have absorbed all her anger, to have spent nine months soaking in rage. She let him cry and cry in his cot until he was as red as his hair and when she caught Rose or another of the maids shushing him she found them a floor to sweep. Her mother popped in on her lunch break most days to find Rayna still in her housecoat smoking with the windows closed while Rose cleaned round her. Six months of boiling tears and unasked questions sent Pieter, who'd dreamt of the pulpit, upcountry to the mines. Rayna didn't try to stop him. For weeks after, she slept with her fists clenched dreaming that when she opened them in the morning she'd find newly pressed diamonds.

There was no question of divorce, not for a young white couple. She couldn't even keep a salesman on the stoep without a neighbour running to her mother. After a couple of months Rayna couldn't take their looks any more. Just as suddenly as she'd married Pieter she moved her and Piet out of Brakpan to one of the new high-rises in Hillbrow by the newly minted Central Business District.

She loved the airy anonymity of her new apartment. It was small enough to make do without a maid, which only shocked her mother more – she dusted and polished furiously banging the hoover around. There were always different faces in the lift and when she looked out across Johannesburg from her veranda on the fifteenth floor she saw the jacarandas bloom, purple roads branching across the city like veins on the back of a hand. The blooms pop-popped under the wheels of the pram as she pushed Piet around, pausing as strangers peered in exclaiming over his straight red hair. Hillbrow was whites only but it was full of whites from all over the world – from England and America, here to cash in. Every evening she stood out on the veranda in the cooling breeze which carried sirens and whistles from the townships. Never as far away as she'd like. The Hillbrow Tower soared over the city – over the whole continent – and she fancied she could hear laughter and glasses tinkling in the revolving restaurant on top. One night she stood out there and let her housecoat slip off. The air held her naked body. The next night it did the same. And the next. Here among all the high-rises she was just another person in the sky. Back in Brakpan everybody knew her, knew her parents, thought they knew her story. After a few months of this she found herself thinking maybe she could pick her son up when he cried and not think about how high up they were, how easy it would be to let him go.

Pieter never sent any diamonds but did pay all their bills so she didn't need a cent from her parents. They made a show of turning up for Piet's first birthday and cheered when he blew out his candle. But she was glad when they left. Every Sunday she visited for lunch – said she'd been to St Michael's in the CBD but never did go. Faith was another thing she'd lost that day. As soon as Elise had taken the dishes through she'd bundle Piet up and head back to their apartment.

This way four years passed. The faces in the lift kept changing but everything else stayed the same. Soon Piet was at school. Rayna answered all the other mothers' questions easily enough. *His pa is upcountry at the mines, yes, it's hard but we all have our cross to bear.* Coffee invitations were issued but she always found excuses, knew she couldn't withstand sustained polite enquiry.

Piet was getting too big for their apartment when Rayna's parents flipped off the N1 at seventy miles an hour. She never imagined them driving so fast. Once her great-aunt had rustled back to Pretoria, predicting that Joburg was about to 'go Kaffir', she moved back into her childhood home and kept on Elise. She had no brothers or sisters to share her grief. Mourning inoculated her against gossip, for a while. She went back to church unsure what she was look-ing for and found the tiny initials she'd etched with her thumbnail on the family pew. She retraced each letter as gently as the pastor made the sign of the cross on her forehead. Otherwise she only left the house to take Piet to school. Sadness shifted beneath her ribs like a deep-sea animal. She seemed to care more for her parents dead than alive. Just as the curtains started twitching – too much grieving was as bad as too little – Pieter came back from the mines. He showed up one Friday while she was serving the dinner Elise had cooked.

She practically pulled him in the door know-ing the neighbours would be scandalised by a man kept standing on what was still technically his own stoep. She made sure to smile as she closed the front door.

He sat at the head of her parents' old table eating macaroni cheese and answered all Piet's questions about diggers and tunnels and cave-ins before saying he was tired. From the inside pocket of a jacket with shop-stiff sleeves he produced a small dull-looking stone, said it was a diamond in the rough. Piet took it from him and cradled it in both hands like an egg that was about to hatch. Elise cleared the table more slowly than usual. Rayna went outside for a cigarette. Of course, Pieter didn't smoke. She stood there alone puffing up into the sky wondering what might happen next. When she went back in Elise was carrying sheets over to the couch. This relieved and enraged her. That night, she thought about going to him. She had her hand on the banister then peeked down and saw a tiny comma curled up by his back. She crept back to her parents' old bed and lay there staring at the plain wooden crucifix looking down on her. She stood up on the mattress, steadied herself against the wall and lifted it off. Where to put it? She'd feel it under the bed and Christ couldn't go in her underwear drawer. Tenderly, she laid it in the bottom of the old dark-wood wardrobe next to her parents who waited patiently side by side in matching plastic urns – she'd collected them from the crematorium, convinced they were still warm. Finally, she slept. In the morning, Pieter was gone and Piet grew quiet as if good behaviour might bring him back.

Over the next few days the neighbours invaded with casseroles and questions – her mother's old friends, mainly. She couldn't keep fending them off. Every casserole taken in guaranteed another inquisition when she returned the clean dish – she couldn't send Elise with them, not if she didn't want to be completely ostracised. Actually, maybe that would be just the thing and they'd finally leave her alone. One morning she even let in the Jehovah's Witnesses because anything was better than waiting for another neighbourly knock or watching the clock till school was done. Rayna started longing for the little apartment, for the city unfolding from her balcony. She caught herself talking more and more to Elise, almost wishing she would sit down at the table with her instead of always being so shamingly busy. Growing up with Elise to do everything for her she'd never really thought about Elise's own children – three of them. Elise explained that it took her two hours to get to work what with queuing to show her pass and all the stops the taxibus had to make, then another two hours to get home. Where did she find the time?

Dropping Piet off one morning she spotted a bright yellow advert on the noticeboard seeking a part-time teaching assistant. Even though she had no qualifications, she was married and a mother, and her parents had been teachers. That seemed to be enough. To spare Piet embarrassment, she volunteered for Year 1, when they're sweetest anyway. She assisted Mrs Bun who clucked and fussed round each new pupil saving her best smiles for them. Rayna tried to help but Mrs Bun liked everything done her way. Precisely her way.

Mrs Brandt picked up her special scissors, felt their reassuring weight and cut out the final star of the day. In the middle she wrote *RAYNA*. As the last bell echoed her thumb fairly ached. She waited for it to stop and reunions to recede before going to get Piet. She planned to surprise him with a stop at that new American burger place he'd pestered her about. Mrs Bun nodded goodbye as Rayna tidied up, carefully slipping her scissors in her handbag so she could cut a star out for Piet at home.

She lifted her coat and went out into the empty corridor. The linoleum was end-of-day sticky and made tiny kissing noises as she walked. By the main doors she spotted Piet. Towering over him was a man. She hurried. As she got closer a dark-haired little girl peeked out from behind the stranger.

'I said I'm sorry, darling,' he was saying, kneeling down. A navy raincoat slid off his arm onto the floor. 'Goodness was late again so your mother has had her hands full and Daddy had to leave the office to come and get you.'

Piet, with his embarrassing tendency to try and charm any potential father within smiling distance, beamed up at him. As Rayna reached them she automatically leant down to pick up the raincoat.

'Thank you,' the man said, his eyes shining beetle-black as he reached out. Rayna didn't let the coat go. Neither did he. Could feelings pass through fabric?

As she started to blush Mrs Bun pushed back through the doors. 'My driving gloves,' she sighed, shaking her head. Then, seeing the two of them, paused and smiled tightly. 'My, what a lovely couple you make.' The man took his coat and his daughter and left.

That night the phone rang – a rare event in the Brandt household. The sound excited Piet, already high from Cokes at the burger place. He hoped it was his pa. But Pieter had never called. It could be the mine boss to say there'd been an accident. Rayna took a deep breath, unclipped her red plastic gerbera earring and snatched the receiver up between rings.

'Miss Brandt?'

It was the headmaster's secretary, Mrs Kurt, the one with the face like the bottom of an apple. She sounded even more pleased with herself than usual. She couldn't be more than five years older than Rayna but dressed like her mother.

'Mrs Brandt … yes.' She felt the line cool.

'Miss Brandt, I'm sorry to have to ring in the evening like this. I did try earlier but –'

'I took my son to that burger place on the way home.'

'Oh.' Mrs Kurt seemed suddenly unsure, shaken by the outrageous everydayness of such an outing. But surely a woman who fed her only child American fast food was capable of anything. 'Oh, well, I'll be brief then. The headmaster has asked me to thank you for your efforts with Mrs Bun's class and to inform you that you're no longer needed.'

'Needed' sounded a lot like 'wanted'. Mrs Bun had come back for her driving gloves but stumbled upon something else instead, had felt the thrill of static, seen the look in the eyes of the pert young helper whose husband was never around. Mrs Bun couldn't be sure, of course, but was the school really willing to take such a risk?

'But … ' Rayna began.

'Of course, you'll be paid until the end of term,' said Mrs Kurt, with the finality of a filing-cabinet drawer closing.

Piet's head appeared around the door followed by Elise lingering to test the air. Rayna twined the curled cord around her fingers until they striped red and white then turned away in case she cried. She began to stutter 'Why' but said, 'Thank you,' then wished she could take it back but just hung up instead. She jiggled the receiver to make sure it was properly down then shouted, 'Bitch!' at the phone. Freed from the cord, her fingers throbbed, which was oddly comforting.

'Who was it, Ma?' Piet asked, stunned. He'd never heard her swear, never heard any adult swear, but of course knew that word, and more. He could say all sorts in Afrikaans, English and Zulu from the garden boy.

'Go watch the TV,' she snapped and Elise ushered him away. Her fingers fumbled as she tried to clip her earring back on and she dropped it. Down on the carpet she leaned against the wall and squeezed back tears.

2

After a week in bed, during which she devoured three whole Danielle Steels, Rayna got up and got dressed. She told Elise to bring her all that week's *Die Burgers* and flicked through them at the kitchen table ignoring news of trade embargoes and townships. She only needed the recruitment pages.

It shouldn't be hard. There were acres of well-paid jobs for people like her. No to teaching. No to secretarial because she couldn't type. She liked the idea of travel but couldn't get away, not with Piet. The school hadn't found a reason to send him home, which was one good thing. South African Railways were advertising for a ticket sales assistant — the hours looked right and the pay okay. She called and explained that yes, she could speak English, and *ja,* she could come in on Monday for a trial day.

That weekend she dug out Piet's old train set and the pair of them let it run round and round the living-room floor. Sitting on the Axminster carpet she noticed how worn it was and tried to remember what colour it had started out as. She looked up at the ceiling and registered cream turning beige. She hadn't decorated since her parents passed away and they hadn't touched it since they moved in when the house was new in 1955. The carpet was older than her. Outside, rooftiles were slipping and guttering slumped drunkenly against peeling walls. Rayna made do with Elise and a girl who took the laundry and a garden boy but they were often late and getting later. She felt ancient when Elise called her *Miesies* but it did no good to be familiar. Her mother always said: you need them to respect you, not like you. They're basically children. She knew they'd all work harder with a man around. She'd use the money from her new job to fix the place up and give the neighbours a little less to talk about.

On Monday morning she drove out of Brakpan and followed signs for the CBD. Her old apartment building rose on the horizon up ahead. Doors locked, windows up, breath held, she sped through Alexandra – plastic bags, whipped up by traffic and dust devils, whooped through the air chased by dirt-black children. It's not votes they need, she thought, it's brooms. How could people live like that? Every roof was corrugated so all of Alexandra sloped like the shoulders of the men standing in packs by the road. If Rayna ever turned off (and it didn't occur to her that there were whole streets, whole worlds out back) she'd see women hanging out improbably white washing, line to line, stretching as far as the eye could see, a river of clean sweet laundry where the road couldn't soil it. This was where Elise, her husband and their three children lived, not that Rayna had ever seen their house.

Rayna's heart lifted when she reached the sparkling streets of the CBD where everybody rushed about their business. She was even happy to wait in traffic as it gave her the chance to admire the men in their suits and the neat secretaries. She opened her window and felt the sun on her arm. The biggest building by far was the glittering granite façade of Johannesburg Park Station. *The Biggest Train Station in ALL Africa* promised the sign. She was shown around by a woman a bit older than her, and a lot bigger, who mentioned each of her five children in the first five minutes. The job seemed straightforward. Rayna nodded lots then gave the woman her papers. She glanced over them then showed Rayna to the ticket desk. Above it hung a picture of the old station, a big Victorian glasshouse too beautiful and fragile for now. Apparently, the government moved it piece by piece to another part of the city. Rayna opened the drawer of her new desk then reached for her handbag. Carefully she lifted out the still shiny scissors and laid them tenderly in her new drawer.

JPS was vast and constantly filled with a fresh tide of people. Still, so many years later, Rayna kept watch for the man with straight red hair. Her customers were always in a rush but one or two stopped to talk, old ones mostly, on their way to visit brothers or sisters – never sons or daughters – on farms. Nowhere-places deep in the country like Bethulie and Ventersburg. Some bought one-way tickets, claiming the city was going down. She just nodded. The city was always going down. That's why she didn't watch the news if she could avoid it. Whatever was going to happen would happen, whether you knew about it or not. Still, she'd noticed prices rising at the Pick n Pay and she couldn't always find the green apples Piet loved. Rayna had a lot of time for the country people, proper old *Boerevolk*. Often, they seemed unsteady as if the world was moving too fast around them. They came in looking lost wearing clothes they'd probably made and she marvelled at their museum accents, kept them talking so she could savour the sounds. They were equally fascinated by this young woman with her make-up and earrings who was exactly why this country was going to hell. Trains went out from JPS to every corner of the great and good and brave land that her parents had prayed for every day and night – to the Karoo, which looked like the moon; to Cape Town, so beautiful she was bored hearing about it and would never go just to spite it, and just up the road to Pretoria, where the business of politics was done. The men in suits with boxy briefcases never stopped to talk.

Until one day one of them did. She'd clocked him before. He was twice her age, at least forty – same sort of age her pa was when he passed away. Like all the rest, he wore a navy-blue suit but his shoulders actually filled it. Maybe he'd been an officer in the Defence Force. Under his trilby he wasn't bald, in fact he had thick black hair but it was very badly cut. Here was a man who could be handsome if his wife allowed him to be. He came to her counter with the correct change so had no reason to linger.

'I'm from Pretoria,' he blurted as the queue shuffled behind him.

'I guessed,' Rayna nodded. 'I just sold you a ticket.' She beckoned to the lady leaning round him. This old goat is looking down my blouse, she realised, so leaned forward to shame him. He blushed goodbye but was back next day. With the wrong change.

'I'm in the Finance Ministry,' he said, reaching through her window. 'Always accounts to settle.' His fingers, nails neatly trimmed, found the ticket but Rayna didn't let go immediately. Their wedding rings tinked.

'I'm Johannes.'

Rayna smiled, pointed to her name-badge and said, 'Next.'

The next day he arrived a bit earlier. With a haircut. He picked their conversation up where he'd left off. 'We're having to come in more and more.' He lifted his briefcase so she could see it. 'Foreign governments just don't understand the need for blacks and whites to live and work separately. We're having to stay late. Do you happen to know a decent hotel?'

'The Paradise Inn,' said Rayna. It sat slowly crumbling by a junction she got stuck at most mornings. Every day she expected the flaking stucco façade to be pulled down. There was so much building going on. Walls were the thing now, and fences. The following Monday, Johannes was back and Rayna asked how Paradise was and he managed a laugh remarking that it was very, er, colourful but the restaurant was surprisingly good, their bobotie more than passable. Would she like to try it?

Every Thursday after that, Johannes had to stay over for business and every Thursday Rayna went straight from work to the Paradise Inn. It was indeed colourful. If Rayna and Johannes realised some mixed couples occasionally checked in they said nothing, not even to each other. Best not think about the laws. Sometimes they even ate the bobotie, the cumin overpowering the minced meat. It was all she could taste when they were safely in their room and he kissed her with an accountant's precision. Johannes had excellent table manners.

Between the two of them they did nothing to prevent Irma arriving. He just assumed she would, although Rayna couldn't ask her uptight English doctor any more than a married man could walk into a chemist and ask for condoms. When Rayna started showing Johannes found less and less to do in Johannesburg. Before she grew indecent, as her boss said, she was put on unpaid leave. At home, she had all the groceries and things delivered and got Elise to take Piet to school but that didn't stop other boys calling him the names he brought home. She grew fat on Danielle Steels and scheduled the baby's delivery date to coincide with Piet's half-term trip to Kruger so she wouldn't have to find a sitter. At the hospital, she hinted at a terrible mining accident and news soon spread so the nurses lavished her with sympathy, which she felt only mildly guilty about.

Rayna was expecting another boy so was delighted by Irma. Piet barely glanced in the cot but Elise was enchanted, fussing with her springy blonde curls. Rayna couldn't afford more than three months off and Elise was happy to look after Irma who was proving to be a very good little girl. Johannes turned up at Rayna's counter her third week back. He seemed surprised to see her. She was even more surprised when he asked to meet again. Same as usual.

For the first time, Johannes didn't get to his feet as she walked towards him, something her father always did for her mother even at home, an old-fashionedness she'd secretly enjoyed. She knew she was a bit late but this wasn't why Johannes remained rooted at their usual table.

'This is Irma,' she said, while the waiter pulled her seat out trying to work out what delicious new drama was unfolding. 'Your Irma.'

'Irma,' repeated Johannes, stunned. He raised his hand and the waiter flitted round. 'A bottle of wine, red, the house will be fine.' He never drank. 'And the bobotie for … ' Suddenly the thought occurred to him that maybe the baby might be hungry too, might eat, might be real.

The waiter hovered as long as he reasonably could, clumping the leather-bound menus closed before buzzing back to the kitchen, freighted with the thrill of impending disaster. Irma slept in Rayna's arms. The man on the next table eyed her like a bomb about to go off but his wife – the woman who'd checked in as his wife – could barely contain her curiosity.

'Ooh,' she cooed, peering into Irma's tiny face then glancing to Johannes oblivious to the tension. 'Just like her father.'

At this Johannes jumped up, threw his napkin down and blustered out muttering 'Excuse me' to everyone just as the waiter arrived with the wine.

'Sorry, dear,' whispered the unlikely wife, sliding back to her table. Rayna started to get up but struggled to hold Irma and push back her chair. Everybody stared but nobody moved. The waiter put the wine down then pulled her up and she half ran across the silent restaurant.

In the lobby, she saw Johannes disappear upstairs and started after him but stopped. Directly ahead was a man she'd not seen for a very long time: still tall, no longer slim. His hair was thinner but still straight and red and as he blinked it caught in his invisible eyelashes. She remembered the cold brush of his steel watchstrap through her school blouse as he reached across to lock her side of the car. The unvisited smell of his house. Her mouth filled with the taste of Kool-Aid.

Rayna backed into the alcove at the foot of the stairs and felt Irma wriggle, willed her not to wake. She couldn't get past him or climb the stairs without being spotted and both actions relied on being able to move. *One room, one night, no luggage,* the clerk said loudly. The man stabbed the paperwork with a pen then paid cash, refusing the change which the clerk pocketed before reaching back and easing a key off hook 27. The man – she would never know his name – turned towards the stairs. Her knees began to give and she held Irma closer as he headed straight for them. He looked like the kind of man she sold tickets to every day. He smiled politely and she felt her mouth mirror his. Then suddenly he was past them and practically skipping upstairs. He didn't even look back. She couldn't move. The next customer, who had been sitting waiting, leapt right up. The clerk didn't pass this young woman a form, didn't ask her a thing, just reached back and slipped the second key off hook 27. Irma grizzled as the girl tottered towards them. Up close she was pretty in that yellow way but Rayna couldn't tell exactly how young. She took the stairs in red heels that gaped at the back revealing raw rubbed ankles. Rayna looked at her hair, imagined taking a pencil from reception and sticking it between thick black kinks she knew it would not slip from. Not everybody's papers matched their face but this girl clearly had no business at the whites only counter.

Rayna hushed Irma then somehow put one leg in front of the other and walked out of the Paradise Inn towards the payphone in the car park. Room 27. She repeated it with every step. 27, 27, 27. She picked up the phone and called the police. *Now I know where you live.*

3

September 1993

Dr Beck is the one man Irma has always known – apart from her brother, but he's long gone. The doctor is a do-gooder from England. She's having to really concentrate because her English doesn't stretch to medical words. The school-blue plastic chair next to hers sits empty. Rick promised. She tries not to look at it, feels it growing emptier with every glance.

Dr Beck double-clicks his mouse with a ta-da and turns the monitor to face Irma who leans across his desk, one hand on her belly that she thinks is fat but which will never be this flat again.

'Here.' He points with the white plastic pen which yells *TRIPTOPAN FOR MIGRAINE* along its length. He clicks it so he doesn't mark his screen and points to a sonar swoosh of black and white: 'Aaand right here. See it now?'

Irma doesn't know exactly what she's looking for but has seen stuff like this on a thousand soaps so nods anyway. The doctor who did her scan at the hospital last week peered into his screen for ages before asking the name of her doctor and saying not to worry.

'So, I'm having twins?'

'No, well … what we see here *now* is a single foetus with estimated maturity of eight weeks and a strong foetal heartbeat … '

'Single?'

'Yes, single and strong, a big heart – *moerse*, you say.'

He pauses, still pleased, decades after landing here, to deploy a local word: 'There is also, you see this black space here, a fluid-filled cavity with the remnants of a second yolk sac.'

Irma sounds 'yolk sac' out in her head rather than repeating his words aloud. She doesn't want this snob thinking her English is not so good.

'So, twins were, ahhhh, a technical possibility but it appears you are now having just the one.'

Dr Beck clicks his pen, turns his monitor around and they both sit back. She feels him try not to look at the clock ticking over the door behind her. He leans forward and scribbles on her file.

Irma memorises the technical words for Rayna. Nodding at Dr Beck she fumbles for the plastic bags by her feet – she spent all morning pushing a trolley round Pick n Pay trying to work out what to cook that would make her mother less likely to flip. She still can't get used to queuing with black people so tries to avoid looking but feels eyes slide over her. It's barely spring but it's good enough weather for a braai and she might feel less sick cooking outside. She feels the weighty coil of *Boerewors* sausage slip and slide in one of the bags as she picks them up and can't help thinking of her own insides, of yolk sacs. Her gums feel sweaty. Rayna's going to go nuts whatever she cooks. Not that she's any right, Irma huffs, two kids with two men, a truth that hangs over their house like the big summer rain. *Tande tel*, Rayna said, when she first asked about her pa. *Not for you to know.*

Dr Beck closes her file and looks up. He knows the girl's mother, has her file in one of the grey steel cabinets behind him, so isn't surprised to see her sixteen-year-old daughter like this. Briefly, he wonders if he's doing any good here and if London is still where he left it. At least the Thatcher woman has gone.

'And it's a boy, *ja*?' asks Irma, her intonation rising with her as she stands. 'You said "he".'

'Ahhhh a boy? Yes, well, we can't accurately determine sex until twenty weeks but he's a fighter, that's for sure. He'll be here mid-April. *Moerse.* Try not to worry.'

In the waiting room, a baby cries, louder as Irma opens the door.

Is it his? Rick knows it could be — he's got one for sure, at school already. He goes to watch her sometimes, perky thing with bouncy dark bunches, never looks back at the gate. The girl's grandma drops her off every day 8 a.m. sharp and he doesn't worry about her spotting him because he was never exactly introduced. The old *wyfie* is watchful. He never gets close enough to catch his daughter's name over all the bye-byes. He wonders if she senses her pa nearby, if some part of her feels a pull.

'Baby, you're not happy?' Irma meows, flopping her arm over his chest to pull him back. She twines his surprisingly dark chest hair round her ring finger and nibbles his earlobe like he likes. 'Baby,' she coos.

He springs out of bed then turns, his right hand automatically raised, shouting 'Fuckin', fuck, fuck!' Irma shrinks back on the queen-sized bed she considers proper luxury, a tuft of his chest hair still wrapped round her finger. Rick, born Eric but Rick to you, is twenty-one: own place, own car, own money. She doesn't ask too much about what he does or why he works every weekend. She might be dumb but she's not stupid and if he doesn't tell her she won't have to lie to Rayna. He half laughs, rubbing his chest, then stomps off to the toilet, hands covering his *piel*, which she thinks is kind of cute.

Rolling into the warm space he left behind she shouts to him over his thunderous pissing.

'So, Dr Beck says I'm two months already… that means he'll be born in April.'

A final forced trickle then silence. No washing of hands. Rick reappears in the doorway rubbing the pink patch blushing among the black tufts on his chest. He's decided not to be angry. He likes this young one, she's a good press and doesn't ask awkward questions.

'He?'

Irma sits up pulling the black duvet up to her chin and nods.

'A boy?'

She nods again.

'And he's definitely mine?'

Irma knows a man like Rick has got to ask.

'He's definitely a he and he's definitely yours,' she says, patting the bed then rolling out of the way as he does a funny little lion walk then dives at her, balls flapping.

4

February 1994

The white leather seat feels deliciously cold against Irma's back but the AC keeps puffing her fringe into her eyes so she has to pffft it out. Onyx Mascara seams her Honey Blonde. It's the middle of summer already and she's not got long. Dr Beck says it's definitely a boy. Rick has bombarded Rayna with more flowers and chocolates than Irma ever got so she's finally allowed him off the stoep. It's not the bribes that swung her, it's his determination to do right by her daughter. He's tried calling her Ma but that didn't end well. Nobody calls her Ma, not even her children. The air conditioning keeps breaking down so the three of them sit indoors cooking slowly rather than risk opening a window. Nobody wants to be one of the stories on the news. Everything is changing.

Irma watches the Winter Olympics in Norway. They cool her down. When she's alone she presses her face to the TV screen and breathes in the cold mountain air. She's learned more about snow and ice than she knew there was to know. The only event she doesn't like is the luge because it makes her think about giving birth, actually pushing. She was two when it last snowed in Jozi — remembers coldness turning all too quickly to wetness as it vanished in her hot hands, her brother trying to gather enough for a snowball. Rayna still says it was the only day a black woman could make a white man.

'Not far now,' says Rick, pushing up into sixth gear. He urges the white BMW through on amber. Proper *spog-motor*. Every rev, every gear, every envious look from all the lazy bastard hitchers. Doesn't do to be sitting at robots now: you're lucky if you just get jacked. Once they're in the car it's all over. The cops are too busy out in Soweto or wherever to help. All the news is full of the election but Rick doesn't think it'll happen, expects a revolution instead. Why not, eh? He watches the history programmes, knows how this stuff works. There's a sawn-off under the new pram in the boot and a machete in the glove compartment and at home a stiletto knife sleeps under his mattress. Whose side will he be on? With the grey old men from the NP sweating in their old grey suits? He's the wrong kind of white for the ANC lovers. He's no Kaffir lover but doesn't hate them either. They're all just customers. Same side as always, only side he knows: his own.

Rick is an entrepreneur who believes his time is coming. Where others see crisis, he sees opportunity. His whole life – no pa, no ma that acted like one – he's survived. Now he's ready to thrive, to hit his luck. And he likes this Irma, doesn't even mind her old ma. He's made enough selling dagga to the rich kids up at Witwatersrand to buy six gears and soon he can move out of his shithole rental and buy a proper house. If they've already been smoking the students ask him to stay and he sits on the floor, the only one not wearing black, the only guy whose ears aren't hiding under curtains of hair, and puffs deep on his merchandise. The beanbag crunches and squeaks as it moulds to his shape and it would be hard to jump up from this position but he could if he had to. He can feel every single one of the million little balls inside the beanbag. The students all talk English with this fake accent but they're as Afrikaner as him. He picks up new words: 'dialectic', 'hegemony', 'guaca-mole'. The guys ask him to do 'street talk' but he doesn't want to do that here and they don't dare push him: moffies never had to win anything but an argument. He listens to all their bullshit *praat* about the pendulum swinging and the new rainbow nation and nods along to their REM and Talking Heads. They're as glad as him that National Service is over – they were running out of degrees to do, starting to think overseas thoughts. But you know what, man, it's still the girls opening the beers. He catches a piece eyeing him, knows he looks sharp even stoned on a beanbag thanks to a hundred press-ups, sit-ups and crunches every morning. She turns away, burned, and her fringe bounces confidingly to her friend. They're nothing like his Irma – she's real. When he looks at Irma he sees himself reflected back in her big brown eyes: only bigger and stronger, a daddy soon. Irma makes him think he can do it all.

He steals a look at her now, seat belt straining across her bump. He didn't stick around to see the last one get this big. Definitely a boy in there, can see him kicking. He likes to lie with his head on her new big boobs and lay his palms across the world of her belly, lure his little man up to the surface like a fish then trace the outline of his tiny limbs. *Gross*, Irma wriggles, *gross,* but lets him touch her any way he wants.

On both sides of the road roll vast dirty yellow dunes, summer sun slides along their smooth ridges casting long shadows. Rick wonders how much it's all worth, this man-made desert dug out of the ground. The land is so poisoned nothing grows. Everybody knows the mess from the old gold mines is proper radioactive, that the blacks in the shacks on them are bubbling with cancers, that their women give birth to smooth dark tumours. Nobody makes them live there, thinks Rick. It's got to be cheap and they're closer to work.

Irma makes a little hiccuping noise as she struggles to sit up in the deep bucket seats. She reaches for the radio and it buzzes with 'Lesotho shooting … Mandela … de Klerk … calm' before Rick slams in The Boss CD and cranks it up. Her ritual 'Not again, Rick' is lost in 'Born In The USA'. But he sings and she joins in the chorus as he pounds the beat out on his white leather steering wheel. The track finishes as the suburbs of Brakpan welcome them home.

'It looks a good one, eh?' says Irma as the next track starts. For a second, he's got no clue what she's talking about so just grins then jumps another light, not liking the car behind. Night is falling, everything is falling.

'Oh, the pram, *ja*! I showed you – it's the Silvercross, trues God, from England. My little man is gonna have the best wheels, eh!'

She leans over as best she can and kisses his cheek, can't believe she got Rick.

'You're for sure coming Saturday, eh?'

'*Ag* … ' he smiles, knowing the chances of him turning up are at best fifty fifty. He doesn't want to be like his own pa. But he needs to be out there work-ing hard for his boy.

Irma beams at Rick and pfffts her fringe from her eyes then rubs the mascara between her fingers and wonders if he'd like her better dark.

5

27 April 1994

The ambulance is going nowhere.

'Can't you move it?' Rayna shouts at the driver who is radioing Johannesburg General. He's not even got the grace to sweat. She mops Irma's brow with a tissue from her pocket, which disintegrates into tiny snowballs that she then picks off.

Irma does her breathing from the classes. She summons the soothing tones of the stuck-up Lamaze nurse: 'Take a big sigh as soon as the contraction begins. Release all tension from head to toe as you exhale. Go limp all over.'

She tenses with the effort of trying to go limp. The paramedic – white, thank God – praises her. 'You're doing great,' he says. Then, to Rayna, 'Some day for it!'

The breakfast news showed pictures of people queuing before dawn at polling stations all over the country: in cities, towns, townships, out on the veldt, in churches, courthouses and huts. Black queues, white queues, ostentatiously mixed queues on university campuses and everybody waiting for it all to kick off. Rayna watched finishing her coffee and wondering what to do with her day since all railway employees had been ordered to stay home. She thought about voting but with Irma so close she couldn't go out and leave her, and anyway, everybody knew the winner. She wouldn't drive through Alexandra that morning for anybody. She knew what was coming and knew they knew she didn't have a man around. She looked out at her walls, the polite three feet of brown brick that was here when her parents bought the house new, the pinkish two feet they added after she left and now the extra five feet of barely set breeze-block. It was hell getting a builder – everybody was making their walls higher – but she paid the extortionate rate. Every brick made her feel safer until she wondered if the men putting them up were building in a weakness only they knew, if every wall could be sent tumbling down with just a single push in the right place. On the news de Klerk cast his vote then they cut to Mandela and that witch wife leering and waving in ANC crowds at a polling station, surprised-looking police the only whites there. Ballots, bullets, both can kill – she was proud of the thought, made a mental note to drop it casually back at work.

'Rayna,' Irma shouted, her voice slipping on the bathroom tiles then across the hallway and down the stairs. She probably wanted a fresh towel. The bigger she got the lazier she got but Rayna only pretended to mind. They'd grown much closer since it was just the two of them – as soon as he could, Piet had followed the man he thought was his father up to the mines. Now Rayna and Irma managed to sit together quietly and it wasn't having nothing to say or a loud sulk. The prospect of a new generation made it easier to think about the future than the past. Gradually, contentment accumulated into happiness. When Rick didn't show for the baby classes then didn't ask her to move in like he promised, Rayna was there to confirm that, yes, all men were the same.

'Rayna!' Irma yelled, panic fanning her intonation. 'MAAAAH!'

Rayna nearly dropped her coffee. When did her daughter last call her Ma? Gathering her housecoat round herself she ran at the stairs two, three at a time, bursting into the bathroom to find Irma marooned. The bathwater looked rusty, old.

'Why so much?' Irma sobbed. Rayna sat her up and kissed her forehead. It was hotter than the water.

'Don't!' Irma cried as Rayna stood and turned towards the door.

'I'm phoning Dr Beck,' Rayna said. 'I'll be right back.'

She returned almost immediately and helped Irma up out of the bath and into a nightie.

'You're having a baby,' she said, kicking a slipper out from under the sink towards her. 'That's all. Think I didn't bleed with you?'

Rayna tried not to look at the towel Irma was holding down there, willed at least a corner of it to stay white. She dashed back downstairs and paced by the front door looking out at the world divided into hundreds of tiny squares by security mesh. Every driveway was full, not a single person in Brakpan had gone to work today and there was no Elise. Not a single maid or gardener had come to work.

After thirty minutes of for ever the sirens brought neighbours out onto their stoeps once they were sure it wasn't the police.

A paramedic carrying a reassuring green rucksack rushed towards Rayna who pointed upstairs. She followed him shouting directions to the bedroom where Irma lay panting.

'Where's Dr Beck?' Irma cried.

'He's gone,' the paramedic said, kneeling down and peeling little round papers off some pads and sticking them on her chest before attaching wires to a monitor which bleeped frantically to life. She tried to pull her nightie over her breasts.

'Gone?' repeated Irma in that old annoying way of hers.

'Gone back to England, gone!' said the paramedic as the heart monitor hurried along and a second, fainter beat struggled below it, like waves beneath wind. 'We can't do this here,' he said, lifting aside the scarlet towel. Rayna nodded, never understood why hospital wasn't good enough for girls now anyway. He shouted downstairs in Zulu and the driver and an orderly appeared with a stretcher pausing almost imperceptibly on the threshold. No black man had ever set foot in this house, the garden boy stayed outside whatever the weather. There was a shed, they weren't cruel. Rayna couldn't look while they got Irma on the gurney, down the stairs and out the house.

In the ambulance the paramedic pumps up the gas and air and hands the mask to Irma telling her to keep breathing. Rayna squeezes Irma's hand and, in her head, does something she hasn't done for years: she prays. She thinks of the crucifix sitting at the bottom of the wardrobe, of her parents waiting side by side in their matching urns all these years. She promises to make it right if Irma and her baby are okay.

Irma breathes like she's learned then pushes when she's told, breathing then pushing, then screaming, muffled by the mask, the clear plastic fogging with pain. 'Jesus!' she screams, pulling it off her face. 'Ma!'

'That's the head,' says the paramedic, somewhat unnecessarily. 'Come now, Irma! Push, Irma, push!'

And so she pushes, feeling muscles she didn't know she had give way to a need that isn't all her own and out he comes, blue and still but beautiful. He gives no sign of having done all that kicking, of having floated up to his father's touch. He brings silence into the world.

Irma drops her mask and looks down as the paramedic clamps the cord, then another contraction crashes over her, throwing her back on the gurney. Why isn't her baby crying? When will this stop? Where is Rick?

The paramedic lays the baby, so much smaller-looking than he felt inside, on a blue hospital sheet and begins massaging his chest. Tiny blond curls press against his head like feathers. Finally, slowly, he opens his eyes and starts to cry. Everybody exhales.

'My baby girl,' Rayna says, kissing the crown of her daughter's head as the paramedic wraps Baba Brandt in the blue sheet. Irma holds out her arms.

Their driver bangs his horn, rolling down his window to tell the guy in the van beside them what just happened in the back, then all across the city, all across the country, a chorus of horns. Welcome, Willem! Welcome, Willem!

You almost can't hear the sirens.

Rick was chilling when his mobile rang. He looked at the Nokia's green and black display: *IRMA*.

'Baby!'

'Don't baby me,' said Rayna.

'Rayna!' he jived in just the same tone, stubbing out his joint.

Her sigh frosted his ear: why did he have to sound so black?

'Your boy's here,' she said, sounding warmer than she wanted to. 'Your son.'

'What!' Rick sat up on his bed and swung his feet to the floor where he felt a Pringle crunch. 'He's here?'

'He's here and she's doing fine now, thank you for asking. You better come. We're staying at the General because … '

He didn't like this pause, a pause meant a deal gone bad, cash lost, a knife pulled.

'Because … ?'

'Because of everything … don't you ever watch that big TV?'

He felt momentarily proud that Irma had bragged about his new wide-screen.

'Oh, right, eeeeverything.' He got up and walked over to the old-fashioned aluminium blinds that came with this place and peeked out. If anything, his neighbourhood was even quieter than usual though everybody was home. 'I'll come then,' he said and the blind tinked closed.

'Now,' said Rayna. 'You'll come now, if you've any respect for the mother of your child, I won't say your only child because – '

Rick held the phone away and stared at it willing her not to give him this shit again. Rayna hung up before he could make another promise he was sure to break.

Rick had some business first. Dagga was only going to get them so far, him and Irma and Willem. That's what they were calling him. Willem Eric. Oh, he was going to love his boy. He'd upgraded to less organic, more profitable stock and worked all the time and that meant missing the baby classes but he still paid for them. He couldn't buy a bigger place *and* grow his business and there wasn't enough room here for three. He was doing all this for them. He'd sort it all soon.

He'd been down to Sandton City Mall to check out rings, didn't know which finger it went on, laughed it off when the fancy counter bitch asked him what the lady might like.

He sold to anyone, money was the only colour he noticed, didn't matter whose face was on the notes. Everybody was buying and the cops were too busy to chase small businessmen like him. Students always wanted dagga but they were getting into coke too, proper marching powder. He liked it best, the cool click in the back of his throat. His sixth gear. The accompanying horn was only fine because it did bad things to his wire but he wasn't alone there.

Rick made his drop and got to the hospital late but blamed traffic and nobody could argue. There he was, snug as a bug in a blue blanket. He wanted to lift him up and unwrap him, to touch the fingers and toes whose contours he'd marvelled at from the outside. Irma's joy multiplied seeing the look on Rick's face and even Rayna smiled at him. They all stayed over: Irma in the bed, Rick in one chair, Rayna in the other and Willem like a chick in his incubator. Willem was no longer as blue as his blanket but still not feeding right. Rayna stayed for the next few days and Rick came at visiting hours with ever bigger, gaudier bunches of flowers. He brought a fluffy Simba which roared when you hugged it. When they were finally allowed home Rick was there – on time – to drive them all and Rayna let him stay over. For the first time. In the guest room. When she took him coffee next morning he was gone. He texted Irma: *Need 2 work. Love my boy.*

Two weeks later he was back looking nearly as tired as Irma, who was happy to hand Willem over to his pa, watched Rick's biceps flex as he held his boy up. She was beyond tired and Rayna was back at work. The always-news just stressed her out and she couldn't drive anywhere alone, not with a baby in the car. Rick said she should stay home till things calmed down. But she was going mad. There was only so much she could say to Elise without it getting weird. As Rayna had done before, she took to spending days in her housecoat smoking, and sleeping when she could. She even tried her mother's Danielle Steels. Her baby weight made itself comfortable. Rick was allowed round for bathtime and Irma got herself up and dressed then and the first week he turned up every night. Then two nights. Then one. *Because you never let him stay*, Irma snapped, careful not to wake the baby: *You don't let him be a man!* Rayna nodded, happy to be the bad-guy.

Rayna has always worked and her kids never went without, nobody can say that: new shoes and uniforms when they were still in school and hair-cuts for the class photo. After eighteen years she's an Assistant Supervisor at Johannesburg Park Station. In all those years she never once had a black come to the *SLEGS BLANKES* window. Now it happens all the time. She thinks they don't even want tickets, they're not carrying bags. She points them down the concourse to their own window. Last month she was briefed by her new, black, boss on the new rules. The *SLEGS BLANKES* and *NIE BLANKES* signs have come down. Still, she notices two queues form.

Mandela has gone from prisoner to president and his new flag flies everywhere but not from the houses in Brakpan where bars grow over every window. Willem's world will not be Irma's just as Rayna's was not her mother's. Everybody is waiting. In Hillbrow, in Brakpan, in Alexandra. Something has to happen. In Rayna's back garden, a clematis climbs the new wall making a break for the top.

Soon, it's Willem's first birthday. Rayna takes the day off and they hang blue bunting everywhere. Elise rustled up yards of it on an old-fashioned sewing machine Rayna found in a cupboard upstairs. Must have been her mother's though she doesn't ever remember her making anything. Willem picks up on the excitement, bouncing up and down in his high chair, banging his spoon harder at breakfast. 'That's my big boy,' says Irma, wiping mashed pumpkin off his face. It's hours till everybody arrives. The two least awful neighbours are popping by and Piet even texted to say he's going to try to come down from Kimberley. Irma wipes her hands on the XL *Little Mermaid* T-shirt she wears as a nightie and wills her waist to come back. She's not seen her brother for years. From what little she hears, he spends his days down the mines and his nights in the bars above them. She wonders if he ever found his pa, if they met somewhere deep inside the world.

Rayna's phone bleeps with a text and she hands it to Irma because she can never find her glasses. 'Roads bad – Piet,' says Irma, handing it back to Rayna who chucks it on the kitchen table. 'Bloody roads! This country!' She bangs open the metal screen Rick fitted for them in his first flurry of fatherhood and unlocks the tinted patio doors. The room brightens. Neither woman realised how gloomy it had been.

'Help me with the braai,' Rayna snaps, rolling the lid back on the half-drum grill. Irma turns to Willem. 'Just bring him!'

Like throne bearers they carry his high chair out into the sun where he blinks his big blue eyes then looks like he might cry until Irma plants a bright red sunhat on his head, the neck-flap covering his shoulders too: a tiny legionnaire ready to march across the desert. She smears sun cream across the bridge of his impossibly perfect nose. Rayna tuts at all these precautions but secretly admires Irma for her care.

The braai gets going and the sun moves round the garden and as the coals finally turn white they hear a car pull up. It's not got six gears, Irma can tell. Dries and Anika, and their shiny little twins, run round the side of the house. They live one street up but drove because that's how it is now. Next door's Alsatian leaps up, its muzzle foaming at the chain-link fence. The boy starts crying and Dries tells him to stop being a moffie then Anika, who is taking social science evening classes, tells him off. Dries swings a bag of meat which Elise takes and Anika makes a bee-line for Willem who is pleased with all this extra attention.

Irma listens for Rick's car all afternoon while Anika tells her about post-colonialism, structural inequality and the new integrated school she wants to put her twins in. Even as they finally start to sing happy birthday Irma is poised to tell everybody to stop, stop, don't blow out the candle, he's here, he's here. But he's not here. He's never here. Willem doesn't know Rick to miss him and she's jealous of him for that. Everybody laughs as he grabs for the candle and nearly gets it.

'Make a wish,' says Irma.

6

February 1999

'There's nothing wrong with him,' says Rayna, as much to herself as her daughter. 'He's just a boy, that's how boys are, trust me. He's no worse than your brother was.'

Irma crosses the kitchen to refold yet more laundry. They'd had to let go of the girl so it was just Elise now and she's getting too old to do everything. Besides, doing something with her hands helps.

'Should I get some colour?' Rayna turns her head in the mirror. She's been more or less grey since Willem was born.

'I've only been telling you for years,' says Irma. 'You should go blonde like me.'

'Maybe,' says Rayna, glancing in the little mirror by the front door, amazed she's made it to grey. Her mother was forty when she died in that car with her father. She's never even seen a photo of her grandmother. For all she knows, the women in her family go bald. She thinks again of the urns in the bottom of the wardrobe and finds she doesn't want to let them go any more.

Irma holds a supposedly clean *Simpsons* T-shirt up to the kitchen window revealing a purple stain. Grape juice. 'See, Ma,' she says, shaking it. 'He's so messy! His teacher says he doesn't pay attention, you see how he is.'

Rayna has let Irma get away with calling her Ma since the day Willem arrived. It doesn't mean she has to like it. 'Irma, he's nearly five, he's meant to be messy, in a world of his own. You fuss too much, it's not good for him.'

Willem arrives at the top of the stairs hugging a once proud lion cub now missing its roar and an ear. He's small for his age, will always be at the front of every class photo, easy to find with his curls. Is now the time to ask the question that's been bothering him all morning? He can't tell from their faces. Ma looks worried and Gran looks annoyed but that's how they always look. Also, faces sometimes lie.

'Can Simba come to school?'

Irma sighs. 'He can come in the car, baby.'

Rayna tuts and mutters under her breath. 'See, that's what wrong. He's not your baby, he's a little man, aren't you?'

'Will, go and brush your teeth for Ma.' He wonders how far he can push this unexpected win. 'Now, Willem, teeth!'

Irma turns to her mother, who is now looking for her car keys. 'What does that mean?'

'You know what it means, you're too soft on him.'

'I'm too soft on him? Me?'

'Yes, you,' she says, lifting and dropping various toys, books and items of clothing. At least she has avoided the unique agony of stepping on Lego today. It's amazing how much space a small person takes up. She doesn't remember Irma or Piet having so much stuff. Most of it was brought by Rick in the increasingly rare moments he managed to come down long enough to remember he had a son. Maybe she should give some of the toys to Elise for her grandchildren.

'Isn't he getting too old for that lion?'

Upstairs Willem hugs Simba closer and tries to remember what he's been told. Teeth, okay, teeth. They take ages. He can't believe he'll have to do this every day for ever. He bounces to the bathroom buoyed by the prospect of the new strawberry tooth-paste his gran sneaked in the trolley after Ma said he couldn't have it.

'You said yourself, he's five.'

'Nearly five.'

'Okay, nearly five.'

Rayna cries triumphantly as she finds her keys then makes for the door. Irma pursues, unwilling to let her win just by leaving: 'He's too old for Simba but not too old for your stories every night?'

Willem was a bit late with everything but walks and talks fine enough now and doesn't even wet the bed so much any more. Each woman spoils him in her own way and blames the other for the way they worry he might turn out. 'Sensitive' is the word Rayna tries to keep from her mind. She remembers those boys from her days in Mrs Bun's class. They lasted about as long as the jacaranda flowers. Pop-pop, pop-pop.

He'd spend more time outdoors if there was a man to throw the mini-rugby ball that's still conspicuously clean or to take him camping in the Bush. They can't do that stuff. A rain-spider got in through the bathroom window last week when Irma was showering and Rayna ran to her screams, thought it was a home invasion, felt their lives becoming headlines. She was relieved when she saw the spider scrabbling up the sides of the bath and was going to squash it but Willem begged her to let him catch it – loves anything he can possibly make a pet of, won't even have flypaper in his room because he can't bear to see anything hurt. He ushered it into an old Strawberry Pops box and took it down to the garden to let it go, laying it on the stoep where it jerked hideously from side to side until Rayna pulled on a pair of proper shoes and jumped with both feet. Willem wept for hours. They'd had to hold a funeral and Elise emptied another cereal box especially.

Whenever Willem is asked to a birthday party it's always by a girl, never more than a couple of streets away and always with Elise holding his hand and waiting to take him home again. And playdates – as modern as the microwave and just as unnecessary, Elise thinks – never last long. On these rare occasions, Rayna and Irma are left alone together with all the things they never say. Secrets expand to fill the space between them like mushrooms in the dark. So they talk about Willem instead, all the places they'll take him – to Kruger to see the big cats, to the new caves found just outside the city where the first men sat round the first fires, maybe even to Cape Town to see if it's really as beautiful as they say. One time Willem came home with a burst lip saying he'd fallen and another time he was inconsolable over a ripped Superman T-shirt. He's getting past that age anyway, Rayna tells herself. Irma is happy to agree.

Rayna deactivates the alarm, undoes the bolts and chains and thinks about what to say next. She's heard plenty of colleagues trade tales of National Service. They laugh about it now: twelve-hour drills, night marches, the war that wasn't. She's glad her Willem won't have to do all that but still wishes he was more normal, for his sake.

Irma goes on, 'I don't remember you telling me any stories.'

Upstairs the tooth-brushing is going well, so well, in fact, that Willem is on his third go. This new toothpaste is delicious and he has to tell them so runs out of the bathroom shouting 'Gran' only the word doesn't come out right. He heads downstairs as Rayna slides the final bolt. She turns to see Willem grinning and foaming pink at the mouth, rabid with strawberry. That vest will never be white again.

'Your son.' She points and Irma turns as Rayna pulls the front door closed silencing the whining alarm.

'Oh, Will-Will.'

7

March 2000

It's Saturday morning and Willem is poised in front of the wide-screen that his pa asked them to look after till he got back from wherever he had to go. Rayna's been called in for more Diversity Training and Irma is still in bed. Elise is hoovering around him and humming along to MTV. Willem's waiting for the beat to kick in. The Backstreet Boys want it thaaaat way and he does too – matches their every move, except the splits. He's not as big as other boys but he's bendier. He wishes he had somebody to dance with but Ma says it's private. Who would he ask anyway? School has a dance every Christmas but he doesn't go because nobody picks him – because he hasn't got a pa, because he can catch a ball, just doesn't want to, because he won't even let the girls be nice to him. He fibbed to Elise when she picked him up after the last one but he knew she could tell (Elise can tell everything) and that was worse. Now he practises every Saturday morning when it's just him and Elise and MTV and fantasises about turning up one year and showing them all his amazing moves then walking out just as the song ends. He would have danced with Lukas – Lukas was really good at Lego. They sat so close for the first few weeks of school they looked like a two-headed boy but dusty old Mrs Bun split them up. Sometimes his ma joins in, says it's her aerobics and lifts him up – before he gets too big, she says. She kisses his face over and over until he wriggles away then she chases him. Soon he'll be six.

The next video is his current all-time total favourite: Britney. He loves Britney. She sits kicking her feet in class and he knows the feeling. He moved on to bigger books with Rayna ages ago, is stories and stories ahead. When the clock hits 3 p.m. the bell rings and Britney's out in the locker-lined corridor and everybody's snapping their hips and bouncing their heels behind her. *Oh baby, baby, how was I supposed to know*, he sings along in perfect time and imperfect English, his accent a bright bubble-gum wish of Brakpan and LA. All the best songs are English, which he knows better than his ma and gran, thanks to MTV and the books Gran buys him. Everybody talks English in the playground. Afrikaans is for class and church but happily he doesn't have to go there. Britney's picking up the pace and Elise is dancing along with her hoover so Willem hops forward between beats and cranks it up. Irma can't even pretend to sleep any more so rubs her eyes and stumbles along the hall to the top of the stairs. 'Willem,' she shouts, but he can't hear, never listens, that boy. Another worry floats up – maybe his hearing's not right, but surely one of the doctors would have picked that up? She plods downstairs yawning, thinking maybe she'll do a bit on her bike. She doesn't hear the front door locks clicking or the burglar bars rattling until Rayna bursts in shouting, 'What's that bladdy noise?' Behind her, almost entirely obscured by a bunch of red gerbera daisies, stands Rick. Elise freezes. Willem is twirling spinning twirling and one day soon he'll brave the splits and everything blurs. *Hit me, baby, one more time!*

Rayna dashes to the TV unsure how to turn it off so clicks her fingers at Elise who just pulls the plug then kicks the hoover off, steering it towards the utility room, being sure to leave the door ajar. Irma and Willem run at Rick who backs out the door and drops his flowers, waving like he's surrendering, scars chasing veins down his skinny arms. Willem wraps his arms around his legs but Rick shakes him off shouting, 'Moffie!' Irma shouts, 'No!' and Rayna shouts, 'Get out!' even though he's on the stoep already. The neighbours will love this. Elise darts out of the utility room and pulls Willem back with her and puts her hands over his ears but he pushes her off and presses his ear to the door. He wants to hear his pa even if it's all just shouting. His ma is crying so he grabs the door handle but Elise stops him.

'A moffie!' cries Rick. 'A fuckin' moffie!'

'Keep your voice down,' shouts Rayna as her across the road suddenly finds something to do out front.

Rick starts towards the front door but Rayna blocks his way.

'You lay one hand on that boy and you'll have me to answer to.'

Rick backs off and kicks the flowers. Irma tries to pick them up and he almost hits her. 'Baby, don't!' she sobs. 'Talk to me.' She wraps her arms around him as he backs away saying, 'What did you do to my boy?' Irma recognises his motor by the kerb and remembers the two of them singing their way home. How did they get here? He peels her off and pushes her away and she almost falls. Rayna runs forward to catch her.

Sure it's safe, Elise opens the door. Rick revs off. Willem streaks towards his ma who sits sobbing on the stoep surrounded by red petals. Elise fetches the broom. 'Go to your room,' says his gran. He runs upstairs and looks down at the garden going through the proper names of everything he can see starting with the tree by his window: *Jacaranda mimosifolia*. Willem knows trees. Jacaranda is one of his favourites. When he was really little he begged his pa to whoosh him along the city's purple streets with the windows down. His pa let him stick his head out, cocked to one side for the *pop-pops*, curls flying, his pa going just a bit too fast, laughing just a bit too much. Can't think about Pa. Arrows of *Dietes grandiflora* glow white and pink in the shade of the jacaranda. The flowers only last a day. Willem's been called a moffie lots but it's the first-time outside school, in his own house, by his own pa. By the time he gets to the blue globes of *Agapanthus africanus* he's almost stopped shaking.

That night Willem can't stop crying. He tries to be quiet because he doesn't want them to hear, to think he really is a moffie, because that's what moffies do. But he can't stop. He stuffs his face in his pillow until it's so hot he can't breathe and when he comes up for air it goes cold and wet. He turns his pillow over and stares at the ceiling. An exact replica of the night sky glows above his bed. When he was a baby his pa stuck it up there for him star by star. He knows them all. The Southern Cross shines right over his head all night, every night. He can't believe they shine on just the same. This thought makes the other side of his pillow wet as well.

Across the landing Irma is two pills deep. It's not Willem's fault, she told herself as she grappled with the child-proof cap. But maybe if he was more like Rick then Rick would want to see them again. Her sleep is dreamless, as empty as her days since Willem went to school. She thought about getting a job but that's not so easy now. Anyway, Willem obviously needs her – after today she can't trust Elise, even though Elise practically raised her when Rayna was out working. Irma needs Rick back.

Rayna lies awake listening to Willem. She's told Irma to stop going to him but still sneaks in, tells herself if she can just get him down she'll have a chance of getting up on time. She's still the breadwinner for as long as she's too costly for the affirmative action lot to lay off – she's so old she's nearly a minority herself, her little joke. She lets Willem cry for ten long minutes then unlocks her door, pads across the landing and lets herself in. The plastic sheets protest as she eases herself onto his bed. She unsticks curls from his face and looks at his features to see who she can see: Irma's mouth for sure and Rick's nose and that must be Johannes' frown. She hasn't seen Irma's father since that night at the Paradise Inn. She waited for the police to arrive then watched as they marched him out, the man with the straight red hair. That night she slept for days. Johannes must be retired now. She still keeps a tiny bar of floral Paradise soap in her underwear drawer. Freckles constellate Willem's cheeks but she doesn't know who they're from. He subsides from crying to sleeping with no in-between as only small boys can. She kisses his cheek, which he would let her do if he was awake – his affectionate nature one of the things she loves and fears the most. Quietly she hums a tune feeling the melody easily but not consciously. The memory of it dances just beyond her. She closes her eyes and sees herself tucked in a single bed with tangled sheets, the window unfairly bright with a summer evening and hears this same rippling lullaby then feels Elise's cool hands laying a damp cloth on her forehead. Rayna watches Willem's breathing steady as the lullaby finds him and keeps humming until his door is locked behind her.

Next morning Rayna has made a decision: a boy needs a dog. Willem's nearly six so she can say it's a birthday present. The Brandts are the only dogless family in Brakpan. Dogs became fashionable right after the first blacks moved in. At night the broad-shouldered Boerboels, big enough to bring down a lion, howl in a chorus. Out on the veldt, not very far from the ever-creeping edge of the city, primitive ears prick up.

As they walk into the pet shop down at the mall Irma still can't quite believe her mother has gone so soft. They are greeted by an air-conditioned waft of warm animal. It's simultaneously sweet and sickening. Willem runs ahead as he has done since they left the house.

'Look,' says Irma, bending over the puppy pen and picking up the nearest bundle. 'Look at his little face.' She holds the black scrap up so they're nose to nose. Rayna peeks underneath.

'He's a she.'

'Okay, look at *her* little face.'

Willem is over in the Small Animal Area. Cruising past the hamsters, all sleepy and boring, he works his way through the reptiles. He can't see anything in the tarantula tank despite tapping on the glass but pauses at the tortoise: *Chersina angulata.* A baby version of the one he saw in a park downtown that he went to with his ma last Christmas. It was a secret. They sat at a picnic table for hours while she looked at her watch. After a while Willem heard this slow rustle–rustle–rustle and the grass trembled like the treetops in Jurassic Park then out walked this massive tortoise. Too big and old to be bothered by them it strolled right past like a clever old rock. They sat there till it was nearly dark. His ma scribbled something on a cigarette packet and stuffed it between the planks of the bench then they left. All the way home all he could do was talk about the tortoise until his ma snapped *Shut up, shut up.* But this one is well in his shell and too small to bother with. In the tank above a chameleon hangs upside down from a bright green branch. Its weird googly eyes flick towards Willem when he presses his face against the tank. He marvels at its stillness and wonders how long it takes to change colour and thinks how pleased his teachers would be if he could stay that still, how happy he would be if nobody else could see him. Mesmerised, he peers closer and sees the branch is plastic, each leaf the exact same size with a rough moulded seam down the middle: *Plasticata fakum.* In the corner nearest his face a desperate cricket pushes against the glass. Willem wants to free them both into a real tree. He'll give the cricket a head start. He reaches for the tank lid, wondering if it's locked.

'Willem!' his ma calls. 'Will-Will!' He wishes she wouldn't call him that here. He turns and tries to tune into her voice. The shop is busy with all kinds of people. He tries not to stare like the chameleon as a white girl pretends to be grossed out by the snakes, turns to a black boy and buries her face in his neck. Irma can't help staring and Rayna tuts too, as much at Irma for being obvious. Willem feels sad suddenly then sees what his ma is holding.

'A puppy!' He bounds over. 'A dog!'

'Sort of,' says Rayna.

'A pug,' says Irma. 'Isn't he, she cute? Look at her little face.'

Willem dances on his tiptoes and puts up his arms.

'Now be gentle,' his gran warns and as he takes the drowsy bundle it yips in recognition.

'She's ours?'

Irma looks to Rayna who looks at Willem, sees his never bigger smile. She nods and he jumps up and down.

'Careful, Will,' Irma says and kisses her ma who takes a sudden interest in a shelf of worming treatments.

'So, what do we call her?' asks Irma.

The puppy licks Willem's face and without hesitating he shouts, 'Britney!'

A boy needs a dog.

8

May 2006

Willem is the only boy in his class who doesn't do sports, which suits him fine: extra time in the library every Thursday morning. He's now tall enough to look down on shelves that would once have towered over him and leave his initials in the dust on top. So many new books to devour!

He sits at the desk by the window on the third floor and looks out at the rugby pitch. Idiots. It's almost worth watching for the chance to see their noses wiped across their faces.

Because he's between *The Order of the Phoenix* and *The Half-Blood Prince* Willem is reading *The Philosopher's Stone* for at least the hundredth time. He still dreams of a letter arriving telling him he's really somebody else, a hero in another world. He's already decided he's going to do English at a university in England. Or become a vet. He's thinking about this when the library door opens and in walks a boy he doesn't know – a boy not in school uniform.

'*Goeie more*,' says the boy. Nobody talks Afrikaans unless there's an adult about.

Willem meerkats to his toes but the librarian must be in the back office. He answers the boy in English, his finger holding his place on the page. 'Hello.'

'Phew,' says the stranger. 'I'm Harry.'

'No way!' laughs Willem, closing his book and holding it up.

Harry rolls his eyes and plonks down opposite. He doesn't have a scar or glasses. He's got brown spiky hair and looks like he should be out playing rugby, not sitting in here. Harry grabs Willem's book.

'Give it back!'

'Relax,' says Harry, flicking through it. 'I've read them all. Not seen one like this though. It's English. Cool.'

Willem has never been called cool. He's been called everything but cool: moffie, faggot, Lil-Will. This Harry has said the magic word. Immediately they begin comparing favourite scenes and arguing over which book is best and what will happen next and before they know it the whistle is blowing on the rugby pitch and the bell is ringing and it's time to go back to class.

'So, who are you?' Willem asks as he packs his bag.

'Err … Harry. Duh.'

'I know that,' says Willem, too ready to be hurt. 'I mean, you're not from here.'

'My ma teaches form two.'

'Mrs Adams!'

'Yeah,' says Harry. 'She loves all that British stuff. I'm actually a Pre-Potter Harry. Anyway, I board at Bethulie and we get different holidays so … '

'How come you're not at home?'

Harry shrugs and turns round. 'My dad's away. Anyway, better go, just wanted to check the library out.'

The next Thursday he's back. The rugby team is doing well so they've gone out of town to play which means a whole day in the library. Harry and Willem talk their way through the entire Potter-verse and after lunch move on to *Star Trek*. Willem is committed to Captain Janeway and convinced she'll get her crew home eventually, but Harry is Captain Picard all the way and does a very good 'engage'.

Harry's snuck his phone in, the new Samsung. He props it in an atlas and beckons Willem round. 'Sit,' he says, shuffling aside.

Willem tucks himself in and peers over Harry's shoulder. 'Vintage!' Willem exclaims as Leonard Nimoy raises an already high eyebrow.

The air between them is charged with the energy of a thousand photon torpedoes. Or at least it is to Willem. Together they sit watching episode after episode exploring strange worlds, seeking out new life and new civilisations.

The bell brings them back to earth.

'Well,' says Harry putting his phone away. 'See ya!'

'Next week?'

Harry shakes his head. 'Our holidays are done, man. We go back next week.'

'Oh.' Willem feels like he's been through a transporter only not all of him has made it back. 'Right,' he says, trying not to look bothered.

Harry walks over and raises his right hand in the Vulcan salute: 'Live long and prosper.' Willem mirrors his gesture.

'Time to boldly go,' says Harry, turning on his foot and tensing as he jumps to warp and whooshes away.

Willem shouts down the corridor, 'To go boldly!' Harry pauses and turns. 'It's a split infinitive.'

Harry shrugs and says, 'Nerd,' then resumes course, laughing.

Willem watches him disappear.

That evening the bus drops Willem at the end of their cul-de-sac. As he stands waiting for the new electric gates to open he hears a familiar yip and looks down to see Britney's face poking through then a flash of a pair of black boots. The lock buzzes and the gate rolls back revealing a sort of soldier. He's standing there just about holding Britney who is determined to get to Willem. His badge says *S4U Security – Jan*.

'Howzit,' he says accusingly. 'This yours?'

9

Taking that stupid dog back gives Jan the perfect excuse to finally talk to that MILF – he knows it's against company rules, he's a lifelong rules man, but he's into her. Jan has never seen a man at number 32.

Seeing a uniformed man on the stoep with her son, Irma rushes to the door. Jan hears bolts and chains rattle. 'I'm coming,' she shouts.

The door half opens and she peeks out from behind. She's in the *Little Mermaid* T-shirt he'd like to get underneath.

'Willem,' she snaps, opening the door. The boy streaks past with the dog yapping at his heels.

'Is he in trouble again?' Irma asks. 'You better come in.'

The house has a weird not-lived-in feel, the whole thing stuck in the 1950s. The carpet is trying to get out the door. Everything is old except the big-arsed wide-screen.

'Just like my parents left it,' jokes Rayna from the kitchen, lighting a cigarette and wafting it round.

Jan coughs conspicuously. Elise polishes the banister again.

'Oh, where did they go? Lot of older folk leaving now.' He makes sure to look away from Rayna as he says 'older'.

'No,' Rayna says, laughing and coughing. 'They're still around.'

'Tsh, Ma,' says Irma, reappearing, having done just enough to her make-up to make it seem she's done nothing at all. Her magazines are full of the natural look. 'That's not nice.'

Jan has no clue what's going on so eyes the coffee Rayna hands him. How old is this mug?

'My grandparents passed away when I was little,' Irma says. 'I don't remember them. Beer instead?'

'I can't, Mrs,' he says. The dog reappears and tries to bite his boots. He shakes it off. 'I'm on duty.'

Irma giggles. 'It's Miss. Call me Irma, please, and this is Rayna and you met Willem already.' She shouts him once, twice and Jan is thinking he'd *klap* any boy of his if he didn't jump first time when Willem appears on the stairs. Kid must be twelve but hardly looks ten with all his curls.

'And you know Britney,' says Irma as the dog attacks his boots again before running to Willem like they've been separated for years.

'Willem, shake the man's hand,' says Rayna, lighting her next cigarette from the last. Jan begins to understand why everything looks yellow.

'Willem, don't be rude,' says Irma, snapping her fingers at Britney.

'Is that your gun?' Willem asks in English.

'He does that,' says Irma in Afrikaans. 'All the American TV he watches and his books. Willem, Afrikaans for our guest.'

Jan lays his hand over the weapon holstered at his side and goes on in Afrikaans. 'Yes, it's mine. You know guns, son?'

'No, I don't,' says Willem, in English again. Irma shoots him a look so severe he proceeds in class-room-perfect Afrikaans. 'What kind is it?'

'My old army Vektor, the Z88,' says Jan. 'Nine-millimetre, semi-automatic, never fails.'

'Have you used it?' Willem asks, now at the foot of the stairs, his hand on the shiny banister.

'*Ja*,' Jan says, looking from Rayna to Irma to help him out here. 'Every day.'

'You shoot people every day?' Willem gasps, making his fingers into a gun and taking aim at this man he often spots just sitting in the car parked outside.

For months Jan has sat in the patrol car with Fumbi watching Irma. She hardly ever goes out except to wave her boy off to the bus tugging at the neck of his shirt. She even cried on his first day at high school – that morning the whole neighbourhood was full of new uniforms. Fumbi had called her a MILF.

'And she's a GILF,' Jan had said, nodding at Rayna who'd run onto the stoep with the boy's lunch.

'Bru, that's not how it works,' Fumbi said, waving politely as he reversed them out of the cul-de-sac to finish their loop. 'A MILF is a mother I'd like to fuck,' he'd gone on, taking one hand off the wheel and grabbing his crotch. 'And I would fuck her. While I admire the older woman, I would not actually fuck a grandma. Would you? Seriously?'

Jan had thought about it for longer than he should have so Fumbi hooted, 'Man, white people are sick! DIR-TY!'

Jan had flinched. This was still new. When he'd done his National Service men like Fumbi, maybe not exactly like him, were the enemy. He'd patrol the surprisingly neat streets of Soweto in one of the dark green armoured vans they all called Hippos checking passes, inviting suspicious individuals into the back for questioning. Not everybody made it home those days.

Now a lot of Jan's old Defence Force mates are in security because people feel safer with a face like their own on the gate. Jan had considered becoming a cop but couldn't get used to blacks in uniform. On the news the other day he'd seen a black judge. It's all rigged now. If you give a white guy a job you have to give a black one too. Fumbi isn't all that black, could maybe even pass for coloured, but definitely isn't white.

'Could be worse,' Fumbi had joked. 'I could be some *kwerekwere* from Zim, coming here undercutting everybody bringing all my black magic and shit.'

Jan had had to agree. At least Fumbi was one of their own. He'd found himself liking the man although he'd never talk to him at his other job. His big plan is to get promoted at the Ford dealership and have his own franchise one day. He sees himself standing on his own forecourt lined with four-wheel-drives that would never see mud and those big hybrids the hot *huisvrous* like cos they sit up high. Everybody wants to feel safe these days.

'Hello,' Irma says. 'Still with us?'

Jan takes a sip of coffee then regrets it. '*Ja*, sorry, I was just – '

'In another world,' says Rayna.

'*Ja*,' Jan laughs.

'Anyway, Willem, what talk is that?' says Irma, stepping over and putting her son's hands by his side. 'Of course, Mr … doesn't shoot people, do you?'

Jan puts his mug on the ringed cork worktop and turns towards the door, doffing his cap at Rayna, the boy and finally Irma. The boy is obviously turning soft in a house full of women.

'You can't have a beer on duty but you could come by for braai, eh?' Rayna smiles. He's hardly touched his coffee but she saw how he looked at Irma. 'Saturday?'

Jan nods and as Elise shows him out Irma does a small squeal. Willem shouts, 'Bye,' in English then flees upstairs. He's halfway to Mordor and has to get back. He wishes for a ring he could just slip on and disappear.

10

November 2007

'It's not so far,' says Irma, looking round Willem's room and wishing it was a bit messier, a bit more normal. She shudders remembering the stiff-Kleenex horror of her brother's room. Maybe not. 'Benoni Park is half an hour max, less if Jan drives. It's got two malls and the school's great. You can come back here any time. Can't he, Ma?'

Rayna is still taking the news in. 'Of course he can, any time.'

Willem has never imagined living anywhere but here, sleeping anywhere but in his own bed where he's watched over by a poster of Legolas, arrows forever set to fly. Peperami, his latest stick insect, does whatever he does in the tiny plastic tank by his alarm clock. All his books are here – all his Tolkien, his notes for an Elvish dictionary, his Harry Potters from England, his entire Encyclopaedia Botanica.

'What about them?'

'I'll help,' says Rayna, who remembers buying each and every one for him. She still lets him read to her, even the elf stuff. 'We'll keep them in the right order, don't worry.'

Willem wasn't planned, a consolation prize Rayna never expected to win and now finds she can't bear to lose.

'You can come back any time you like, son,' says Rayna. 'We'll leave your room just the same.'

Willem thinks briefly about running away but where? How would he get there? He can't upset his gran.

'You want a Coke?' Irma asks. 'Come on, let's go downstairs, get you a drink.' She takes his hand which he shakes off and they all go down to the kitchen where Britney raises her head in greeting but doesn't get up.

Irma produces a can from the fridge and Willem wipes the top with his sleeve. For once she says nothing about how he gets with sugar.

'The complex has a pool and there'll be loads of other boys your age,' Irma goes on. 'Cool, eh?'

Nobody says 'cool' now. Even Willem knows that. He can't swim, avoids changing-room situations for reasons he's avoiding working out. He's still behind the other boys, waiting for hair. He shrugs and slugs the Coke knowing he could get away with a sizable burp. He crushes the can with an ease that surprises and pleases his mother then drops it in the recycling bin he forced them to buy. If everything really is going to crap, if the world really is ending, he wants something left for the animals after. Willem believes we are in the Holocene Epoch of man-made extinction.

Irma gets her phone out and pulls up pictures of the duplex. It's a puddle of melted pink ice cream. Classic Johannesburg Tuscan. Seemingly plastic yellow roses clamber up the standard super-high walls surrounding it. Brakpan might not be what it was but Rayna can't imagine living anywhere so new. She's staying put, not that they've asked her.

'Look,' says Irma, zooming in, her new gel nails tapping the screen. This sound, like so many others, makes Willem want to scream. He picks out the tiny echo between the fake nail and the real nail below, plastic atop dead protein. 'Look, lots of room for Britney.' She taps the screen again and Willem frantically tries to find a more positive association, that's what the school psychologist said to do: he conjures the jacaranda outside his window tapping the glass in the wind. Then he remembers the time he thought he could control the weather after he saw a tiny dust storm whirl up from nowhere then fall to nothing in the playground.

'Willem,' sighs Irma. 'See,' she says to her mother. 'Jan goes to all this trouble for us and he can't even be bothered to look at the pictures.'

Willem grabs the phone from his mother and holds it right in front of his eyes. 'See, I'm looking right at it, I'm basically in it.'

She snatches it back, wiping it on her T-shirt. His skin is getting oily. Jan has cleared her skin right up. She's going out now, joined the new Virgin Active at Benoni Park, that's how they found this place. The gated complex is plenty big and has 24/7 guards so she can jog outside — finally lose her baby body. Maybe even make some friends. Get a job, who knows.

'Look, Elise,' says Irma. 'Come see.' She holds her phone in front of Elise who glances at it and sees tiled floors that will never quite look clean and classic bad white taste.

Britney heaves herself up from her basket, waddles over to the screen door then plonks down. Rayna opens all the locks and lets her out — she doesn't bother making a show of finding a place, just squats by the door and doesn't even look away.

'I won't miss this,' says Rayna, wafting her nose theatrically and fetching a plastic bag from the kitchen drawer. But she will.

'We won't land you with her, Ma,' Irma says. 'Don't worry.'

11

June 2008

Every morning Willem does push-ups on his bedroom floor because he wants arms like Hicks from *Aliens* but nobody knows this. He never lets Ma or Jan see him anything less than fully clothed and he's got his own bathroom now so it's easy to keep his new body under wraps. One day he might casually stretch in front of Jan who swears he got a six-pack doing National Service – drank one, more like.

'Oh, come on, Will,' says Irma, tying the Day-Glo laces on her ludicrous new Nikes. 'It'll be fun!'

'No, it won't,' he says, refusing to look up from his phone where he's about to launch a full attack with ten battalions in order to finally become Hero of Sparta. He's been building up to this for days and was up all last night training archers. His thumbs ache and he's about to ATTACK but his instinct tells him to PAUSE just as Jan meat-paws his phone.

'Thanks,' says Willem, planting his hands in his pockets, not even bothering to raise his voice.

'Stop mumbling,' says Jan, dropping the phone in with his gym kit and zipping it up like a body bag. 'You and that thing. Maybe use the actual phone to ring some buddies? Oh, that's right –'

Willem stares at the landline which he only submits to when it's pressed into his hand. Who talks on the phone?

'Jan, don't tease,' chides Irma, retying her laces so she doesn't have to clamber off the treadmill halfway. Jan says you should never interrupt your cardio. Irma likes the view from their gym. It's on the fifth storey of the mall so she can see Jozi rising in the distance. Her ma used to live in one of the big white towers over on Hillbrow. Nobody goes there now. It's gone Kaffir. Jan says the balconies are all bursting with trash they just chuck down on the street. Last year a social worker got killed by a falling fridge or something. The whole CBD is basically no-go. The gym windows are tinted and make her feel like she's wearing shades indoors. She wishes Willem wouldn't do that, misses seeing his eyes, his daddy's eyes. She still wonders about Rick. Where he is, how he is, if he still is. Maybe he hit his luck. Likely he's in one of the white townships littering the road up to Pretoria. Jan says they're shameful, a stain on the country. He pointed one out on the way to the Voortrekker Monument which Willem's school said was no longer appropriate to visit.

Irma and Jan's gym is mixed. Mixed is all Willem has known. He's at Benoni Park Academy, one of many fee-paying schools that popped up post-1994 but even these are increasingly subject to state intervention. Jan likes to tell Willem he wouldn't last a day in a real school, never mind National Service. Rayna pays the fees because she knows Jan's right even if she'd never say so. Willem's got black kids in his school and a coloured boy in his class. Irma's still getting used to mixing, catches herself looking in the gym mirrors. The changing rooms have cubicles and the showers have frosted screens but Irma still glimpses curves through the steam, wishes she could get glutes like that, briefly wonders how she looks to them.

'If you're not coming with us what are you doing?' asks Jan. 'He's fourteen, Irma, he should be out, the fridge is full of beers I don't count. When I was his age –'

'When you were his age, God was a boy,' half laughs Irma, worried Willem will kick off. He's been so angry lately. She's not sure he's taking his Ritalin. 'You boys, come on, Jan, let's go.'

'I was sneaking out, parties down at Braamfontein, making the best of what God gave me.'

Willem wanders over to the big cushion in the corner of the kitchen where Britney spends more and more time sleeping and farting. He sits on the cool tiled floor next to her and rubs her ears and she snuffles to his touch without waking.

'We had to have our fun before National Service, all the drills and marches and … ' He runs out of words and stands there staring. 'The time of my life, it was. You don't know how good you got it.'

'Come on, Jan the Man,' says Irma, bouncing to the door aided by the bubbles trapped in the soles of her Nikes. She pecks his cheek and he comes to, startled. 'Don't want to hit the rush. Will, phone your gran, see how she is? She loves when you phone.'

Irma pulls Jan out the door and they're gone.

Willem sits where he is until each lock clicks into place and the alarm bleeps into life. Britney sleeps on as he wanders over to the phone. His grandma had a mini-stroke six months ago – just what those bastards were hoping for, she said. Rayna swears in front of him all the time now and doesn't even apologise, which is one of the ways he knows he's growing up. They laid her off just short of her pension but she's fighting them. Willem helps her research other cases online and sends links by email which she's surprisingly good at for an old person. She now spends whole days getting angry online. To distract her he registered her on a family-tree site. His ma only goes online to book gym classes and beauty appointments. He picks up the phone and listens to the tone, summoning his gran's number as easily as he remembers all numbers, except the ones he's meant to. His maths grades are not good but neither is his maths teacher. His only As are in English and biology. Willem's fingers dial the familiar digits but he puts the receiver down, decides on email instead. This means missing her voice but also means he can end the interaction when he wants without upsetting anyone. Anyway, he's staying next weekend. She's kept his room exactly like she promised and Elise still cleans it every week. Willem freed Peperami into the jacaranda the day they moved out, instantly losing him among the leaves. He died, he told them. How could you tell? Jan had laughed.

Instinctively, Willem dips in his pocket for his phone but it's gone to the gym with Jan. He opens the fridge and considers making a massive sandwich then feels exhausted at the thought so grabs a six-pack of crisps instead.

His new room – he still thinks of it as new – is bigger than his old room and he's got his own bathroom but hates it on principle. Even if he couldn't hear his ma and Jan through the wall. His bed he reserves for sleeping, everything else he does at his desk or underneath it, although it's starting to get quite cramped. There's an outhouse but that's for the garden boy.

Willem wanders into the family bathroom, opens the medicine cabinet and rattles the bottles made out to his ma. The one with the big purple pills is half empty. One time he saw her take three. Willem had been shouting at Jan for walking into his room and Britney was barking and Willem ran at him pushing him out but Jan didn't budge, just laughed, and said, *That's more like it.* Willem had landed a sort of half-punch and Jan was raising his fist when Irma got between them then fell down clutching her belly. Willem went to her but Jan told him *stay back and shut that fuckin' dog up.* When his ma could talk she'd said *It's all right, it's all right.* Willem looks at the bottle now and thinks about taking one just for something to do but puts it back exactly right because Jan doesn't miss a trick.

They won't be back for ninety more minutes and if they're gone longer than two hours he's to ring the front gate. Their door is open so he looks in at the huge bed and shivers in the AC. Too gross.

He goes to the living room and flicks the TV on to kill the quiet and Britney joins him. He hopes for more riots because that means less school – he loves class, just hates his classmates. But no, the newscaster says, the police have got the Situation under control and illegal Zimbabweans are to blame. Mbeki appeals for calm and refuses to quit. Same old. Willem clicks the TV off and wanders over to Jan's 'library'.

It's always locked even when he's in there. He won't even let their helper – that's what his ma says to call the maid now – in to clean so every day she bumps the door with her mop leaving a tideline of resentment.

Willem tries the door. This time the handle turns all the way. It swings open. He half expects an alarm but nothing. Straight ahead is a big old lawyer-looking desk with an office chair behind it. For a second Willem sees Jan sitting there. He should pull the door closed now and if he does he won't have to lie when they get back. Everybody can tell when he's lying. You were just born honest, his gran says. He leans forward but can't reach the handle. He holds on to the door frame and lunges for it grabbing only air. He can't leave it because then they'll know for sure he opened it. He'll have to go in. Willem takes a deep breath and steps forward as if the air in there might not be breathable.

The wall to the left is galleried with framed photos. Who knew Jan had been a boy? A fat boy at that. Fat Jan is on an elephant then at the zoo with a snake draped round his thick neck. Willem thinks Slytherin thoughts and wills the coils to tighten but they don't. Fat Jan is getting his matric and in the next picture he's swapped school uniform for khakis and a crew cut and regulation smile and he's looking fitter. Willem has to look close to find him now: saluting in a parade, giving the thumbs-up from the back of a big green truck, blacked up and laughing. Willem has never seen Jan smile so much. In the most recent picture Jan is standing in front of a red, white and black flag that Willem knows you won't find in any atlas. It's a flag from the news: the AWB. Terre'Blanche and all that. Proper old-school Boer dumbness. Classic Jan. Willem wonders if his ma knows and makes a note to discuss it with his gran next weekend.

The wall behind the desk is floor to ceiling shelves but there are no books. Jan only reads online. Willem looks over his shoulder then pads over to the desk and sits in the chair. The leather sticks to the bottom of his back where his vintage *Star Trek* T-shirt rides up. He leans into it tilting till he's almost lying down then sits up again. It tips him forward so hard he knocks an empty box of man-size tissues off the desk and bumps the big old desktop PC. TitsNTyres. com pops up. Willem reaches down to pick up the box and wonders if there's such a thing as woman-sized tissues. He tries the drawers: locked, locked, open. He slides off the chair onto the carpet. The bottom drawer rolls open, deeper than it looks, and he reaches in feeling round without looking (tries to forget that scene from *Dune*). His fingers find paper (probably bills), glossier paper (maybe a photo) and then the rustle of magazines. He fishes them out. On the cover of *MANSVOLK* there's a guy in complete camo gear standing in an empty shopping mall wielding a glossy black assault rifle. It includes features on Building the Perfect Panic Room and Self-Defence: Your Youngest Can Learn. *LOSLYF* features a black woman his ma's age on the front wearing a tiny zebra bikini. Her mouth is wide open and secret pink. Anton Kiekbusch snuck a copy in once and made all the younger boys look at it in the changing rooms. This one falls open in the middle showing a topless white woman standing in front of the Voortrekker. She looks bored. He closes it. As he lays the magazines back in the drawer he finds a box. It's heavy and cold but not old – a shiny red cash tin. He lifts it out carefully. The key is in the lock. It turns. Before he can unsee what's in there, he closes his eyes and turns it over: a photo of his ma sprawled naked on their bed. He feels his face flush – he'll never be able to lie about this. He should never have looked, he shouldn't be in here. Then he registers what's beneath the photo. Careful not to turn it over again, Willem reaches for the gun. Jan's old friend – his Vektor Z88. It feels dense yet surprisingly light. Willem walks over to the wall of photos and takes aim at Fat Jan on the elephant, Fat Jan getting his matric, Army Jan on patrol. *Bang! Bang! Bang!* He takes them all down, making sure to miss the elephant. He squints like you're supposed to and imagines the kick, wonders how much it really takes to pull the trigger. As he takes aim for the final time he glimpses a dull fatal glint in the revolver's chamber. The gun slips from his grip. He closes his eyes and braces for the bang. Nothing. He opens his eyes again slowly, desperate to avoid any sudden movement. He looks down at the gun as if from a great height and watches fear run down his trousers and puddle onto the carpet. As he falls to the floor he hears a key in the front door.

12

March 2009

Willem is naturally drawn to the middle of the mini-bus, more than a punch from Anton and his crew but still behind the actual retards. No luck. Mrs de Vries sits him up front next to her.

'You're a good boy really aren't you, Willem?' she says before reminding him to buckle up. He's not a boy – he's nearly fifteen. From behind somebody mewls 'Lil-Will' before subsiding into hilarity. They both ignore this. It's going to be a long day.

Mrs de Vries has read the psychologists' reports, has his Ritalin in her bag, his mother on speed-dial. Willem can see actual molecules of stress pushing the overheated air towards the roof of the packed minibus. When he gets back home he'll try to build an atomic model of it, wonders what the chemical formula of stress is.

Grade 12 are bumping their way down to Bloemfontein to visit the Anglo-Boer War Museum.

It's a non-compulsory history outing organised and paid for by the headmaster, Mr de Villiers, who stands at Assembly like he's still in the Defence Force and expects each and every pupil to carry his – or indeed her – self like a soldier. As he never tires of telling his wife: we are at war, just not officially. She knows all about this. Mr de Villiers has other things to do on a Saturday which don't involve his wife or school. So, this trip is being supervised by Mrs de Vries, who the pupils call Bush Baby because of her bulging eyes, and their classroom assistant Mthunzi, who is at one of the new teacher training colleges and doesn't want to be here any more than they do (and had to cancel a date). As a small rebellion, Mthunzi is wearing nail polish – imported Chanel Jade, she explains, fanning her elegant piano-span fingers for the benefit of the teenage girls buzzing round her.

Fifteen of the sixteen pupils in Grade 12 are present – Siyanda is the only absentee. His parents wouldn't sign his permission slip and have booked to come in next week to share their reservations with Mr de Villiers who is puffing in anticipation. He finds this annual conversation tiresome but also comforting because he gets to repeat himself and that's always nice. He schedules this outing for a weekend to pre-counter such objections, certain most parents will welcome a Saturday without offspring. Not Siyanda's. These people are all the same.

Of course, he will tell them over coffee and biscuits, we teach the history of the Struggle – he will capitalise the Struggle by saying the word slowly. As per the new Department of Education rules we now cover in detail: The Rise of the National Party and Apartheid, the Emergence of the ANC, the Sharpeville Massacre, the shooting of Hector Pieterson. He will pause after Pieterson knowing they will have the famous image in their heads: the bare-legged small-for-his age twelve-year-old with blood already crusting his face, cradled in the arms of a dungaree-clad student slack-mouthed with terror, his older sister running alongside pleading, palms raised. He'll give Siyanda's parents that moment. Then he'll hurry through the big names: Malan, Verwoerd, de Klerk, Mandela. Finally, he'll place his hands on the seemingly blank piece of paper that's been sitting on the desk between them. Warning them that they may find it shocking, but giving them no time to object, he will turn it over to reveal seven-year-old Lizzie van Zyl: her joints thicker than the bones they barely hold together, her eyes twin graves in a skull crowning through fevered skin. A living skeleton. *This little girl died on 9 May 1901 of typhoid – which is what killed Anne Frank, you know.* He has other arguments prepared – 28,000 Boer women and children killed in British concentration camps, more civilians dead than soldiers. *Really the Boer Wars are the root of all our present-day difficulties.*

Lizzie's photograph usually does the trick.

After two hours in the minibus Willem is bored – they weren't even allowed to bring their phones. Plus, he really needs to go to the toilet again. The bumps in the road keep giving him a hard-on so he covers his lap with his hoodie – all the other boys will be having the same problem, he thinks, then worries this thought will somehow be picked up by Anton.

'Miss,' he says, turning to Bush Baby who feels queasy from trying to read. She loves the Outlander books, dreams of Jamie in his kilt. Her eyelashes brush the inside of her glasses.

'Yes, Willem?'

'Can we stop please, Miss? I need to go.'

'You need to what?'

He blushes. 'I need to go.'

Lil-Will needs to go, Lil-Will needs to go, sing-songs Anton before abruptly stopping, thanks to a devastating eye-roll from Mthunzi. Because the back of the bus is starting to hum a bit and they can't open windows on these roads, Anton changes his tune. 'It stinks, Miss. Can we stop?' The others applaud what is now his idea.

Mrs de Vries leans forward to the driver whose name she didn't quite hear the first time he said it and is now afraid to try and say in case she offends him. Was it Zam?

'No, *Miesies,*' he says. '*Yingozi. Gevaarlik.* Too risky.' He takes both hands off the wheel and gestures at the wide empty world framed by the windscreen. It feels like there should be farms but there are hardly any houses, barely any trees, no billboards even. It's a film set tired of waiting for the actors to return. The driver knows all too well you don't stop upcountry, even for cops, especially for cops. If a cop car flashes you just flash back then drive to the nearest busy place, say a petrol station, and stop there so you have witnesses and CCTV. If you see a body in the road you drive round it or over it if you have to. You never slow down to look. You certainly do not stop a private-school minibus with fifteen white kids and a white lady and a pretty black girl in the middle of nowhere. He shakes his head definitively and Grade 12 groan as one. 'We'll be there in twenty minutes, *Miesies,*' he tells Mrs de Vries, who is starting to look forward to the lavatory herself.

'Just twenty minutes now, class!' she calls over her shoulder. 'Now, who can tell me the dates of the First *and* Second Boer Wars?'

Willem knows, he's good with dates, but says nothing and leans against the window and crosses his legs. Focus on something else, that's what the psychologist told him. The tinted glass cools his face but as it warms he pulls away and his cheeks stick. Out to his left an ostrich stands up like it's being pulled on strings then shakes orange dust from its feathers. *Struthio camelus.* Without squinting too hard he can see the dinosaur still inside it.

Right on time, their minibus rolls in to Bloemfontein where the buildings struggle over two storeys, except for some crappy block they'd knock down in Jozi. Every pair of eyes they drive past stares in as their driver tries to find the museum. Every bump in the road sends a message to Willem's bladder. He's not lost it since that day in Jan's library. He's determined not to at school. Bad enough being Lil-Will and all the rest.

'Bloem is a shithole,' mutters Anton and everyone giggles agreement. Bush Baby pretends not to hear. It's not the most impressive town she's ever seen.

'Left here,' Mrs de Vries insists, poking at the map sliding off her knees as they jump a junction.

'No, right,' shouts Mthunzi, holding up her iPhone. 'See?'

Mrs de Vries can't see so Mthunzi passes her phone forward and Anton shouts, 'PICS!' which Mthunzi ignores while mentally inventorying exactly what photos she does have on there. The phone reaches Willem who looks at the blinking blue dot and points right.

'Right it is then,' says Mrs de Vries.

Once you knew what you were looking for you could actually see the museum for miles. A soaring white obelisk pierces the relentlessly blue sky. Willem loved the Pharaohs and remembers begging to be a mummy and his ma using up all the toilet rolls and Rayna shouting like crazy after she got home from work and ran upstairs bursting. The gods with wings and beaks seemed more real than the one they had to pray to before every school assembly, before every meal. Willem hated Jan's praying voice – it was like his ma talking to the bank on the phone.

At the museum gate, a khaki guard taps the driver's window with the barrel of his machine gun and talks rapidly in the usual combination of languages but, Mrs de Vries notes, with more Afrikaans than usual. Their driver shows their paperwork. The guard checks it walking the length of the minibus peering up through the windows, so they all look down on his khaki cap. Eventually he ticks their papers then goes back in his sentry hut, makes a call and raises the barrier admitting them to the mostly empty car park.

Their driver unlocks the door and as he slides it open Grade 12 pour past Mrs de Vries into the open air. Willem gets out last and carefully. Unbuckling his seat belt felt dangerously close to release. He's got to get to a toilet.

Mrs de Vries herds her cats up to the front of the museum with Mthunzi following. In front of the main entrance sits a giant black ball pierced by two huge spikes. Like something from a scrapyard.

'It's a ball of wool,' trills a bright young female voice from behind it. Stepping out she points up:

'And those are knitting needles. If you look closely you'll see the "wool" is actually barbed wire. This sculpture represents the suffering of the brave Boer women you'll meet today.'

'I am Alison de Vries from Benoni Park Academy,' says Bush Baby, extending her hand. The frisson that accompanies a teacher using their first name runs through the class. 'This is Grade 12 and this is Mthunzi.'

'Well, everyone, welcome to the Anglo-Boer War Museum. I'm Anna Vorstadt, a curator here, and I'll be taking your tour. You all have Afrikaans, *ja*?' She smiles cleanly at Mthunzi who nods once then turns to Mrs de Vries who chirps '*Ja*' on behalf of Grade 12. Everybody prepares to tune in to the frequency of the classroom.

Once inside Willem bolts to the disabled toilets because he doesn't want to have to stand next to Anton who hisses 'Spaz' as he rushes past. Then the tour begins. Anna hands each of them a piece of folded card the size of a bank card. She starts with Mrs de Vries then the boys, then the girls and hands the last to Mthunzi. 'Fucked up,' Anton sniggers, pointing at a wax figure of a Boer commando holding the old Orange Free State flag above him, his gesture of defiance undermined by his peeling grey moustache and missing eye. A *Bittereinder*. When everyone has their card, Anna tells them all to open the first page. Willem looks down:

Camp Record: BF/01/125a
Name: Master Frederick Philippus J. van
              der Watt
Other Names: 'Fred'

'You each have a copy of an official camp record,' says Anna, holding hers up. 'Inmates never saw these but the British kept careful notes on every man, woman and child in each of the camps.'

'What men?' asks Anton. 'Weren't they all fighting?'

'Not all,' says Anna. 'Older men who were injured in the first war of liberation, boys too young to join their fathers on commando and, of course, hands-uppers.'

'Moffies,' mutters Anton to stifled giggles.

'It's a little more complicated,' says Anna. 'But yes, they were considered cowards. Hands up if you know what a hands-upper is?' She waits for the usual laugh and it comes dutifully from one of the quieter girls. Nobody raises their hand.

'Hands-uppers were traitors,' says Willem, the words out of his mouth before he knew he was even going to speak. Not his words, Jan's maybe. 'Traitors who went over to the British.'

'That's right,' says Anna. 'Well done. Hands-uppers literally put their hands up in surrender and signed the Oath of Allegiance to the British Empire.'

Mthunzi raises her hand but Anna doesn't seem to notice. 'Did the British keep records in every camp?'

'Not in every camp, no, as we'll see. Very little is known about the black camps.'

'Ah, the black camps,' says Mrs de Vries as if she'd just remembered something while rolling her trolley out of the Pick n Pay. Something she couldn't be bothered going back for.

'I'm Helen Grobler,' trills Anton, waving his card, hands on hips, swishing imaginary skirts. 'Unmarried!' He winks at Willem who ignores him.

'We allocate cards randomly,' says Anna over the laughter. 'To make you think about gender.' More laughter. 'And identity. Does anyone know how many camps there were? How many civilians were imprisoned? 116,000 in forty camps. And how many died in the two years before the war was lost and the camps closed? 28,000 women and children – 22,000 were sixteen or under. That's about your age but most were much, much younger.' The laughter stops. Anna is satisfied. She pulls the patchwork cardigan her fiancé says is too ethnic around herself and makes a note to ask the janitor about fixing the AC. She opens her card to the next page and Grade 12 follow, glad of something to do.

Willem's says:

Name: Frederick van der Watt
Born in Camp: No
Age on arrival: Six years
Gender: Male

Race:	White
Marital status:	N/A
Nationality:	Orange Free State/Boer
Registration as child:	Yes

He tries to remember being six and finds he can very easily. It was when they got Britney, when his pa turned up and caught him dancing with Elise in front of the TV.

'Willem, please pay attention,' pleads Mrs de Vries. The rest of the class is halfway up to the next floor and here he is staring at the one-eyed *Bittereinder*. Has she missed his pill? The others were too drawn by the horrors anticipated ahead to notice him lagging. Anton leads on, head and shoulders above everyone else, his taxi-door ears visible for miles.

Upstairs there's plenty more to see. Willem thinks the British have the coolest uniforms, one is the same scarlet of the Imperial Guards in *Return of the Jedi*. Like birds, the further south the English fly the fancier their feathers became. One red-velvet-lined case is filled with medals and badges. Willem covets the Duke of Cambridge 17th Own Lancers insignia, a silver skull and crossbones. Also cool is the bronze acorn of the Cheshire Regiment. He imagines planting it and giant bronze oaks bursting from the dry red soil, leaves glinting in the summer sun before burnishing into autumn.

'Willem, don't touch,' says Mthunzi, gently lifting his hand from the glass cabinet where it leaves a hot print which quickly evaporates leaving a ghost hand. He blushes then pulls his hand away, wiping it on his trousers. He starts to say sorry but she's already turned back to the girls who are freaking out at some creepy old dolls.

Anna moves them all along to the life-size tableaux which aren't quite as crap as downstairs. 'This is a farm burnt by the British,' she says, pointing at the scene behind glass which looks like the shacks Willem passes on the school bus. Blackened timbers lie where they fell from a singed thatched roof but the whole thing is lit by flickering fluorescent light. An old Singer sewing machine lies on its side by a big Bible with the pages ripped out. He remembers seeing one like it in the bottom of Rayna's wardrobe when he was snooping for birthday presents, next to a pair of dusty old plastic pots. 'The Scorched Earth policy was supposedly intended to cut off support to men fighting on commando but the real aim was to break Boer morale by forcing their women and children onto the open veldt or concentrating them into camps like the one right here at Bloemfontein.'

Mrs de Vries nods. 'Yes, class. My great-grandmother was in the camp by the Vaal at Vereeniging. It was terrible, terrible, poisoned meat and dirty water and flies everywhere. All her sisters died.' She shivers as if cold was creeping up from the river.

Anna leads them over to a low table encased in Perspex. Inside sprawls a huge-scale model: hundreds of tiny white tents arranged in neat rows separated by white boulders the size of biscuit crumbs. Like World of Warcraft, only dusty.

'This is Bloemfontein Concentration Camp,' says Anna, pressing a button so a firefly-sized light comes on by a rectangular tin hut. 'And that's the hospital which many women called "the death house" because so few patients left alive. The cemetery is not featured because it would take up too much room but it would be right over … ' She walks across the room and stops. 'Here.'

She goes on. 'Mourners were only allowed ten minutes to say goodbye to their loved ones. Wood was a luxury needed for boiling the river water to make it safe to drink so often coffins contained more than one body. Many mothers cut up their dresses to make shrouds for their children. They were not permitted to go to the graveside so many burial sites remain unmarked.'

Willem presses a random button and a light comes on in another corner of the model. Anna walks back over. 'That's the camp prison, a prison within a prison. They called it the Bird Cage.' Willem squints into the tiny corrugated-iron hut, is sure he can see someone in there. 'And right next to it are the latrines. Happily, our budget doesn't run to immersive odours.'

Anton guffaws and makes farting noises. Anna goes on, 'We only know all this thanks to the bravery of Emily Hobhouse, an English lady who travelled here in 1901 to see conditions for herself. She kept detailed diaries, which the inmates were forbidden to do. This is one of her most famous entries: '*I call this camp system a wholesale cruelty ... To keep these camps going is murder to the children. Thousands, physically unfit, are placed in conditions of life that they have not the strength to endure. In front of them is blank ruin ... If only the English people would try to exercise a little imagination – picture the whole miserable scene. Entire villages rooted up and dumped in a strange, bare place. It can never be wiped out of the memories of the people.*'

'Did she visit the black camps?' Mthunzi asks.

'No. There were, of course, at least as many black camps but they were not thought safe for a lady.'

'But Bloemfontein was?'

'Yes, well, there were many black people coming and going here – some women kept their servants but there were also black people working in the laundry and as guards.'

'Because their homes and jobs went up in flames with the farms and the British charged them for their tents and rations,' says Mthunzi. 'Right?'

'Yes, that's right,' says Anna. 'They reported directly to the British and were carefully... managed.'

'Managed,' mutters Mthunzi. 'Right.'

'Yes,' Anna nods tightly. When she started at the museum there was no acknowledgement of the black camps. Now, thanks to her, there is a whole display. A bit of gratitude wouldn't go amiss. She banks this moment to share with her boyfriend then decides against it because it would only confirm his suspicions and he's even worse when he thinks he's right. She buttons her cardigan up and goes on.

'Miss Hobhouse was hated by the anti-Boer government in England and when she returned there few believed her initially. Here you can see a copy of the *Daily Mail*.'

Willem walks over and looks at the yellowing paper which reminds him of his gran's kitchen, all old with smoke. In huge letters the front page screams '*WOMAN:THE ENEMY!*'

'Soon other observers and wounded soldiers sent home confirmed what Miss Hobhouse had seen. Remember, there were no iPhones then – photography was still very new so this was the first time people could see the front line. Were it not for Miss Hobhouse's bravery and charity many more women and children would have died. She had conditions and rations improved and got the camps closed when the Peace was signed in 1902 although many thousands had to stay on because they had no farms to go back to. Her ashes are interred beneath the obelisk out front.'

Mrs de Vries shuffles awkwardly and looks around. There are no other visitors. Distant corners of the room are in darkness and most cabinets have no lights. From a speaker somewhere, a jaunty English voice bursts into song:

'I have come to say goodbye, Dolly Gray,
It's no use to ask me why, Dolly Gray,
There's a murmur in the air, you can hear it
everywhere,
It's the time to do and dare, Dolly Gray.'

She suddenly feels very alone and wishes she was
back in her classroom or the arms of her Jamie.

Anna leads them over to another case. 'Diaries were
forbidden in case they fell into enemy hands and
letters were censored but one or two women kept
diaries in secret. The most famous, which you may
have studied in school, is this one.' She points to a case
which contains a tiny blue book. It's propped open
and the curling pages are crowded with ant-size writing that looks more like sheet music. 'This is the diary
of Sarah van der Watt who arrived in Bloemfontein
on Thursday 10 January 1901. Now, who got her son,
Fred? Willem raised his hand. Anna tilted her head at
him sympathetically then continued.

'Like most Boer women, Sarah refused to sign the
oath but she paid a very high price.'

'Did she die there then?' asks Anton, pointing to
the model of the camp.

'No, she did not,' said Anna. 'In fact, Sarah was
eventually reunited with her husband.' Here she
looks directly at Willem again. 'Samuel van der Watt
surrendered himself at the camp on the 5th of April

1901 injured but recovering. Like many men, he couldn't bear to see his family suffer any more. He signed the oath and records show they left together. We'll learn more about their fate in a moment.'

They've arrived at another of her new displays, the one about the *agterryers* – freed black men who scouted for the commandos and sorted supplies. All part of the new history.

'Why weren't they given guns?' asks Mthunzi, reading the display.

'I suppose there just weren't enough for everyone,' says Anna, turning away. 'Right, I know you've all been holding on to your questions but I also know your teacher will be wanting a cup of coffee so before we head down to the café I'd like you all to turn to the final page and find out what happens.'

'Freed!' shouts Anton, waving his card as if he's won a prize. 'Helen Grobler: freed on the 7th of April 1901!' Mrs de Vries opens her own and coughs. 'Typhoid, I'm afraid.' One of the most popular girls bawls and the other girls fly to her side like iron filings to a magnet in science.

'And you?' Anna walks over to Willem. 'You got Fred, yes?'

Willem nods but doesn't want to find out his fate at the same time as everybody else. He unfolds the final page.

'Aloud please,' says Anna and the others stop exclaiming over their results and listen as Willem reads:

'Date arrival: 10/1/1901
Date departure: 4/4/1901
Reason departure: Death, malaria – ?'

The girls look at Willem like it's his fault.

'Samuel van der Watt got here the day after his son died,' says Anna. 'We don't know if he knew Fred was dying or if this was simply tragic coincidence.' She pauses and Willem hands her his card, eager to be rid of it. 'We do know Samuel and Sarah left Bloemfontein a couple of days later on the 7th of April to return to what was left of their farm. Sarah buried her diary not far from here where it was discovered in 1988. They left the same day as her friend Helen Grobler, who appears extensively in her diary. It's possible she even accompanied them. We can't know. However, we do know Sarah and Samuel went on to have another child – a girl – because her descendants have visited the museum and very kindly allow us to continue exhibiting Sarah's diary. Now, who's hungry?'

'I hope the coffee's good here,' says Mrs de Vries to Mthunzi. 'Do you drink coffee?'

The road home seems straighter and smoother but slower. Everybody's quiet, even Anton. They've taken that special museum hush with them. Most are drowsing. Willem peers out into the not-quite-night and wonders about the ostrich he saw earlier, hopes it's safe. Then he remembers there aren't any lions or anything, not really, just the memory of them. It probably lives on a farm anyway. Every few miles a pair of orange eyes flash but when he blinks they're gone.

A couple of the girls have drifted to the back of the bus so Mthunzi has planted herself there. Willem can't tell if she's sleeping or not without looking back. It might only be him and the driver still awake. He makes a cushion from his hoodie and slumps against the window wishing it had been this cold on the way down. He closes his eyes and thinks about the museum. He doesn't know any Freds. What actually is malaria? You got it off mosquitoes but did they lay eggs in you or what? His hand goes to his pocket but comes back empty. This is the problem with not having your phone, you can't know things.

He's the last to wake as they pull back into Jozi, which earns a round of applause. He wishes they'd not seen him sleeping. He drank a load of juice when Mrs de Vries gave him his Ritalin back at the museum so he really needs to pee again. He crosses his legs, thinks about the dust that came off the ostrich, about bones in the soil. The oldest human bones yet found were uncovered in a cave their minibus passed five minutes ago. Their ancestors were right there all this time. He tries to do what the psychologist said – breathe slowly, take control. He starts to panic, wonders if he could do it into an empty water bottle – not water, don't think about water. He puts his hoodie back over his lap and subtly undoes his trousers which brings some relief.

'Can we stop, Miss?'

'We're nearly there, Willem,' Mrs de Vries answers with the last of her patience. 'So, no.'

'Please, Miss.'

'Why?'

'I've got to … I need to … ' He can't bear to say it so just nods at his lap.

'No, you can just hold on, we're only ten minutes away.'

Ten whole minutes from the gates of Benoni Park Academy where his ma and Jan are waiting to pick him up. He closes his eyes and starts counting down from 600 – that's all ten minutes is, 600 seconds. At 442 the minibus hits a big bump and then another.

Mrs de Vries shrieks, her bug eyes falling out of her head. The girls fake-scream and Anton starts chanting, 'Moffie! Moffie! Moffie!' Only Mthunzi comes forward, asks if he's okay, producing woman-size tissues from her handbag. Willem can't speak. Humiliation blooms warm then cold across his grey flannels. It trickles into his good school shoes.

Mrs de Vries's shushing isn't working on the hyena pitch so Mthunzi stands as tall as she can in the minibus and shouts, 'Shame!' Grade 12 look far too quiet as their minibus pulls up to the school. The mild guilt of the waiting parents who'd enjoyed a teen-free Saturday is turned to anxiety by the pale, quiet faces behind the windows. Word spread faster than the stain.

The next day Willem stays in his room building and rebuilding atomic models of the noble gases: Helium, Neon, Argon, Krypton, Xenon, Radon. Odourless, colourless, simple: unreactive under normal circumstances. He could do them with his eyes closed and has, in fact, tested himself to be sure.

He can't go online because of yesterday, his Facebook – tumbleweed anyway – is now papered with SpongeBob and other yellow insults. His ma told his gran who emailed but he couldn't handle her being nice. Jan and his ma are pretending not to shout so he sticks his earbuds in and starts the audiobook of *The Philosopher's Stone* again but can't focus so drops into a *Star Trek* spiral on YouTube, watching the Enterprise escape over and over. He wonders what Harry is doing now.

When he finally ventures out for lunch Jan tells him to put his uniform through the wash. Willem fetches his still damp trousers from his bathroom then stuffs them in the machine and slams the door.

'Easy!' Jan warns. 'That cost money.'

Willem shrugs while his ma opens the machine drawer and pours in something that smells like the ready-made cocktail she sometimes drinks at home on a Saturday night.

'There's no point,' says Willem.

'Why?' she asks.

'I'm not going back.'

'What?' says Jan, looking at Irma who looks back to Willem.

'You've got to,' said Irma.

'No I don't,' says Willem. 'I can't.'

'You need your matric,' says Irma, who barely got hers.

'You're going back,' says Jan. 'And that's that.'

'You can't make me,' says Willem, turning to his mother. 'He can't.'

'No,' she sighs. 'He can't.'

For a second Willem thinks he's got away with it. He begins to imagine a future where he just stays in his room reading or better still goes back to his gran's and reads to her and maybe works on her garden.

'But you've got to go, Will,' says Irma. 'You need to finish school. You need your matric and your gran paid all that money.' Willem turns to leave as the washing machine fills with water and starts to churn. 'You can't let her down.'

'C'mon, Lil-Will,' says Jan, buddily punching him on the shoulder just hard enough.

Monday comes and Jan drops Willem off at the gates and watches him walk in then waits for ten full minutes. Willem knows what's coming, knows what Anton and his crew will say, knows they'll hold their noses in the corridor and say he stinks. Maybe he does. Willem knows some of the girls will give him pitying glances which he mustn't let settle because that would be truly fatal. He endures English, which he usually loves because it's the one class where they're supposed to speak English. He is grateful to Mrs de Vries for ignoring him. They're doing *Romeo and Juliet* and he watched the Baz Luhrmann film online where they both look like girls. He lets the soundtrack spool through his head as class rolls by: 'Young hearts run free, never be hung up, hung up like my man and me.' He's extra careful not to sing along. The song in his head drowns out most of the hissing pissing teasing.

The toilets at lunchtime are usually safe.

'Made it today, Lil-Will?' Anton steps out from a cubicle. Willem turns to leave but the rest of Anton's crew pile in from the corridor. They're all older but Anton fits right in because he's so tall, only his eagerness marks him out as not yet final year. One of them pushes Willem right into Anton who spins him away shouting, 'Get off, piss-moffie!' Another pin-balls Willem away and he slips on the wet floor and falls. Willem looks up at Anton who is reaching for his zip as the others chant, 'Do it, do it!' This isn't happening. Willem crawls into the nearest cubicle and is kick-closing the door when Anton bursts in. It happens fast, what happens next, it always does. Willem didn't mean it. They are all silenced by the dull thunk of bone connecting with cold, hard porcelain. Anton lies where he lands, head slumped in the toilet bowl, blood blooming in the water.

Afterwards the boys tell their teachers and the police that they saw it all: *Willem was always weird, he's got no friends, we always knew he would end up doing something like this.*

13

September 2010

'Two more chances than me, son,' shouts Jan, waving the contract in Willem's face. On the front it says *X Military Leaders* and beneath *STRENG VERTROULIK – HIGHLY CONFIDENTIAL*. It looks like a bad photocopy. It is a bad photocopy.

'I'm not your son!' cries Willem. Jan hasn't tried 'son' for years so he must be desperate.

'Don't I know,' smirks Jan, shaking his head. 'No boy of mine – '

'It'll be good for you,' says Irma opening the fridge, where as usual she hopes to find answers. She pops back up, a strawberry in her mouth. 'Shall I make us a fruit salad?'

Willem and Jan both stare, even Britney gives her a look from her cushion. She disappears back into the fridge.

'Listen to this,' says Jan, reading from the contract. '*We instil: faith, discipline, rules and regulations, respect, hard work, hard education, tough physical exercise, bearing, literacy, numeracy, efficiency, reliability, team work, animal care and conservation and community defence.'*

'So?' shrugs Willem. 'What do I care? I'm not going.'

'So, what are you going to do now? Eh, Mr Clever? You've been hanging round here for a year. Driving your mother mad. You think she needs this? All the shrinks and the pills, expelled because you – '

'I. Didn't. Do. Anything,' shouts Willem, pausing between each word and wishing that he had, that he'd grabbed Anton's big stupid ears and smashed his head on that toilet over and over.

'*Ja*, so how come he ended up with twenty stitches?' Jan had been secretly proud when Mr de Villiers rang. He'd never felt remotely proud of the boy before but he continues to deny the one right thing he's done.

'You didn't do this, you won't do that,' sing-songs Jan. 'I didn't want to do National Service but look at me now, eh. You couldn't take the real deal, let me tell you, getting *opfokked* – drilling till you puke blood. But this place is *lekker*, it'll sort you out – see?' He holds the contract up and reads aloud: '*We make men out of boys.*'

Willem sneers and folds his arms.

'It's not funny,' says Irma, closing the fridge. 'You've no matric, how will you get work? It's not like how it was, you can't just walk in, there's all the affirmative action and … what will you do?'

'We're not made of money,' Jan says. 'You're lucky you're not in jail.'

'You were the one always telling me to "man up",' says Willem, walking over to the fridge wishing he could just climb in and close the door and slip into a cool sleep for ever. Go into stasis like in *Aliens* only with no monsters when he woke up.

'Not like that, you don't fight dirty,' says Jan, putting his fists up. Britney leaps off her cushion as fast as her little legs can carry her and stands growling between him and Willem. 'Easy, tiger,' says Jan, raising his hands in mock surrender.

'They do all this scuba and trekking and teach you all about the animals so you get a job as a ranger at the end,' says Irma, who imagines being taken on a safari by her son wearing a proper name-badge and a gun over his shoulder. 'It's not a punishment, Will – it's a treat. You love animals! It'll be good for you. You'll be outdoors all the time with other boys like you.'

Willem gulps. There might be other boys, but they won't be like him. He's never met another boy like him, who likes the stuff he likes. Except Harry.

'The General is a good man,' says Irma, pointing to the photo of him that came with the contract. His shoulders fill his uniform. He's a bit like Tom Selleck in *Magnum, P.I.* with that big moustache. Even Jan says he's solid, proper, *moerse*. He's helped hundreds of boys like Willem. And he's right, things are terrible – she can't watch the news any more. Willem needs to toughen up. This man can sort him.

'And it'll get you away from your computer and that phone,' says Jan. 'Get you right.'

Willem shrugs. They wouldn't understand, they never understand. Then it hits him: 'I'll go back to Gran!'

Irma opens her mouth but Jan shakes his head.

'What?' says Will. 'She doesn't like being in that big house and I can help with her pension stuff and her family tree.' He imagines the pair of them sitting up late reading to one another. Suddenly he really needs to be back in his old bed looking up at the stars.

'Listen,' says Jan, as if Willem had any choice. 'We talked about this as a family and your gran agrees – '

'As a family? What?'

Irma looks puzzled, is trying to speak when Jan raises his hand. 'Your gran agrees it's best –'

'Best for who? All you ever wanted was me out the way so you can have her all to yourself. Now you're sending me to some fucking –'

'Don't talk to your mother like that!'

'To some FUCKING … what even is this place? I Googled it, I can't find it, where isn't on Google…?' His voice, not yet fully broken, sounds like a radio trying and failing to tune in. He shakes his head and big hot tears roll down cheeks still some months from a proper shave.

Jan turns away.

'Will, it's for your own good,' says Irma reaching into the back pocket of her jeans and holding up a familiar brown bottle. She rattles it. 'Will-Will, baby.'

'I don't need pills, Ma,' sobs Willem. 'No more, please.'

'They calm you –'

'I don't need to calm down!'

Jan clenches his fist, closes his eyes, starts counting down from a hundred in his head.

'Don't make Mama cry,' begs Irma, drying her eyes. 'You know I hate it when you make me cry. Now, you gonna be a good boy?'

Jan continues counting down. He really doesn't know what he'll do if he ever gets to zero.

Willem balls his eyes with his fists. 'Okay, Ma,' he gives in, the skin beneath his eyes taut with salt and heat and hurt.

Jan pauses at 58 and opens his eyes: 'So, you'll go?'

That morning he'd shown Irma where to sign on the contract before transferring the non-refundable deposit to New Dawn Safari Rangers Ltd.

Willem shrugs. Even his gran is on their side. He wishes for his pa then realises there's no point. 'If it's what she wants.'

Irma looks at her two favourite boys in the whole wide world and thinks of the test she did that morning in her en suite, the jacaranda-purple stripe promising a new beginning for them all.

PART THREE

I

1 October 2010

The gate snaps closed. As Willem glances in the wing mirror two khaki-clad boys bolt forward to chain it. Their pace suggests imminent invasion. Geldenhuys jerks the handbrake on. Willem is thinking about getting out when somebody flings his door open flooding the cabin with all the heat and light of the day.

'*Uit!*'

Willem looks to Geldenhuys who nods urgently. Before he can move two sets of hands are on him and he's out on the ground blinking up at a dozen pairs of dusty black leather boots. His duffel bag crashes too close. As he pushes himself up another, spotless, pair of boots lands right between his hands. The boots are so shiny they reflect his face back. He looks pale.

'On your feet, son,' says the owner of the boots in Afrikaans in a low, gentle *there, there* voice, as if Willem standing up is the one thing in this world that would truly make him happy. He extends a man's hand, sack-rough and outdoor-brown but silvered with scars. It hoists Willem up so effortlessly he bounces slightly. Willem squints against the sun which is moving out of the man's way. His ma would call him 'handsome', a big Boer right out of 'De La Rey' – the only song Jan likes. He's got a clipped cigar-brown moustache and a surprising mullet the exact same shade. He appraises Willem with the rapidly assessing eyes of the diamond dealers down from Kimberley that you sometimes see in Sandton Mall, briefcases chained to their wrists. Medals march across the expanse of his chest. At his side hang a radio, a black-handled knife and a gun like Jan's. Apparently, he doesn't need a name-badge.

Geldenhuys slams the door of the bakkie then stands to attention between them: 'B-Brandt, sir.'

'I know who this fine young man is,' he says with-out turning. He's used to being heard. Then, slowly to Willem the way his ma used to talk to Elise, 'Do you know who *I* am, Brandt?'

Willem shrugs. He runs his fingers through his hair, his curls feel even curlier than usual. In front of him stand ten boys in identical khaki with identi-cal buzzcuts, all white and evenly spaced like skittles. They're all about his age. Their boots occupy the bit of the world they press upon with recently assumed confidence and they stare straight ahead. Their uniform only draws attention to their differences.

Some still have the bird-like ribs of boys while others boast wheat-field stubble and brand-new shoulders. Sixteen hits everybody differently but this lot are all taller, shorter, fatter, thinner than normal. He thought there'd be more of them and that they'd all be like Anton.

The man steps closer to Willem who takes a sudden interest in the ground. Gently he takes Willem's chin in his hand and tilts his face up then reaches for his shades and slips them off. 'That's better, eh?' He flashes denture-perfect teeth, laughing over his shoulder to the other cadets who all laugh back, all except Geldenhuys. They fall silent as soon as he starts to speak.

'*Ja*, now we can see each other proper.'

Without being asked, the most normal-looking boy steps forward and pockets Willem's Oakleys then slots back in line. His nametag says *Volker*. Willem opens his mouth but Geldenhuys shoots him a look so full of fear he stops. A braai is getting going nearby and Willem's stomach remembers he refused the pancakes his ma made special.

'I'm the General,' the man says, as if Willem hadn't guessed. He pauses then raises his arms like a politician on the news. 'And this is New Dawn.'

2

That first night Willem feels famous. Everybody calls him Brandt, claps him on the back, *Hey hey, howzit, Brandt?* He's never really noticed how strong his second name is. He can be Brandt now, he thinks, sitting up straight around the fire with all the other boys who left their first names outside the fence.

This place is smaller than he'd imagined. Ahead sag two rows of tents like the ones in that museum in Bloem – cream canvas worn and patched with years of scraps. Dragonflies F16 across a man-made pond and next to this rises a giant cotton-bud flag-pole. Willem recognises the red, white and black flag from Jan's library. Past that is a low concrete sty of big dirty pigs. Some busy white chickens bustle around, but there are no other animals, not even an ostrich. So much for conservation. In the centre stands a guard tower covered in the same camouflage netting that's draped over the fifteen-foot barbed-wire fence surrounding the whole compound. Who are they watching for?

Looking through the flames at the other cadets, it's clear nobody in here was getting picked for any teams out there. Except maybe Volker. Corporal stripes adorn his shoulders making him their commanding officer. One boy is so tall and thin he looks like a folded razor. Spreading next to him is his opposite. Several have taped earlobes covering piercings and even Volker has a tattoo peeking from his sleeve, black tendrils creeping down his arm. Willem can't identify the leaves in the dark. We should all still be at school, he realises: we're all problems here to get fixed. He doubts any of them had a buzzcut before. He wonders when his curls will come off. He's never liked them, threatened them with scissors a hundred times but his ma always pleaded. Maybe he'll move faster without them.

Everybody knows his name but nobody knows anything else about him – nobody knows Argon is his favourite Noble Gas, nobody knows he's almost memorised *The Philosopher's Stone* and *The Return of the King*, nobody knows his best friend is his gran. Willem is suddenly average, maybe even slightly above, and it feels glorious.

Bottles of Castle bob in a blue cooler filled with melting ice and beer is the perfect thing to wash down the meat. Willem's tongue probes his molars for burnt bits. The braai is still smoking and he thinks of the cigarettes he nicked from his ma confident they'd make good currency. They're all speaking Afrikaans even though it's just them.

'Smoke, boys?' he asks in English, jumping up and shoving his arm deep in his duffel. He *ta-das* the pack out like a magician. Nobody moves.

'No? Awww, c'mon.'

Silence. He offers the pack to Geldenhuys who shakes his head and knots his arms. Volker jumps up and snatches the pack tossing it on the fire where it catches straight away.

'What the – ?'

'Rules,' says Volker in Afrikaans. 'No smoking. No smoking, no drugs, no mobiles, no – '

'That was all I had!' cries Willem, staring at the flames.

'And quit with the English,' Volker spits – actually spits. 'This is South Africa, man. Not England. Not your fancy school. So, we speak Afrikaans! Search him!' Two of the bigger cadets grab Willem and start slapping him up and down. He braces for more but they drop him, disappointed.

'Enjoy that?' laughs Volker, rubbing himself all over. 'You.' He snaps his fingers at Geldenhuys who jumps up. 'His bag.' Without hesitating Geldenhuys fillets Willem's duffel, spreading the contents by the fire.

'Get off my stuff.' Willem starts towards him but again Geldenhuys's face says stop.

'No English, no smoking, no alcohol,' intones Volker.

'Oh yeah,' says Willem, turning round and necking his beer, already feeling Brandt fall back into the shadows away from the warmth and light of the fire. Volker snatches the bottle from his hand and tips the last of it hissing onto the fire. The others just sit and watch, relieved it's not them.

'Zero alcohol,' he says, tapping the bottle before dropping it into the embers where it soon begins to crackle. 'Can't you read? Don't you know? We're soldiers now, gotta stay sharp, gotta be ready.' He turns and points at the guard tower where a watchful light has come on.

'For what?' Willem turns to the others. They look away.

Volker is about to speak when Geldenhuys squawks, 'C-contra.' Willem knows he's found his phone and is about to beg Volker not to throw it on the fire, when Geldenhuys hands over a second pack of cigarettes. His ma must have squirrelled them.

'Naughty boy,' tuts Volker, unsheathing the pack from the clear plastic which shrinks to nothing as it hits the flames. He then empties the cigarettes in one by one so the air is briefly smokable. Nobody moves.

'Now, let's get you looking like a soldier,' says Volker as the tall thin cadet appears handing him a heavy pair of shears. Willem recalls the cut on Geldenhuys's head and runs his hand through the curls his ma promised he'd love when he was big.

Volker points in front of him: 'Kneel.'

Willem turns to the faces glowing round the fire and laughs but they just keep looking down. This is no joke. He thinks about making a run for it, but where?

'Kneel!'

Volker snaps his fingers and Willem feels two sets of hands on him and when they can't get him down as easily as they thought they kick the backs of his knees. He falls forward and they hold his shoulders. Volker gets a handful of his curls and jerks his head forward. He feels the night air whisper on the back of his neck.

'Hold still,' says Volker, snipping the air in front of his face. 'Don't want any accidents. Soon have you right for the General.'

As curls fall around his face Willem imagines he is Argon – still, inert, invisible. *Don't cry*, he tells himself, *you hated your hair*. 'Cut! Cut! Cut!' chants Volker with each snip and the boys clap as the shears snap. Soon Willem feels the heat from the fire tight on his scalp and there's a big cheer as the final curl falls. Willem watches it catch on a breeze then shrivel in the flames.

'That's better,' says Volker, extending a hand. Willem refuses it and pushes himself to his feet. 'Suit yourself.'

A tired trumpet sounds from beyond the fence and the boys jump up pairing off to their tents. 9 p.m. Lights Out. Volker pisses luxuriously on the fire then turns to Willem as he zips up. 'Bedtime, Will. You're in with G-G-Geldenhuys.' He purses his lips. 'Night, night.'

3

'We know they're coming,' insists the General. No good morning, no breakfast, just the same thready trumpet in the middle of the night. The sun is still only a suggestion at the bottom of the sky. Willem searches blearily for the Southern Cross and tries to wake up. In summer, the nights are as cold as the days hot. He shivers in boxers and a T-shirt. The others are all dressed. They must sleep in their boots.

'And this time we'll be ready. That means we need to be up and dressed for Reveille, eh, Brandt?'

Even in the half-light Willem can see Volker's grin. He doesn't know what to do so just stands there. The General steps towards him.

'Haircut, good. Ma not here to dress you? Shall we call her up and get her to come and help you?' He leans in and sniffs. 'Maybe give you a bath too, eh?'

Blushing makes Willem feel a little less cold. Blue smoke wisps up out of the embers of the braai and he wills the warmth over.

'So, boys, who can tell Brandt our rules?'

'I know some already,' says Willem, determined to stop the slide in his popularity that Volker started last night, desperate not to be Lil-Will any more. To be Brandt.

The General raises an eyebrow and Geldenhuys nudges him. 'Sir! I know some already.'

'You do, eh? Quick learner. Not what your step-dad says – he's a smart guy, known him since way back. He says you got problems, got chucked out of school, sent to a shrink.' The General paces round him looking him up and down. 'Let's hear it then.'

'No English, no smoking, no alcohol.'

'Good,' says the General, genuinely pleased. 'Soldiers need to be fit and sober. What else?'

There is a pause then Volker shouts, 'No mobiles, sir!'

Willem still can't believe Geldenhuys found his cigarettes but missed his phone. He tries not to even think about it in front of the General. He plans to dig it out of his duffel then find a proper hiding place but Geldenhuys is always around.

'Why no mobiles, Brandt?'

'I don't know, sir,' Willem says. 'Distracting?'

The General fixes him with his eyes. 'Volker, why do we forbid mobiles and unauthorised radio use?'

Volker steps forward and the General's words march out of his mouth: 'Information is ammunition, sir.'

'That's right, Corporal. At ease.'

Volker puffs up, out-glows the embers of the braai.

The sun makes a break for it as the General paces in front of them like a lion in the zoo only there are no bars between them and him. 'For years we underestimated our enemy – we credited them with the intelligence of beasts because they acted like animals. We treated them as any good farmer would. And how did they repay us?'

He pauses to consider this speech. He's delivered it for over fifteen years to hundreds of boys in dozens of camps like this. Boys who now do good honest work guarding white farms from Cape Town to Johannesburg. After 1994 the supply all but dried up but as the headlines got worse cadets started coming through again. The National Service ban is a disgrace so it's up to him and what's left of the AWB to train these boys up. If they survive, South Africa survives. This latest batch is the worst yet – freaks and moffies. That Geldenhuys had longer hair than his wife. But he'll get them all up to Volker's mark. He'll build another army.

Freed from the horizon the sun springs up and in the clean early light the camp is even shabbier than Willem realised. The General points to the sun and goes on. 'We brought light to darkness but now we're the last white men in Africa. The Belgians fled the Congo, the French left Algeria, the Portuguese, Italians, even the Germans are gone. But we're still here – we are still here! Why? Because this is our land!'

He pauses in front of Willem. 'So, in here we speak only the tongue God gave us – not the cockroach click–click we beat at Blood River, not English lies. Afrikaans!'

Volker cheers and the others don't miss their cue. Willem remembers all the locks on all the doors, all the bars on all the windows, all the headlines: car-jackings, gang-rapes, farm attacks. He realises that last night was the longest he's ever spent outdoors. Jan threatened to take him camping but never did. In Jozi most of the stars are too scared to make an appearance but out here he can find stars he's only ever seen on the ceiling over his old bed at his gran's. Out here the stars are free.

'It wasn't always like this,' says the General. Willem has heard a lot of this from Jan and even a bit from his gran when she showed him how low her walls used to be. 'The blacks were better off before too – before we let the terrorists out and called them freedom fighters and let them ruin our country.'

The General pauses and remembers Colonel Terre'Blanche, the night he was beaten to death in his own bed with lead pipes by two boys raised on his own farm, boys he'd trusted, indoor boys who will quietly disappear the day they get out of jail.

'How many farmers have died defending their homes? How many? One thousand – one thousand! And how many murderers have gone to jail? Not one! Because now the Kaffirs run the courts. Justice has fled our land!'

He swallows conspicuously. Boys this age will do anything, anything, to avoid embarrassment. If he can get them now then that's that. 'They steal our farms and can't even care for the animals, the crops die so we have droughts and our shops are empty. Free houses, free water, free electricity – they want it all for free! They can't even keep the lights on!'

Willem remembers the power cuts – long dark hours without the internet, long hot nights without air conditioning and windows you can't open, the constant bleep of alarms, the panic button by his bed, the razor wire with roses growing through it, the neighbours with the perfect garden they never go in because it's full of security snakes, according to the sign they had to put up. He's only in this place now because he got expelled but what happened with Anton only happened because of what he can hardly bear to remember on the minibus. And that only happened because they couldn't stop on the road because of what might have happened if they had. If it had been safe to stop he could have got out and had a piss and that would have been that. He could have been at home right now.

The General points to a big shed by the gate. 'In here we have our own power, our own water, our own language. It goes dark when I say! We are well supplied and there are many like us. When the Kaffirs call their Uhuru and rise up, when that Red Day dawns we will be ready and this time we will not stay our hand, we will take back the land God gave us!'

He pauses for more cheering led by Volker.

'*Bloed roept om wraak* – blood calls for vengeance! We call for it as our fathers did. We are the Israelites in the desert. We are the chosen people!'

The birds singing for the dawn reach a new pitch.

'You're all brothers now. You're all my sons and I'll give you what the army gave me: a father. Now, Brandt, what are the rules?'

Willem no longer feels cold. Maybe this is Helm's Deep, the Last Stand of Rohan against the darkness of Mordor. Maybe there really are Orcs at the gates. Maybe he just needs to get through this shit and get back home.

'No smoking, no drinking, no English and no mobiles, sir!'

'Very good, Brandt,' says the General, walking over. He licks a finger and draws it across Willem's fore-head leaving a clean mark in the soot from last night's fire, reverse war-paint. 'Maybe there's hope for you yet. Clean kit, clean body, clean mind. Yes?'

Willem nods vigorously, finds he wants to please this man or at least not displease him. 'Yes, sir!'

The General walks over to the edge of the pond and spits in it. 'Good, good. Now, boys, what do you say we baptise our new recruit?'

4

They didn't know, Willem tells himself. They didn't know I can't swim. Flies billow around the tent as he dries himself and he wishes for that sticky paper his gran used to hang in the kitchen.

Geldenhuys doesn't know where to look, so lies on his sleeping bag with his back to his new tent-mate. The dorm at school was one thing but he's never shared with just one other and hated camping when his parents dragged him to the farm. He'd rather have stayed at school, the only boys left for summer were *Uitlanders* and not so bad. Nobody wanted to share when he got here which didn't bother him though it was meant to. He listens to the rough towel saw across Willem's back then slow between his toes and else-where. He imagines Willem's skin blush beneath it.

'You can turn round,' says Willem, wrapping the towel twice round his waist while he roots in his bag for boxers.

It was Geldenhuys who'd thrown him the rope. The pond was deeper than it looked. Willem didn't touch the bottom, not even when he went under the second time. He flailed for the edge and when he found it Volker nudged his hands off with his boot. The General stood watching. Somehow, Willem kicked back up and as he gasped a rope splashed next to him and he grabbed it pulling himself out to clapping. As soon as Willem was out Geldenhuys dropped the rope. They cheered as he coughed up pond and the General thumped his back and he laugh-choked with them.

'So, what do we actually do here?' Willem asks, turning away to pull his boxers on under his towel. He got changed like this the one time he'd gone to the gym with Jan just to shut up his ma. Jan had swaggered and swung about.

'Drill, digging, h-h-history,' says Geldenhuys over his shoulder in English.

'Afrikaans only, Geldenhuys,' says Willem, only half joking. His tent-mate half laughs.

'My name's Victor.'

'Not according to your badge,' says Willem, enjoying the feel of his new khaki shirt as he does it up leaving the top button undone, as always. 'I'm Willem, Will. You can turn round now. I'm dressed.'

Geldenhuys rolls over and sits up.

'How do I look?'

'Same as everybody else,' Geldenhuys says, looking at his watch. 'Two minutes till drill, best run.'

'Okay,' says Willem, putting out his hand to help Geldenhuys up. 'Thanks again for the rope by the way, I can't – '

'Swim, I guessed,' Geldenhuys interrupts, refusing his hand. 'I better show you how before we start scuba.'

'But I can run,' says Willem, dashing out, leaving Geldenhuys wrestling with the tent flap.

'Glad you could join us,' says the General as Willem arrives at the Assembly Ground, Geldenhuys panting behind.

In his right fist, he holds a clipboard:'Morning drill 0700–0900.' He reads on: 'Then Volker to allocate grids and shovels for digging 0930–1230. I remind you each pit must be four feet deep and filled in immediately after inspection, yes? We can't have any more accidents.'

He looks up. 'Then fodder.'

A stagey groan greets this news so the General lets the new arrival in on the joke:'She may not be the best cook but she's my cook, so enough insubordination.'

A dozen voices answer as one:'Yes, sir.'

Someone makes a small gagging noise. Instantly the General locates the sound and beckons the offender over. Willem remembers him from round the fire, Connor. In any class, in any school, he'd be the fat boy. Connor ambles over, each breath a labour.

'Fodder not gourmet, eh?' says the General. Connor covers the remaining paces as quickly as he can. 'Rather sit on your fat, lazy arse? That's the problem with this country now.'

Connor bows his head. The back of his neck is red and getting redder. His collar shifts revealing the top of his spine, paper-white and stooped from a lifetime looking down.

'What you see there, eh?' asks the General. He leans down and makes a show of scanning the ground before looking right up into Connor's face.

'What? Eh? *Koekies*? Stand up straight!'

Connor can't move.

'Look at me, boy!' Just as Connor lifts his head the General klopps him with his clipboard. Connor cries out but doesn't cover his gushing nose, just stands there. Willem puts his hands to his own nose and Geldenhuys elbows him.

Nobody moves, not even Volker. The General shakes his head, his face a mask of genuine disappointment, then takes a perfectly white square handkerchief from his pocket and wipes the blood off his clipboard in three efficient gestures. His wife can't cook but she loves to iron, likes the clean whoosh of steam, even if she's the only white woman for a hundred miles doing such a chore. It gives her dignity.

'*Opfok* for you, Connor. Corporal, you know the drill.'

Volker cracks his red, ready knuckles and sucks a deep breath in through tight nostrils.

The cadets form a neat square round the flagpole, three each side. When Volker blows his whistle they drop as one: twenty press-ups, twenty squats then twenty seconds running on the spot. If you don't get your knees up high you get a slap from Volker who walks round looking like he could drill all day. Willem is glad of all the secret exercises he did in his bedroom and thinks it's a shame Jan can't see him now. He quickly learns to inhale on the ascent so he doesn't suck up dirt and imagines himself back home, feels the carpet slip beneath his palms. Volker watches closely but can't fault him and this pleases Willem until he sees that anger, like lightning, must go somewhere. He winces as it strikes Geldenhuys whose arms tremble after two sets – he's swim-team fit but he's been here a month and it shows, the skin on his high cheekbones is taut and brown like paper on a tightly wrapped parcel.

After another set Volker blows his whistle again: five laps of the inside perimeter while he stands with his stopwatch taking notes. Every time Willem passes Volker shouts, 'Boo!' and every time Willem flinches and hates himself for it. The chain-link fence jinks merrily as the boys run past and when he gets up to speed Willem trails his fingers along it feeling it spring to his touch.

After five laps, they huff back to the flagpole and do another three sets of push-ups, squats and running on the spot. Connor wheezes back last so they're forced to watch him huff until he flounders to his knees and pukes. *Opfok.* Then it's the leopard crawl: a shallow hundred metre trench of soil and rock. You lie on your front and when Volker whistles you crawl, not like a baby but flat on your belly, pulling yourself forward with your hands and feet. Like a leopard stalking bok. At speed. You can't get up because the trench is criss-crossed with barbed wire – Geldenhuys's back, glimpsed in the tent, is proof of its sharpness. You can't even look up, so you don't know how far you've got left. You can only go forward.

After drill the General reappears. 'Special tradition for new cadets,' he says, and marches them to the latrines. They're at the back of camp screened by rusting sheets of corrugated iron. Flies billow as they arrive. In the depths, Willem can just about pick out a scrap of familiar green. 'All it's fit for,' says the General, holding up a fresh South African flag and spitting on it. 'How many colours in this rag?'

Everybody knows it's six. Volker steps forward: 'Five.'

'That's right,' says the General, tossing it in the mire. 'Blue, red, green, yellow and white. Black is not a colour. Black is darkness, ignorance, want. Black is the absence of light!'

He orders the boys to step forward one by one and piss on it. Volker's hips jerk as he marks out the Y. Willem waits till last and everybody watches except

Geldenhuys. But now, irony, he can't go. He closes his eyes and strains. Nothing. Volker sniggers. *Come on, come on.* The flag is Jan and Anton and this place and Willem is surprised by how good it feels when he manages to let go.

Finally, fodder. The gate opens and the General drives the bakkie in with a cool box on the back – a couple of boxes of Strawberry Pops and some sliced white bread and some old ham. Geldenhuys grabs a loaf and shares with Willem. They eat without talking sitting in the shade of the bakkie. Volker makes a show of chewing biltong he said the General gave him. Before they've even finished there's another whistle and everybody jumps up: digging. Each pair of cadets is issued a laminated gridded map of the camp. Every square on the grid is outlined in black. Each pair is to dig a pit four feet deep and four feet wide in their designated square. After Volker's inspected it they are to fill it in putting every plant and rock back exactly where they were. This is a conservation project, the General reminds them. Afterwards you mark it off with a red cross. There are many more black squares than red crosses. It's going to be a long day. It's going to be a long three months.

Willem and Geldenhuys collect their shovels again and swing them as they follow the map to the next square. As usual, they are a pair. Geldenhuys hardly stutters when it's just them. They talk over and through each other. Always in English. About school and how stupid it is. About their parents and how stupid they are. After half an hour they reach their destination. Willem was told he'd be looking after animals in here. It's been a week and chickens are the most exotic specimens he's seen.

'It's like *Holes* without the funny bits,' says Willem as they assess today's square.

'I loved that book,' say Geldenhuys. 'That makes you Zero.'

'Or you,' says Willem. 'What exactly are we conserving?' he asks poking around with his boot.

Geldenhuys shrugs.

One plant occupies most of the space: spikes of orange flowers stick up from fleshy tongue-shaped leaves.

'*Aloiampelos striatula*,' says Willem.

'Right,' says Geldenhuys, a little impressed. He points to a big scrubby tree nearby which, for some reason, the weaverbirds have shunned preferring to hang their nests round the base of the guard tower. They've still not seen anyone go up there.

'*Combretum imberbe*,' says Willem. 'Leadwood. It's super-dense and takes ages to burn. You can use the ash for toothpaste.'

'Or you can just use toothpaste,' says Geldenhuys lifting his shovel. 'We better start before Volker comes.'

'Right,' says Willem, tuning in to the danger Geldenhuys is used to.

The soil is red and crumbly and whirls off in the little winds that whip up out here. Every morning they wake up full of dust, their eyes gritty, mouths dry. The General says they'll know what they're digging for if they find it. Carefully they lift the aloe. Willem bends down to shift the roots and gasps. 'Look!'

All Geldenhuys sees is soil. 'What?'

'Look!' says Willem, pointing to a small, particularly smooth, rock. '*Lithops* – Living Stone. They're really rare in the wild now.'

'It looks a bit like … ' Geldenhuys tilts his head. 'An arse!' Willem laughs then cups it carefully and replants it to one side where they won't tread on it. As they start lifting the aloe something black scuttles out. Geldenhuys swings with his shovel.

'Don't!' shouts Willem, staying his hand. '*Parabuthus transvaalicus.*'

'A scorpion, I know,' says Geldenhuys moving closer to Willem. '*Grossus hideousa poisonoso.*'

They watch until it disappears under a rock to wait for the night then get back to digging. The aloe clump was hiding a waist-thick tree stump. It's so old it seems impossible it was ever actually alive. Willem can't identify it from what's left. How many boys have been on this treasure hunt? They hack the soil around it and as the hole gets deeper they talk less, hopping in and out to shift rocks. It's just Willem and Geldenhuys and the scrape of shovel on soil and stone. Every now and then Geldenhuys gets his inhaler out and takes a puff holding each breath for as long as he can.

'Want a go?' He holds it out.

'Sure,' Willem shrugs. As he puts it to his mouth he sees a wet mark on the blue plastic where Geldenhuys's lips were but takes a puff anyway. He can't hold it and coughs. Geldenhuys claps him on the back and they laugh. After another hour Connor rolls by on a rusty bike leaving them water and a slice of pap. Willem wishes for his gran's macaroni cheese. His stomach rumbles at the memory of the braai that first night. His ma says she should put a swing door on the fridge. She can talk.

They stop to eat. They're nearly done for the day. Soon it's history. He looks past the fence to the giant steelworks on the horizon. It could be a mile away, it could be a hundred. There's nothing but veldt between him and it. There's nobody out here. He feels his T-shirt stick to his back as sweat cools. The sun is getting ready to go but it's still hot. Even stones small enough to throw now cast shadows – soon they'll all stitch together to make the night and then he can try to sleep.

Another whistle goes and they down tools and march back to the flagpole. There the General sits them in rows on low rickety benches, worse than church, round the pole where the red, white and black flag flies. The blackboard is so old it's grey. There are no books. Chalk squeals as the General writes *FREEDOM, POWER* and *PURITY!*

'This right here is where mankind started,' says the General gesturing all around. 'South Africa is the cradle of man. Not his coffin.'

Willem nods. He knows all about the remarkable finds in the caves just outside Jozi, so close to the motorway they echo with cars. Caves where you might find a sleeping dragon, a Smaug atop his hoard. At the very back, where the sun has never reached, are long narrow shafts a man like the General could never get down. At the very bottom of one of these, piles of bones were laid to rest with love long, long ago. And on the walls above flicker ochre paintings of the world they left behind: antelope frozen in eternal flight, tigers stripe-deep in the long grass that still grows outside and elephants with tusks so great they hold all of time in their beckoning curve.

'We were here first, we moved from those caves to the veldt, perfected hunting then farming. We nurtured this land. They stumbled in from some-where out there and saw what we had. They got jealous, like Cain. Covetous. They began to ape us – dress like us, talk like us, pray like us. But they are not us. They can't farm because they can't plan and they're cruel – know why they eat goats, not sheep? Because sheep don't scream when you skin them.'

Willem thinks of Elise, the only black person he's ever really talked to. He tries to imagine Elise skin-ning a screaming goat and it's ridiculous. All he's ever seen her do is sweep, dust, smile. Willem got the Struggle in school but he's never been to Soweto. His ma can't believe they do tours there now, refused to let him go to the Apartheid Museum in Year 7. What does Willem really know?

'If we don't want to end up as another pile of bones in a cave then it's survival of the fittest, right now, this moment. *Ja?*'

Ten sets of shoulders shrug. Only Volker shouts, '*Ja!*'

The General goes on. 'You need to hear this! You need to know the truth! Not the politically correct bullshit you get out there. AIDS is God's work but there are still more of them and interbreeding weakens our genes. We must not forget who we are – history is on our side.'

On the blackboard, the General scrawls: *Job 6:11: What is my strength, that I should hope? And what is mine end?* On the last word, his chalk snaps and falls to the ground where he crushes it, white into red under his boot.

After history their official duties are done. As always, the General's favourites get fed first. This time the cool box is filled with brown paper bags of cold McDonald's. Willem and Geldenhuys and Connor wait while Volker and his pals take what they want then run for what's left.

'My parents didn't pay 22,000 rand for this shit,' says Connor, stuffing some saggy fries in his mouth.

'Why don't you fill out a complaint form?' says Geldenhuys, snatching a burger. 'Your pal Volker can get you one.'

'He's not my pal,' says Connor. 'He's – '

'Scary?'

'Yeah.'

'Ugly?'

'Yeah!' Connor laughs and walks with them as they head over to their tent to eat. Geldenhuys lets the flap close in his face.

'What did you do that for?' asks Willem.

'Somebody's got to be lower down,' says Geldenhuys. 'And it's not going to be me or you.'

Willem and Geldenhuys share whatever they get and promise that when they're out of here they're hitting the food court in Benoni Park Mall and eating till they're as fat as Connor who they reckon must have been Jabba-like when he arrived.

After dinner it's the latrines and then the 'shower': a cold-water hose and a bucket round the side of the tool shed. There's no floor, so you stand in a puddle of mud, your feet dirtier than before. There's no cubicle or curtain so everybody can see you. Volker showers every evening and doesn't care who watches. Connor is sweaty as always and decides to brave it. Volker and his crew watch him strip then laugh as he gasps under the cold water and tries desperately to tempt foam from a brick of red soap. Every time he turns away they duck in front of him until eventually he bursts into tears and grabs his towel and runs to his tent. Willem turns to go after him but Geldenhuys shakes his head: 'N-n-not worth it.'

After Lights Out Willem and Geldenhuys whisper into the gap between their sleeping bags. Geldenhuys isn't that into sci-fi but is deeply into listening to Willem talk about it. Willem remembers his afternoons with Harry and wonders where he is now. They fantasise about pushing Volker in the latrines and laugh into their pillows. Willem never knew he was funny. The only book they're allowed is the Bible so they recount over and over their favourite bits of *The Lord of the Rings*, argue the merits of Legolas versus Aragorn, the films versus the books (they agree the books are superior but plan a marathon when they get out to be sure). Most nights they fall asleep mid-sentence.

'Shhh,' whispers Geldenhuys as he lifts his hand from Willem's mouth. It's warm and wet, cooling quickly in the night air. 'It's me.'

Willem sits up and rubs his eyes. Geldenhuys walks over to the flap of their tent and peeks out while Willem wriggles out of the fug of his sleeping bag and steps into his boots.

'What you doing?' Willem whispers. 'Don't!'

Moonlight or maybe starlight floods in as Geldenhuys steps out. For a moment Willem is alone and unsure what to do then Geldenhuys pokes his head back in and says, 'C'mon!'

When they're both out Geldenhuys raises a silencing finger to his lips as if Willem needs to be told and jerks his head to say 'Follow me' as he heads towards the parade ground. Willem is acutely aware of every sound – all the night noises that air conditioning and the city normally drown out. There are crickets, as always, but also the high chit of swooping bats. Probably *Tadarida aegyptiaca*, the Egyptian Free-tailed, notoriously anti-social. They flit their way to and from the guard tower which is, as always, lit. Willem suspects it must be empty. There will be scorpions too and other things you don't want to stand on in the dark but they are all predator silent.

Above all this the stars shine. Willem pauses for a moment and feels the world turn as he struggles to pick out the Southern Cross among the interstellar static. He's never seen a sky so big or bright. It's dizzying and he spins slowly to take it all in, stumbling as Geldenhuys comes back to take his arm and pull him along. They stop at the pond.

'Lesson time,' whispers Geldenhuys pulling his T-shirt over his head. His chest is smooth and silver in the starlight like a knight's armour. Willem looks back at the tents then turns to find Geldenhuys already sitting down with his feet in the water. 'Get in,' he urges and pats the side of the pond. 'We need to get you scuba-ready.'

Willem thinks back to the ducking he got when he arrived then kicks his boots off without untying the laces then undoes his trousers so they slide down at the same time as he pulls his T-shirt over his face. He leaves everything in a pile where he can easily grab it from the water. His white boxers glow embarrassingly. As he sits down his friend slips into the pond barely breaking the surface. The water seems to welcome him.

'It's not cold,' says Geldenhuys, who does seem to be shivering. 'Promise. And there are no leeches, probably.'

Willem pushes himself off the edge and as his head disappears below the surface he kicks and comes up panting. 'Shhh!' says Geldenhuys reaching him with just a few strokes. 'Don't panic. Hold the edge if you want. Or my arm or whatever. Just breathe. And shhh.'

Willem keeps one hand on the muddy bank and his friend holds the other and amazingly he's not drowning. They stay like this for a few minutes as the ripples clear and the silence settles again. Geldenhuys stays high in the water keeping an ear out for Volker or the dogs. The surface of the pond mirrors the sky so they float in stars. Willem doesn't want to move.

'Right,' says Geldenhuys. 'I'm going to let go – '

'No,' Willem pleads. 'Don't, I'll – '

'You'll float,' says Geldenhuys. 'You know you will. Don't panic. I'll let go and then you let go with your other hand and just lie back and keep breathing and you'll be fine. Like this.' He pulls his hand away and Willem splashes for it but Geldenhuys is already out of reach.

Mud blurts between Willem's toes as he pushes himself off the bank into the middle of the pond. He holds his breath and starts to sink and splutter but Geldenhuys is there and it's okay and suddenly he's breathing and floating. They're breathing and float-ing and even though they can't see one another each knows the other is there.

'Okay,' says Geldenhuys, who could have captained his school swimming team if he'd cared. 'Now kick your legs, quietly, that's it.'

Willem can't believe it's this easy.

'Now, flap your arms, no, smoothly – imagine you're a bird trying to take off. There – backstroke!'

Willem manages a sort of circle and doesn't even mind when he hits the muddy sides, just reaches back to wipe his head and knows he'll be all right if he just keeps breathing. He kicks back to the middle and bumps into Geldenhuys who is floating quietly on his back. In the water, in the dark, it doesn't matter whose fingers find whose toes. Nobody can see. The stars are saying nothing.

They better get back. Just one more minute. Breathing and floating.

6

It doesn't take long to break a boy – the General has got it down to about two weeks. Break them down then build them back up right. Whatever's left.

Willem has been at New Dawn for nearly three weeks. He's no longer the boy who had his picture taken at the gate with his ma.

'Brandt!' shouts Volker. Willem stands to attention as best he can and drops his shovel. He should probably lean it against the ancient tree stump he and Geldenhuys have been digging round for days. The handle is brown with blood from blisters. How many splinters are in his hand? The first one went so deep he couldn't pick it out. Geldenhuys said to suck it out instead. Willem shoved his hands in his pockets as Geldenhuys demonstrated on his own hand. Willem copied. It worked.

'One-to-one time, Lil-Will,' sings Volker, picking up Willem's shovel and swinging it so he has to duck. Volker whoops and marches off.

'We all get one,' Geldenhuys says. 'It's like an evaluation. Connor says he got to call his parents.'

Willem tries to scuff the muck off his boots scraping one against the other as he passes the inner gate and heads over to the old homestead. Volker spits as he passes, the gob drying immediately in the dust. 'Lift those feet!' Willem's right ankle has been swollen for a week. Is it broken?

Could he get a signal here? He's snuck his phone to various corners of the camp but no luck. Too late now, it's buried under his sleeping bag. Willem lifts his sore foot onto the stoep which creaks with his weight even now and catches his reflection in a window. It's not him, can't be. He looks stretched somehow. Older. He remembers the way Geldenhuys's shirtsleeves flapped round his arms. The whites of his eyes are the only clean bit of his face. At least his right eye is open again. His palms are a crust of blisters and his back is criss-crossed from leopard crawl. His feet are mad itchy and raw. He tugs his shorts out where they've bunched up – his arse burns from the shits because what food he gets is crap. He's so hungry. Last night he sneaked out after Lights Out and raided the bins to see if he could find something from the General's house but nothing. One of his front teeth is gone – Volker knocked it out after catching him talking English again, said that would shut him up. He didn't even bother trying to find it. His ma will go nuts. Bruises mottle his body. To start with he could have told you how he got each one but not now. The newest ones hurt most but are least spectacular, the brown of his gran's kitchen table where she's left a cigarette burning. The bruises on the way out are purple and orange screensaver sunsets. They're all merging to make a new camouflage pattern, perfect for this new world of pain.

'Done admiring yourself?' asks the General from a round black speaker mounted by the front door. Wires snake up along the frame and into the house. The door is open and leads into a square hall with a door in each wall. Canned TV laughter bursts from behind one of them. A sound from another planet. Only the door ahead is open. 'Don't just stand there, Brandt,' says the General genially. 'Come in!' Waxed floorboards squeak beneath Willem's boots and he skirts the faded rug. The house smells of clean fresh pine and Willem is suddenly aware of his stink.

'Come through,' shouts the General. 'Sit down.'

Like Jan's library, the General's study is dominated by a heavy old desk which he sits behind in a high-backed executive leather throne. He points to a low stool. Willem sits. Bookshelves stretch floor to ceiling filled with leather tomes and trophies. The General is used to winning. Somebody must polish them for him, probably the wife none of them have ever seen, not even Volker who's been here longest. Thanks to the General's lessons, Willem recognises the flag occupying one whole wall: the red, white and black of the AWB, the Brotherhood sworn to preserve the Boer land and ways. It flies over their Assembly Ground but not where anyone passing on the road could see, not that anybody out here would bother.

The General taps the microphone on his desk. Reading upside down Willem sees three buttons: *Talk, Reveille, Emergency.* So that's why the trumpet always sounds exactly the same. Next to this sits Geldenhuys's inhaler. In the centre of the desk, in a clear Perspex case like the ones at the museum only not dusty, rests an old gun.

'Beauty, eh?' asks the General, not waiting for an answer. 'Mine as a boy.' He takes the case off carefully and, with shocking tenderness, lifts the gun out. He points it towards Willem. 'Touch it, if you want. Go on, Brandt.'

Willem rests his eyes on it. The only beautiful thing in here. The word 'beautiful' joins a series of dots in his head which lead to Geldenhuys. He dismisses his friend and reaches for the gun then stops. Is this another trick? Is he about to break another unwritten rule? His hand trembles mid-air.

'It's cherry,' says the General. 'Good for carving because it's soft, but soft things don't usually last so long. I show this to all the cadets but only my special boys get to touch it. Go on, son. It won't go off.'

Time has made the wood strong and dark. Willem runs his hand along the barrel. It's smooth and somehow warm. Gently the General lays it down then puts the case over it like a blanket over a sleeping baby. He leans back.

'Carved by my great-grandfather for his son when we were fighting the British in the Second War of Liberation. Handed down ever since. Proper antique,' he chuckles. 'Like me.'

Willem tries to remember how to respond. There is an awkward pause. The General stares at him.

'So, what's turned up on your digs?'

Willem shakes his head. The General mimes opening and closing his mouth.

'Nothing, sir.'

'Know what you're digging for?'

'No, sir.'

There is a plain glass jug of what looks like lemonade on the desk. The General reaches over and fills a glass offering it to Willem. It clanks with ice. Willem's lips are split so the lemon stings but he drinks it anyway while the General watches. He's careful not to gulp.

'You're digging for history,' says the General when Willem has finished. 'Our history. When the British came, my great-grandmother buried our family silver here.'

So, it *was* about treasure. Actual buried treasure. Willem wonders where to put the lemonade glass, daren't put it on the desk so rests it between his knees.

'Our soil is full of secrets. The world needs to know what the British did – their lies, their camps. That silver is proof!'

Willem glances at the photos behind the General. There are none of his wife or the daughters he occasionally mentions. Only men. White men in green uniforms. The General flicks through a file.

'You've been here nearly three weeks now, Brandt. What do you think? Fitting in?'

Willem doesn't look directly at the General because you don't unless ordered. What does he think of New Dawn? He hurts in ways he didn't know he could. He stinks, he knows he does but they all do, except Volker who doesn't care who sees him shower. He dreams of food. He can't believe his ma sent him here. Jan must have talked her into it, maybe even he doesn't know what it's really like. He's been here for ever. He's never going home. What does he think of New Dawn?

'Tiger got your tongue?' The General pounds his desk and the gun jumps in its case as if the trigger's been pulled.

'N-No,' Willem stutters.

'C-c-caught G-G-Geldenhuys's st-st-stutter, eh?'

'No.' Willem shakes his head. 'No.'

'No, what?'

'No, sir.'

'Caught any more bad habits off him, eh, Brandt?' The General leans forward and winks. 'You a moffie too?'

'No, sir,' says Willem. 'I'm not like that.'

'Aren't you? He is. He's a moffie, eh?'

'No, sir, no!' As the cold lemonade hits Willem's bladder, he fights the urge to cross his legs, knows the General would hate that.

'Don't lie to me, Brandt, his own mother told me he got caught with another boy at school and they chucked him out. You don't want to be like him. Soft boys don't last.'

Moffie. Faggot. Lil-Will. Willem's never been like other boys and long ago gave up wanting to be. Other boys are stupid, literally. But where does that leave him? He recalls that first day when he felt Geldenhuys trying not to look at him getting dried in their tent. All through school Willem tried not to look – he didn't want to see himself reflected back. He became almost invisible. Now he's not even sure who he wants to look at. He really likes Geldenhuys and he loves that Geldenhuys likes him. It's a new feeling: being liked, being seen. They're friends. He's just not sure he feels exactly the same way.

'I'm not lying, sir. I'm no moffie.'

'And Geldenhuys?' The General pauses and looks down at a checklist. 'Does he look at you? Touch you? Try to get in your sleeping bag? What about the shower?'

'No, no, he doesn't look at me. We don't look at each other.' Willem really needs to go the toilet. Is there one in the house? There must be. Maybe the General would let him go. Better that than –

'You don't look at each other? You share a tent, you drill together, you dig together, do you walk about with your eyes closed? Is that why you're so slow? Is that why your ma sent you to me?'

Willem tries not to think about home. He'd give anything to be back in his bedroom under his desk. In that moment he decides he's moving back in with his gran when he gets out. Maybe she'll take Geldenhuys too.

'No, we don't look, I don't – '

'But he does?'

'No, he – '

The General gets up and walks slowly round his desk. Carefully he pulls a folded handkerchief from his trouser pocket and it's the cleanest thing Willem has ever seen. Willem feels the familiar impossible pressure build in his bladder. Not again, not here, not now.

The General hands him the handkerchief. 'Open it,' he says, moving one hand to his belt which he slowly starts undoing. The big brass buckle is a lion's head. 'Open it!'

Somebody turns the TV up in the other room and it's a game show with lots of applause. Willem's hands shake as he unfolds the handkerchief. It feels empty. What's inside is so familiar but also so out of place he can't fathom it. He puts one hand to his head where the blond curl came from.

'Seems your boyfriend kept a little souvenir.'

'He's not – '

'Shhhh,' says the General, raising his hands as if Willem is an animal he doesn't want to scare off. Willem closes his eyes. His legs are shaking. He can't hold on. He feels the heat of the General's hands close around his neck then suddenly they're gone leaving the strangling tightness of his top button done up. Laughter erupts from the TV next door.

'That's better,' says the General, stepping back, his belt swinging lazily like the tail of a cheetah about to run. 'Now, Brandt, up.' Willem can't move. He tries to slow his breathing, to stop whatever is going to happen from happening.

'Up! Stand up and take it like a man!'

The General grabs his collar lifting him up off the stool, which clatters backwards. The lemonade glass leaps off his lap and smashes. 'Pick that up!' The General drops Willem and pushes a boot in the small of his back forcing him onto his belly. 'Leopard crawl!' So Willem drags himself across the snapping sticking shards and as his palms slip and slide red on the slick wooden floor the air above him rips. The noise and force are surprising. Willem feels bonds between individual atoms break for ever. Down here, with his face against it, he notices the floor glows the same deep red as the old toy gun. He can't hold on any more but he's wet now anyway. For a moment he smells cherries and then that's all.

7

Rayna didn't expect to like the internet. At JPS she'd supervised the transition from writing tickets by hand to printing them from beige plastic boxes that looked more past than future. That first computer got so hot in summer she had to train a fan on it which left her sweating. Just before they finally got rid of her she was upgraded to a biscuit-thin laptop which slipped nicely into her handbag on her last day. It burbles into life now on her kitchen table and, as always, the sound is a tiny triumph.

She types in her password: Willem1994. Each tap on the keys is a victory over the boredom she resists, a protest at the accumulated quiet of her big empty house. Her screensaver springs up and she reaches out to stroke Willem who is almost managing to smile in his Grade 12 class photo. She doesn't do this every morning but often enough that the screen is smudged where he sits in the front row, out of trouble next to his teacher, his tie loose and his top button undone.

Rayna waits for her coffee to cool on the table that can easily seat six but never has. Early summer wafts through the screen door. In every border, improbably green arrows of agapanthus shoot up, fleshy buds held atop surprisingly slender stems and each one ready to burst as soon as the bees arrive. The jacaranda is finishing, the ground beneath it wet with purple bruises. You're not supposed to look up at jacarandas, something in them can blind you if it falls in your eyes. You just had to know they were beautiful without looking too close. Who told her that? It's not the sort of thing her mother knew. Her father only cared about history – preferred the past. She's getting sentimental in her old age. But Willem loves all nature. He can name any tree from a single leaf and even tell one kind of ant from another. Underneath all that curly hair is order, taxonomies, great cabinets of glass with feelings carefully pinned to velvet. It's one of the few things she knows for sure about her grandson and because it's one of few certainties she treasures it. He especially loves books where nature runs wild and, she has to admit, Tolkien does keep you going, though he's no Danielle Steel. She still feels guilty about the day she stamped on the rain-spider that Willem caught in the bathroom. His sunny little face clouded with betrayal. She can see it now. Sensitive.

This camp sounds like three months of being forced to do all the things they – and she includes herself – tried to make him do. The cupboard under her stairs bursts with their failed ambition: rugby balls, cricket bats, even football gear. All almost clean but not quite pristine – the odd grass stain or scuff. It's these markers of his willingness to try that break her heart. Why has she not got rid of it all?

It would be easy to blame Jan. Too easy. Irma's dim but she's not dumb – she knows what she wants even if what she wants is not what she actually needs. Rick was a druggie and he's probably dead but at least he had something about him, exploding into the house high with crazy gifts: huge bunches of flowers, giant teddies, boxes of chocolates the size of a TV. Outsized affections. Jan goes to the gym before work every morning, drives with an eye on fuel efficiency, calls her *Ouma* – *Ouma*! What goes on below that crew cut? Nothing, Rayna, always thought. But lately she sees something. Sometimes he just stares off into the distance. Irma says he wakes her up shouting in his sleep about patrols and ambushes then denies it all in the morning. Britney never liked him. She misses that dog and can't believe she misses her.

Her coffee is plenty cool now so she takes a luxurious slurp, one of the few benefits of living alone. She's slipped into old habits, sitting in her housecoat at nearly noon. Elise has been and gone. Elise still comes every day before she's up and cleans rooms she's not been in for months. Willem's room is just as it was. Rayna keeps her promises. Elise does too

– she remembers the day the boy's father came back and all the trouble about that dancing, she thinks the *Miesies* should never have let him go to that place and it shows in the way she asks after him and how she stacks the dishwasher so Rayna's favourite coffee cup is never quite clean.

Willem was gone a week before they told Rayna. A whole week. 'I've got room for him!' she'd screamed – actually screamed. It was too late then.

'It's for the best,' Jan had said in his calm voice, which only enraged her.

'Best for who?'

'He needs to grow up, Ma.'

'Like you have?'

'That's enough,' said Jan.

'Don't "enough" me in my own home,' said Rayna, patting her pockets for cigarettes. 'You've no business sending him anywhere, he's my – '

'Grandson,' said Irma. 'He's my son.'

'Oh, and you know what's best for him?'

Jan retreated looking relieved. Rayna found her cigarettes in a drawer and lit up. She slammed the pack back without offering Irma one.

'He didn't get his matric, no school will have him and we paid a fortune for Benoni Park – '

'We? I did. I paid his school fees. And why? Because you don't work, you've never worked.'

'I couldn't, I had Will – '

'I managed to hold down a job with you *and* Piet.'

Irma shrugged. 'He might as well be dead and buried in that mine.'

This only riled Rayna more. 'What? The truth hurts?'

Irma walked over to the drawer and fumbled for the cigarettes, hands shaking. She stuck one in her mouth. Jan started to protest but thought better of it. Rayna gripped the lighter so Irma went to the cooker and leaned over the gas hob, pushing her fringe out of the way. She stood up and inhaled deeply turning to face her mother. Jan checked his watch.

'Willem needed me, Ma,' said Irma, shaking less. 'You needed me, I couldn't just go out and get a job.'

'You couldn't?'

'I couldn't.'

'You could! I didn't need you.'

'You … you were never there, you just left me with Elise.'

'I left you with her because I had to go out and work.'

'And why was that?'

'Because nobody else was going to do it.'

'Because we had no father – '

'What?'

'Because you,' and Irma stressed the you, flicked her eyes at Jan who was edging towards the door whether he meant to or not, 'because you couldn't keep a man!'

It's true, Rayna thought, she couldn't. There hadn't been a man of this house since her father, not unless you counted Willem. 'I never needed one,' she said. 'Maybe I wanted one, sometimes, but I never needed one. Not like you.'

There. She'd said it. Not what she feared she'd say – not about Johannes: *Your father was already married and dropped me the moment he laid eyes on you.*

Irma said nothing.

'We should go,' Jan began. 'Cardio class.' Both of them turned to stare at him. He collapsed into silence.

'This place,' said Rayna, blowing smoke at Jan. 'Where you sent my only grandson, what's it called?'

'New Dawn Safari Rangers,' he coughed. 'You can write to him.'

'I'd rather hear his voice,' said Rayna, scribbling on the notepad with a picture of a round dial phone which had waited by their phone for twenty years. Phones didn't even look like that any more. Irma winced.

'You can't, Ma, they're not allowed calls for the first month, till they're settled, right, Jan?'

'Email?'

'No email,' said Jan. 'No phones.'

Rayna had never seen Willem without his phone. As far as she knew, he could not actually live without it.

'What if something happens?'

'It won't,' said Jan. 'It's *lekker*. He'll be safe there.'

8

Willem is starting to think like a soldier. Padding across the parade ground with Geldenhuys all they hear from the other tents is snoring, the odd cough. The gate is bolted and chained but it's easy enough to scoop the soft red soil out from under. They work quickly but quietly, freezing when their shovels scrape a stone. After half an hour Willem scrambles under, ripping his shirt on the chain-link as he pulls himself through. Geldenhuys hesitates, looks back at the guard tower which they've worked out is probably just for show. Willem turns to leave and Geldenhuys drops to his belly. Slighter than Willem, he slips through and they leopard-crawl the rest of the way. Up ahead is the homestead. A single light shines in the General's study. Willem freezes so Geldenhuys almost crawls over him.

Wordlessly, Geldenhuys places a hand on Willem's good foot and squeezes lightly. Willem turns his face from the lit window and starts crawling again, practising excuses in his head: *It was a dare, we were testing security, we were going to come back.* Excuses won't work but it's comforting to pretend they might. Over in their kennels the dogs bark. They bark all night because they're forced to be quiet all day. Every night they hope for a reply. Willem misses Britney. He reaches the gate where Jan made him pose for a picture with his ma. How long ago? Days, weeks, for ever. The wire hums with electricity but next to the gate is a battered old tree and one of its branches hangs over. If they can climb it, they can drop down the other side. Geldenhuys slip-scrabbles on the smooth bark and Willem boosts him up. The dogs bark louder. Still only one light on. Geldenhuys is up now. As Willem rushes at the tree his ankle gives but Geldenhuys catches his hand and helps him up. They don't have time to worry about getting down. It's not so far in the dark. They edge along the branch and Willem feels it flex, lowering him, so the last three feet is easy. Geldenhuys follows and the branch springs him a bit further.

The world outside seems bigger than before. Over on the horizon the vast steelworks burns all night, silhouetted dark against darker. Blue and green flames flicker here and there. Somewhere in its shadow is the big red barn Willem saw when he arrived. There will be people there and a phone. They have to get to it. Fireflies dance just out of reach guiding them away from New Dawn, through the waist-high love-grass, crisp now at the height of summer.

Willem is running, limping, as fast as he can, as fast as he dares. He channels a cheetah: *Acinonyx jubatus*. His gran said they used to be everywhere too. When he gets home they're going to Kruger to see the big cats. Without stopping he looks over his shoulder to Geldenhuys. He's coming as well.

Running, limping, running. Like Sigourney Weaver at the end of *Aliens*. Away from Anton at school. Away from Jan. Every step shoots pain from his right ankle up his shin through his thigh into his belly. Keep going.

'Come on!' he urges over his shoulder, between breaths. Can't be too loud. Are they far enough away not to be heard? When will their tent be found empty? Who will find it? Volker, of course. He's always bursting in, pulling off their sleeping bags, trying to catch them. One night, Willem was so bored he read his Bible by the moonlight milking through the canvas and Volker stormed in and Willem could tell from the way he snatched it that he'd never read a book.

Willem peers at his army watch glowing dimly: only fifteen minutes till the General presses the Reveille button and the fake trumpets herald another day, only fifteen minutes till the sun comes up and shows everybody where they are. If they'd left any earlier they risked getting lost in the dark. Now they risked getting caught in the light.

How far now, how far?

Willem leans on his left foot and turns to Geldenhuys whose rapidly appearing outline makes a show of speed: true of foot Legolas bounding forward, arrows ready. Geldenhuys staggers and stops with his hands on his hips and his head thrown back.

Willem limps back and grabs an arm pulling him forward. 'Come on,' he says, turning. 'Come on!'

'I can't,' gasps Geldenhuys. 'My … a-a-asthma.' Willem pats his friend's pockets for his inhaler then remembers seeing it on the General's desk. He stands Geldenhuys up straight, lays both hands on his chest and feels his heart thudding out of it. 'Slower,' he urges, pushing against his ribs like the shrink did for him at school the day Anton fell, before the police came and told her to stop fussing. 'Slower.' He peers over Geldenhuys's shoulder into the disappearing dark. Is that another light?

How long now, how long?

'That's it,' he says encouragingly even though the other boy's breathing is ragged. 'Deeper, slower, thaaat's it.' Geldenhuys's heart begins to feel like it might stay put but he can't run any more. Willem puts his right arm round his friend. Together they step forward. Up ahead a dog barks – they hope it's a dog. The sun is nearly up and the fireflies are fading and they can see the big red barn. They're going to make it.

Not far now, not long.

Geldenhuys pants against the gate while Willem reaches through feeling for the bolt. He's never seen a fence so low. His fingers find the rusty bolt and shuffle it across. It protests loudly and they brace for dogs. Nothing.

The gate swings open on its own weight and they limp through together, just able to walk side by side along the neat paved path that leads to the farm-house crouching at the side of the barn. It looks like it always has, since the sun first rose behind it as it's doing now. Small pink roses fuss around the door which opens as Willem reaches out to knock. A doughy old woman draws it towards her. Her white hair is pulled into a neat bun. She inspects them over half-glasses then steps aside. A storybook *ouma* up and ready to greet the day.

'You best come in,' she says, in country Afrikaans. Willem enters and Geldenhuys follows. They brush past her full black skirts. She closes the door not bothering to lock it.

'*Dankie*,' says Willem, suddenly worried about his boots. Old women hate dirt. The walls are covered with framed faces. Here and there is a husband or brother. They all have her mouth and look unduly pleased.

'*Dankie*,' says Geldenhuys as soon as he can talk. He does a little boarding-school bow towards the woman who goes into the kitchen leading off the hall.

'You'll be wanting breakfast,' she says, clanking a black iron skillet on an antiquated stove. It begins to smoke lightly and she cracks eggs in two at a time.

'Sit,' she urges. They take a seat, unable to believe that moments ago they were out there in the dark. Now they're sitting at a scrubbed pine table while somebody's *ouma* cooks them breakfast. Willem pats his pocket as he has done every second since their escape. He feels his phone, wonders how much battery is left, realises there's no point asking for a charger.

The kitchen smells of freshly baked bread. She turns the eggs and talks over her shoulder: 'I saw you coming, sight for sore eyes.'

Geldenhuys looks to Willem who shrugs.

She reaches for a bread knife and cuts two door-stops from a big loaf then butters them richly before sliding on the fried eggs. She lays a plate in front of each of them. Melting butter pools around the yolks. They have never seen anything so good.

'*Dankie*,' says Willem again, grabbing a fork, but she stays his hand.

'Grace!'

Geldenhuys mutters his old school prayer which seems to satisfy her.

'Don't thank me,' she says, pointing to the cross on the wall by the stove. 'Thank the Lord, He's the one putting breakfast in your belly. I'm just a means to His end. We all are.'

She looks past them towards the window and out to the veldt where the sun is now right up. Had it ever been dark?

'Excuse me,' says Willem, pushing his chair back. 'I didn't wash my hands. Where's the bathroom?'

The old woman puts down her coffee cup and it takes a second for Willem to realise she's laughing. It sounds like a hand clearing cobwebs.

'Bathroom eh? City boy. The toilet's out back. Leave it as you find it, thank you, I've no girl here.'

As Willem gets up Geldenhuys stares at him with the universal terror of all teenagers left with an old person then takes refuge in his breakfast which he's embarrassed to see he's almost finished. He takes smaller bites and chews slowly to stave off conversation. Their host eyes him over the rim of her cup which is wreathed in the same pink roses growing round the door.

Out back a tin bath hangs on the wall of the windowless toilet which has an old-fashioned chain pull. Lace doilies drip everywhere. Willem pulls his phone from his pocket and presses *ON* then *MUTE* as it bleeps to life. No such sound was ever heard in this house. He holds it up: *NO SIGNAL*. He walks to the far corner and wills a signal to reach through the air and find him. In desperation, he climbs on the toilet seat waving the phone around and there, one bar! Gone. Back! Gone again.

He pulls up his gran's number and hits *DIAL* but it doesn't ring. Email, he'll email her. What to say?

A knock at the door.

'All right in there?'

'Yes,' shouts Willem, trying to sound like he's squeezing.

'Don't be long,' she chides. 'Your eggs are getting cold and nobody wants cold eggs.'

'Coming,' he says, pulling the flush. At the same time, he holds his phone out, snaps a selfie and hits *SEND*. Hoping, hoping, hoping the email's gone, he pockets his phone and opens the door almost walking right into the old woman.

'Sorry,' he says, pretending to dry his hands on his trousers.

'I didn't hear you wash,' she tuts. 'Let's see.'

He holds his hands out and starts to apologise but she just lets them drop and shuffles back to her kitchen. Willem follows.

There sits Geldenhuys. Behind him stands the General.

Willem turns to run but Volker blocks the front door. The General shakes his head.

'You should take better care,' sighs their host. 'That's the third lot this year. Look at them, they're filthy, like Kaffirs.'

'I'm sorry,' says the General. Geldenhuys flinches as the General grips his shoulders. 'Thank you for keeping them here. It won't happen again. I'll be sure to send over some eggs. We'll be no more trouble, Mrs Kriel, I promise.'

The General orders Geldenhuys up but she raises a hand, her fingers made of pastry. He halts. 'Let the boy finish his eggs,' she says, pointing to Willem. 'Waste is a sin.'

9

'Well, I can see that,' says Rayna, surprised it took Irma this long to tell her. The thought occurred as she stormed off last week but she's not picked up Irma's calls since. She avoids guessing how far on her daughter is in case she gets it wrong. Irma always was touchy about her size.

'Three months,' says Irma. 'We wanted to be sure, didn't we, baby?'

Jan puts his arm round Irma and pats her shoulder. She looks up at him as if he's just rescued her from a burning building and in a way, he has. This place is beyond past it. Everything looks faded thanks to the old *wyfie*'s industrial smoking. The carpet meets you at the front door. Cork is peeling off the kitchen walls. The living-room wallpaper is a garden run riot – he's convinced it's actually alive. One day its tendrils will trap him. Jan decides there and then that when this museum comes to them they're selling – you couldn't renovate it enough. And this neighbourhood is getting way too mixed for his little man – it's bound to be a boy. A proper little soldier. *Ja*, he'll flip this place whatever Irma says. The thought makes him smile which Irma mistakes for paternal pride. She kisses him and turns to Rayna.

'Aren't you chuffed, Ma?'

Rayna picks up her cigarettes and Jan coughs and stares at Irma's bump. She slams them into a drawer. Her laptop gives a tiny chirrup as it goes to sleep and her screensaver comes on – a photo of Willem hugging Britney the day they got her. She still can't believe they sent him away. She's tried Googling the camp, nothing much comes up. Just photos of teen-age boys in khaki and none of her grandson. The phone number on their website just rings and rings.

'Of course I'm pleased,' says Rayna, a little too loudly. Then: 'What does Will think?'

Straight away she can tell he doesn't know. Are they expecting her to tell him? Is that why Jan has finally remembered to bring the big ladders to prune the jacaranda that's trying to climb into Willem's old room?

'We've not told him yet, Ma.'

There's something else. They haven't seriously come over to give her news she can see with her own two eyes. What? Which of them is going to say? Should she make it easy? The screensaver scrolls through photos: Willem button-bright on his first day at high school.

'We tried phoning but we can't – '

'They're out on manoeuvres,' snaps Jan, for the thousandth time that week. 'Probably to the lake to start scuba.'

Irma remembers how Willem loved *The Little Mermaid*, how they sang all the songs together, how he held his breath in the bath that time and scared her. '*Ja,* scuba, he'll love that.'

Rayna isn't buying it. 'He could have come here,' she says, again. 'I'd have taken him, you knew that, his room's upstairs.'

Irma turns away as Jan says, 'He said he didn't want to – '

'Didn't want to?'

'And we didn't want you having to run about after him and his mess.'

'He'll be back soon and he'll be better,' says Irma. 'Won't he?'

Rayna doesn't want him 'better', she just wants him back. And now here they are saying they can't even get hold of him.

'Well, did you phone the man?'

'The General,' says Jan reverently.

'Yes, the General,' says Rayna, looking at her daughter for answers. Never wise.

'*Ja,*' says Irma. 'We tried but he never answers.'

'He's a busy man,' says Jan. 'They're on manoeuvres. Willem's having the time of his life.'

'The time of your life,' says Rayna. 'Do you even know the boy?' She pauses and wishes for a cigarette.

'He'll be fine,' says Jan. 'Just the same as always, giving cheek and fighting.'

'Willem doesn't get into fights,' Rayna gasps. 'And he doesn't talk back. To you maybe. Not me.'

'That's not fair, Ma,' Irma chimes, putting both arms around Jan who looks like a bear in a circus. 'You don't know how bad he got – the shouting, the swearing, the disrespect – '

'A teenage boy shouting and swearing? I can't imagine it.'

Irma and Jan sit in silence. They swap a look and Irma shakes her head. Jan goes on anyway.

'He did other things.'

'Such as?' Rayna says. 'I raised a boy of my own, shock me.'

'He broke into my library –'

Rayna raises an eyebrow. She's never seen Jan and a book in the same room.

'And went through my things, private things … Magazines.'

Irma blushes.

Rayna laughs. 'So, you sent him away because he found your dirty magazines? He's a teenager! And they're your magazines! You were always worrying how he'd turn out, I thought you'd be glad!'

Rayna had worried too and felt ashamed, yes, ashamed. But only because soft things don't last in this world. She understands the old hate but not the new one. Everybody is angry now. You can't build walls high enough. These days they don't just take what you've got. Now it's knives and acid and boiling water. The news is a never-ending horror movie and nobody knows how it's going to end. Rayna knows she won't always be around so she's been to see a lawyer. The house is Willem's already. And she's moving him back in as soon as he gets out.

Irma pulls a pleading face at Jan which Rayna hopes to God she didn't get from her. Jan goes on anyway.

'And he … '

'He?'

Irma sidles over to the door. Jan stands his ground.

'He jimmied my desk open.'

Irma turns her back to the two of them.

'And there was a photo, you know, private.'

'No, I don't know,' says Rayna, instantly regretting it.

'Of Irma.'

'Ma, I – '

'And he'd been looking at it.'

'No, he had not, you – '

'It's true, Ma,' Irma insists.

'I don't believe it,' says Rayna, shaking her head. 'I don't.'

Rayna's screensaver rolls on and here is Willem taller now, taller than her, squinting into the camera, his blond curls catching the sun.

'I don't believe it, any of it,' she says.

'We should go,' says Irma, grabbing her handbag. 'The traffic.'

'Sit down,' orders Rayna. 'It's Sunday, there's no traffic.'

Jan takes a deep breath. 'And he'd got hold of my gun.'

'Gun?' Rayna gasps and prods Jan in the chest. 'You left a gun lying about?'

'He got into my lock box,' Jan protests, backing off. 'I don't know how.'

'He was just lying there,' says Irma, starting to cry.

Rayna gets the cigarette packet out the drawer and crushes it. 'Did he, was he … ?'

'No,' sobs Irma. 'No, thank God. 'I ran over. The carpet was all wet and I shook him until he came to. Then he went crazy lashing out. After that he stopped sleeping and threatened to run away. I was scared he was going to hurt himself.'

Rayna walks over to her laptop. They are not describing the boy on her screensaver.

'We had to do it, Ma. For him.'

10

How long has it been now? Three days? Four? The door shows no sign of opening. They're locked in a box made of rusty iron sheets. Willem and Geldenhuys watch the sun come and go in the gap under the door. One day half a Mars Bar appears there, a crescent bitten off one end. It looks like Connor's smile. The ants find it first but Geldenhuys cleans them off and shares.

The General had loaded them onto the bakkie in silence. Volker was posted with them to stop them jumping off. The old lady waved them away. Back across the veldt. Back through the gates. The others stood waiting by the flag. The General gave them all the choice: either take their turn or Volker would beat them all one by one. Connor cried. So, the General watched as each of them took their turn. He called a halt when he was satisfied they'd all contributed. Then he handed Volker a *piele wapper*. The thick rubber hose was as long as a man's arm. *The strong take the weak, it makes the pack stronger, they're broken already.* Volker only stopped when it slipped from his hands.

Now they're in here. The Bird Cage, the General called it, as he chained the door. In a faraway corner of Willem's memory, a tiny light comes on. He remembers the trip to the museum, the scale model of the camp, the prison within a prison. This can't be real. It hurts to sit. It hurts to stand. He's lost more teeth. There's a rough narrow plank they take turns trying to sleep on. Geldenhuys is having trouble breathing – he can just about lie down but can't rest knowing Willem is on the floor. Forget blankets. It's a freezer or an oven. They're sweating or shivering. The air tastes like it's been locked in for years. In one corner there's a bucket of water and another for whatever comes out of them. Flies commute between the two. Willem's throat burns and his belly ripples with cramps. He dreams of opening the fridge at home and being bathed in light and cool and plenty. By day two or three they just brush the dirt off whatever is shoved under the door. Soon they're feeling in dark corners for scraps rejected on day one. Willem knows what lives out here and would normally be pleased to identify a millipede but there's something about not being able to see. Geldenhuys takes over, pattering his fingers around like a blind man reading a face. He'd screamed as the door was closed. Willem found him in the dark and held him: *It'll be okay, I promise.*

Outside life goes on as usual. Every morning they're woken by Reveille and every night they hear Lights Out. Whenever Volker passes he kicks the door so the chain rattles and coos kissy noises, calls them 'lovebirds'. The General hasn't been back.

They talk in English and don't bother whispering any more. Willem can no longer stand on his right foot. He spends most of his time slumped on the floor with his knees by his chin.

'This isn't real.'

'No,' says Geldenhuys.

'Do you think they knew?'

'Who?'

'My ma, your parents, you think they knew?'

Geldenhuys has avoided this thought since his mother dropped him off. He'd imagined this place couldn't be worse than the boarding school he was expelled from for 'immoral conduct'. His mother couldn't look at him when he arrived home with his trunk. Mercifully his father was away, as usual. He stretches his arms and feels his breathing slow a little as he confirms that no, he can't touch two walls at the same time. Like an old man, he groans to the ground and puts an arm round Willem's shoulder. Willem lets it rest there for a moment. It feels good and nothing has felt anything but shit for so long now.

'Get off!' Willem snaps, flinging his friend's arm off and blinking back tears. 'Fuck you!'

'I was j–j–just … ' says Geldenhuys quietly, hoping Willem will stop shouting, not give Volker any excuse. Things can always get worse here.

'Shhhh,' he pleads. 'They'll hear and – '

'And what, eh? And what?'

'I-I-I, I don't know.'

'You don't know sh-sh-shit, do you? I should've gone on my own, I could've got away but I had to drag you. And now what, eh? Happy it's just the two of us?'

'No, you're upset. You need to be q-q-quiet or they'll – '

'They'll what?' Willem punches a wall and it dings like a bell and he reckons he could knock it down if he was still half as strong as when he got here. And then what? Volker? The General?

Geldenhuys stands in the corner he's retreated to without realising, an auto defence learned long ago. He steps towards Willem again and bumps one of the buckets. It swills and slops. The space between them hums like the electric fence.

'I'm s-s-sorry,' says Geldenhuys. All he wants to do is stroke the head that had all those beautiful curls, to kiss Willem's face until he stops crying.

But Willem can't stop. His face is a slick and he's glad it's dark so Geldenhuys can't see. He drags his sleeve across his nose which only makes it worse then sits up quickly because he starts to choke and leans forward sobbing onto the ground which sucks up tears as it has always done never questioning who is crying or why.

And now Reveille is sounding. The chain on the door is rattling. A new dawn is pushing under the door.

Somebody's coming.

Rayna is waiting for her coffee to cool.

It's a week since her fight with Irma and Jan and she still can't believe the things they said. After the door slammed, she went up to Willem's old room and sat on his bed straightening his impossibly faded Harry Potter duvet. She buried her face in his pillow. It didn't smell of him any more.

She feels her cup again: cool enough. As she picks it up her inbox opens with days of mail. In among the special offers and spam is an email. From Willem. A picture.

Her cup falls to the floor.

PART FOUR

1 March 2015, Ventersburg

Judge Violet Khwezi does not approve of theatrics. But this doesn't stop her engaging in them when they suit her. This morning she has huge sunglasses clamped to her face – she excused the luxury of them to Charles by tapping the black frames lightly and saying 'Prescription'. He nodded knowing she was really convincing herself. The Judge is the first from her family to finish school, never mind go to university. Sometimes she still can't quite believe that this is her life, that she's familiar with the view from the back of a car, that she has people to do all the work done by her mother and all the mothers before – all the Letties that scrubbed and swept and smiled so she could be Violet. Comforts and discomforts she is the first in her family to feel. She wears her sunglasses even though the car windows are tinted in case the camera flashes get through again. She wears them because today she doesn't want to see even more than she doesn't want to be seen.

Her car pauses at the gates of the courthouse. On one side, professional mourners picket in black T-shirts bearing that final grim photo of the boy and his date of birth: so young, *Nkosi*. They're mothers themselves, as they'll tell anyone with a microphone or a camera. Black, white, all united by grief. Feasting on sadness. Four of them carry a life-size cardboard coffin on their shoulders. Defiant rainbow flags flutter in the breeze despite the mother's insistence in interview after interview that her boy was normal. Each time her story gets neater, her grief shaping itself to the news. Across the road stand what's left of the AWB, their assault rifles as glossy as her sunglasses. They are soldiers in an army that no longer exists, defending a country that vanished in 1994, but they're still not used to having to shout to be heard. The Judge knows this from countless 'domestic' cases. In rigid unison they chant their initials: 'A – W – B! Free the General!' Each side almost drowns the other out. The gate swings inwards. This is how it feels to go to prison, she thinks, not for the first time.

Judge Khwezi has been sentenced to Case SH 219/10 for four years. Some days she finds herself almost wishing for a jury – trial by jury was done away with when she was at school. But selection would be impossible. Prejudices would need to be balanced because they certainly couldn't be left at the door with the guns daily detected by the scanner. It's all down to her.

The defendant's lawyer (his third) has already said they'll appeal. The Department wants the maximum sentence: life for a life. Child abuse, neglect and murder are the charges. It's four years to the day since the boy died – a fact the media reports with glee when they know fine well the courts couldn't organise anything so neat. The coincidence lends today's proceedings further charge, as if they needed any.

Since police raided the camp, three more bodies have been found – all male, all around sixteen. Those boys will not be her concern. New Dawn Safari Rangers Ltd continues to operate at least three 'Training Camps'. TV cameras were invited in to show healthy boys enjoying healthy outdoor activities, healthy food and healthy horseplay. Boys will be boys.

She tries not to think about all the other cases piling up. Crime is the one thing this country has no shortage of. Her neighbours in Hyde Park are fitting private generators because what use is a laser alarm with no spark? Others ship in private water in case the mains are poisoned. She resists these latest lunacies.

Today she will deliver her judgement. Over fifteen years she's watched thieves, rapists and murderers walk free, even from shame. Still, she's never seen injuries like this, never taken so long to read out a coroner's report, never lost so much sleep even on the increasingly rare nights the air conditioning works.

She finally discussed it with Charles one Friday after Faith – who noisily emptied the glass recycling bin – headed off to her taxibus. Not talking about the case was ludicrous when every paper, programme and blog in the country was taking sides. Charles, Professor of Political Science at the University of Witwatersrand, would normally be wheeled out to comment on such a state of the nation case but recused himself. He barely moved while they sat finishing the last of the Shiraz they'd bought after a long tasting lunch in Franschhoek. She didn't say anything prejudicial, nothing that could get her in trouble, of course. As she described the boy's broken broomstick arms, his unseeing eyes too big for his shaved head, Charles reached for her hand. It was this small tenderness that finally made the tears come. His hand on hers hadn't been an official crime since the miscegenation laws went in 1985 – was it only then? Charles offered to come with her today but she said no even though part of her wanted him to. He would just end up looking angry in the papers, angry and white.

One good thing: this case has brought her closer to her children who are far away which is exactly where she wants them to stay. Zee, on a Rhodes Scholarship in Oxford, and Violet, interning at the UN in New York, phone her more often now, and not just when they're walking between appointments or about to eat. She hopes the calls won't stop when all this does.

She gets out of the car, thanks her driver and steps into the hot hushed courtyard, crossing quickly into the shade of her private chambers. Chambers sounds grand – like University College in Oxford where Zee is. She feels proud that a part of her sleeps in the neat single bed beneath the sloping lime plaster ceiling where Shelley once dreamt. In reality, her chambers are as municipal as the rest of the courthouse. Beige carpets, beige walls, the compulsory portrait of Zuma. She doesn't think it will hang there much longer but nothing surprises her any more. As she lifts her robes from the coat stand she tries to distract herself by planning a holiday. Maybe she'll surprise the children – meet them in Rome, she's always wanted to go. She fixes her hair in the small porthole mirror screwed to the wall: four years greyer and thinner. *Die Burger* always runs the photos that make her look most tired, most angry, because nothing baits their readers out in Brakpan more than an angry black woman. Except, perhaps, an angry black woman with power. Her own mother wore a wig. Her daughter, Violet, has changed her name on Facebook to Lettie – enjoys the shock value of going by a maid's name. It's part of her great reclaiming. She rejects wigs as a symbol of oppression and queens herself up with a range of loud dhuku headscarves and talks earnestly about post-post colonialism.

The Judge picks up the folder containing her verdict. In it sits the boy's pathetically thin file. From his prenatal scan to his first day at school to a phone shot snapped at his wake and sold online. She still can't believe the mother insisted on an open coffin. *Let them see what he did.*

She wishes she could unsee the broken, ancient-looking boy. The forensic pathologist's report: multiple recent injuries – twelve in total. None more than two months old including both wrists broken, multiple contusions and bruises. Various opportunistic infections explained by exposure, malnutrition and severe dehydration. The lining of his mouth was burnt – any boy 'talking shit' was allegedly forced to eat his own faeces then wash his mouth out with detergent. Wound #12, impalement by longitudinal object, constituted final cause of death.

She thinks about her own son when he was sixteen, not so long ago really – chipping away at his International Baccalaureate, ambitious amber-flecked eyes following her gaze overseas. He had to have his appendix out and she remembers the hand-wringing terror of waiting for the doctor, worrying he'd be carjacked for drugs, and then the terrible speed of diagnosis, the acronyms hurried into his phone. Zee, his boxers pulled down for the examination, pulling the covers up and shouting at her to get out, get out, then vomiting. He was too far gone for keyhole, boiling to burst, so now sports a long diagonal scar along his hip. It's the only mark the world has imposed on the perfect body she made.

Judge Khwezi sweeps into her courtroom and everybody shuffles to their feet, the General last. A pre-show hush descends. The press gallery has been extended again with folding chairs and the floor writhes with cables. The public gallery brims and, as usual, she mentally ticks off who is present.

The General's wife looks dressed for a line-dancing competition, perhaps a regional final. Her red gingham shirt dress is plastered with red, white and black badges demanding *FREEDOM!* She is never off the television, cannot believe her loving husband and father of their three daughters is being persecuted like this. It's a witch-hunt, she says, racism. When she tottered to the dock she kissed her husband extravagantly. Not once did she speak directly to the Judge who, with satisfaction, forgot to offer her a stool. She gave all her answers in Afrikaans.

We married at sixteen, it's his family farm, been there a long time. No, I never had another job, I'm a wife and mother. He's a good man, a patriot. No, I never went through the gates, that's my husband's business – he treats them like the sons we wanted, no I never heard screaming.

No, she didn't know. No, she didn't know. Know, she had to know.

In four years not one person has turned up for the Volker boy, except his social worker who spends most of her time fretting over her phone. Volker never even checks the gallery and this pains the judge as much as the facts of his case. He's jail-pale now and his face is framed by hair so luxuriously black it appears almost wet. He looks like a model from one of the trashy magazines Faith leaves in their kitchen. His testimony was chaotic. When it became clear, even to him, that he was being blamed, he panicked. For the first time he looked his age.

I was living out, you know, I had no place. The General took me in, I worked hard. It was lekker. *He was good to start. Promoted me. No, I didn't do that, it wasn't me. I was their commanding officer but he was in charge. I just did what I was told.*

The General sits back like a man with all the time in the world. He's in fresh-pressed khakis, the folds never sharper. How does he keep so smart in custody? She doesn't want to know. Lots of soldiers became police – to many this man is a hero. Posters of him look down from the walls of shacks in the white townships. Judge Khwezi has as much trouble getting used to the idea of these places as the people in them. His shaving-brush moustache trembles with terrible restraint. His mullet has greyed from the roots out over the course of the trial. She knew it must shame him for people to know he dyed it. When he was shown the coroner's photos he shuffled through the pile considering each one carefully then shrugged. Like his wife, he spoke only in Afrikaans.

Ja, it's my place but these pictures are nothing to do with me. I was a captain but everybody calls me the General. I've trained thousands of boys, set them right. No, I don't know what a conversion camp is, no. Listen, my other places are still running, go see. No, we never had any black cadets. They'd be welcome to apply. Volker was a tramp when I took him in, dirty like a … like an animal. These parents send their boys to me because they're desperate. They can't toughen them up. Brandt had attitude from day one. He wouldn't shower so he stank and had toilet problems, his own mother said. He wouldn't eat but was skinny anyway, I reckoned AIDS. We caught him eating trash. That's how come he got jippo guts. He was not popular. Geldenhuys followed him round like a girl. The lads called them moffies. That's boys. Anyway, is that what you want for your sons? Brandt didn't want to change. He and his little friend were stubborn and lazy – always whispering. They ran away to buy smokes or drugs maybe. Sure the army's tough. This was no torture, it was discipline. Every farmer keeps a piele wapper *to hand. It flexes, ja, goes pwoot when you swing it. Stings real bad. Volker stole mine. I should have kept a closer eye. I didn't know all he was up to. I trusted him. I was a father to those boys, like the army was to me.*

Mr and Mrs Geldenhuys huddle together by the door like birds on a ledge. Unbearable responsibility tugs at the corners of their mouths, weighs down their shoulders, cloaking them so that even in the crowded courtroom no one sits close. They talked about their beautiful boy, his gentle nature, his difficulties because of his stutter, the wonderful opportunities the General promised. The father gripped the stand with both hands, knuckles white. The mother's hands kept fluttering to the fine gold cross at her throat.

No, we never went there but we spoke to him, to the General. He was very persuasive, said he had a one hundred per cent success rate, promised to look after Victor, treat him like one of his own. Yes, he was expelled. No, he was not a homosexual. Girls loved him, he was only sixteen. No, we don't hate anyone, they're just not —

No, they didn't know. No, they didn't know. Know, they didn't want to know.

Irma Brandt and Jan Smit now occupy opposite ends of the same bench. Their little boy has grown from baby to toddler in this courtroom. He slides off and on his mother's lap so she gives him her phone to play with while she fans herself with a laminated photo of her son. In it Willem is about fifteen and standing in his bedroom doorway. He's wearing a white T-shirt with faded out New York street signs — *Bleecker, Bowery, Broadway*. Blond curls bounce away from his face and even he has managed a bit of a tan. He grips his phone in one hand and clearly can't wait to get away. As Miss Brandt fans herself the Judge notices she's no longer wearing her engagement ring. The cameras will spot this too and it will make a good sidebar.

No, he's not Willem's pa, I don't know where he went, he left when Will was six, he was sick, drugs. Ja, I missed him. We lived with my ma. Oh ja, Willem was good, a beautiful bubba, I was gonna have twins but the doctor said there were problems, it never happened, so Willem was everything in one. He started to have issues at crèche. He still wet the bed, ja. He lost his concentration and, like, okay, we would start to read and then he's tired. All the kids have ADHD now. Jan was our security guy. It was hard for Willem because before it was just us and ma and the dog. Jan spoiled him rotten. Bought all the cricket kit and stuff but Will always lost interest. For sure it got worse when he was a teenager and he wet himself, you know, when he was stressed. The kids called him names, Will told me, but you know what, there's so many things my mind blocks them. It's hard for me to remember. That place was Jan's idea. We were getting married, Willem was going to give me away, he didn't even know I was expecting. Everything looked so good there. Nice old place, proper lekker. Listen, my president could be standing here and I won't even know who he is, I'm not interested in politics, I never voted. Jan was into all that. The General says Willem was fighting and hurting himself. No, my boy's not like that. They wouldn't let me see him. I don't know what power that man has with his mouth, he's either the devil himself or I don't know. I didn't want this. My Willem was no moffie. That's the General's lies. He said they make boys into men. He promised to fix my son, help him get a job so he would be okay. But he tortured him. It's nothing to do with gay anything. I just want my boy back.

No, she didn't know. No, she didn't know. Know, she knew now.

Mr Smit gave evidence straight after.

303

No, we're not married, we were going to. Ja, I was in the South African National Defence Force 1982–86, last National Service lot. Tough, ja, sure. I made corporal. Sure, I kept my service gun. In a safe box. Willem broke into it. We're lucky we came home when we did. Yes, I have my picture with Terre'Blanche. It was at a rally at the Voortrekker. So what? I heard good things about the camp from a guy whose cousin got sorted there. Willem was lazy, weird, always on his own. This spectrum stuff is rubbish. He was just spoiled, soft. A moffie? For sure not normal. She was the one who couldn't take him any more, said we just needed alone time. I was only trying to help. I treated him like my own. I'm sorry how it all turned out.

No, he didn't know. No, he didn't know. Know, he knew enough.

From day one the grandmother arrived on her own sitting nearest the defendants, her hands pressed prayer-tight in her lap. If looks could kill she'd be on trial. She speaks to no one – not Press, not the mothers outside clamouring for some of her glamour-grief and especially not to her daughter. Once, her little grandson ran up to her tugging at her hand and that was the only time she cracked, rushing out before anyone could really see, her daughter hurrying after but returning almost immediately. She seems to have aged less than the others. Rarely has the judge seen any witness display such steel.

Yes, Irma is my daughter, she was. No, she's never met her father – I was married but not to him. I'm still in the house I was born in. I worked at Johannesburg Park Station from 1976 until I was forcibly retired in 2006 – they stole my pension. Willem was born on the big election day in the back of the ambulance. I was there. He was always quiet, hardly cried. Pretty boy, yes. Lovely curls. He was reading way before school. I bought all his books, they're still in his room. He wasn't slow, just took his time. He was getting over the toilet thing. We were all right until Jan turned up. I wasn't jealous, no. She just didn't have time for Willem any more. Then things went wrong at school. I was the one who changed his sheets, not the maids, I never told his ma. Maybe I made it worse. I don't know. He wasn't the same as other boys, no, but so what. I loved him for that. Homosexual? I don't know, I don't care, I've never met one, he's not like them on TV. It's not important. They should never have sent him there – he could have come to me. They never asked. When I got that picture I didn't recognise him. It wasn't my Willem. He was all bones and bloody. I just grabbed my keys and started driving. It's not far. I stopped at the shop there and called the police then when I got to the place I was just shouting his name and banging the car horn at the gate and all these dogs came running and then the sirens but it was too late. I was too late.

No, she didn't know. No, she didn't know. Know, if only she'd known.

They are all here.

The rest of the court brims with anti-abuse NGO volunteers, who look vulnerable without their plac-ards, and khaki-clad copies of the General, who keep feeling for their guns. All are equally angry. They've fed their rage for four years until it's filled her court-room and spilled out into the land. Don't they have jobs? Families? Competing chants make it through the security glass from outside. Judge Khwezi sits down sending a waft of settling through the room. Everybody follows.

'The defendants will remain standing,' she orders and the General struggles back to his feet, leaning on the bench as if in pain, appealing to weakness now. Volker, ever obedient, leaps up. He's developed a habit of scratching one thumb with the other so both look raw.

'State your name and date of birth for the record,' the court secretary asks.

Volker brushes a forelock from his eye and no longer waits for the General: 'John David Volker, 2nd of March 1994.'

The General speaks calmly. 'General – '

His little army erupts and Judge Khwezi bangs her gavel. 'The gallery will be silent and I say this to all of you, I will have no further interruptions. This court does not recognise the rank – '

One of the younger khakis, born after the coun-try he's nostalgic for was already dead, leaps the gallery running towards her. *This is it*, she thinks, *they've missed a gun, the guards won't get to him*. She's glad she told Charles not to come today. She closes her eyes. A strange old song visits her, a comforting almost-forgotten lullaby from for ever ago that her mother used to hum when she couldn't sleep. But there is no shot. Only shouts. As she opens her eyes, the man unfurls the AWB flag and the General raises his right fist for tomorrow's front page. A guard bundles the man out. Her mother's melody dances back to the past.

Judge Khwezi bangs away with her gavel but silence only falls when the General coughs like a conductor before a concert. Everyone is desperate for the end now. Even him. Yes, after this she will definitely go to Rome with Charles and the children. She raises her gavel one final time: 'I will order each and every person in this courtroom bound overnight. Enough!'

Satisfied, Judge Violet Khwezi puts on her reading glasses and begins to read her verdict.

'John David Volker and Samuel Frederick van der Watt, you are charged with multiple counts of child abuse, neglect and with the murder of Victor Geldenhuys. How do you plead?'

Epilogue

1 March 2015, Johannesburg

Willem is propped up in bed waiting. His gran said she'd be straight back from court. He's way too big for this bed now and has been for years but doesn't want anything else to change. He wiggles his toes under his Harry Potter duvet which is now so worn Harry is almost invisible. Dinner smells drift up from downstairs. Macaroni cheese. Elise is busy.

He remembers all those weeks and months in hospital. They feel like one long moment. He wasn't really sleeping but wasn't awake either. He wasn't really dead. He wasn't really alive. He couldn't move – couldn't even blink. There were no clouds, no angels. It wasn't even all that dark – he wished it had been. There was always a light right above him shining pink and hot through his eyelids so he could trace his capillaries like rivers on a map. Whenever he started to remember he followed those branching forks until he forgot again. *I got away,* he reminds himself over and over. *I got away.*

In hospital he was never alone and it was never quiet. All day and night people were coming and going poking and prodding. Early on he remembers a man murmuring and felt the sign of the cross on his forehead. People talked in front of him because they thought he couldn't hear. *He's a fighter, he won't make it, the mother should be jailed.*

When they let his ma in, she rushed at his bed wailing then stopped. Even in his state, Willem caught the sharp smell of sick and heard the nurses give her something for her nerves. He felt her cheek wet against his hand and wished he could pull away. Every day she was there. Never with Gran.

After how long of trying – trying so hard – he managed to open his eyes. But they were stuck shut. He started to scream but couldn't because something was choking him. Then there were voices and faces and he was blinking into an even brighter light and his throat was full of dry and his mouth tasted of hospital.

He was in a medical coma for six months. *Now you're back you've got to help us,* the detective said. *Leave him alone,* his gran pleaded. But no.

Only you can answer our questions. What happened that day, son? What happened?

The chains come off at Reveille and the door swings out and everything is bright. They can't see. Volker drags them out under their arms and chucks them on the ground. Dimly Willem feels his shins rip as he skid-lands. It takes Geldenhuys a minute to sit up and when he does one side of his face is mince. Fresh blood trickles into his shirt reviving old stains. He looks like a red marble statue. They're both so weak and light they might blow away.

Everything is quiet. There's no talk, not even the usual shuffling. The morning air is thick with weather about to happen. All the boys stand tall, boots shiny, eyes fixed. Connor looks away when the General orders them both to get up. Willem can barely move his right leg. Geldenhuys crawls over but he pushes him away and half stands alone. The General smiles.

'You've caused me a lot of trouble.'

He circles them slowly as he talks.

'A lot of trouble. Not eating, not washing, fighting, running away like that, bothering my neighbours.'

Geldenhuys slumps back moving his lips but no sound comes out. The General pauses by him.

'W-w-what?' He leans down. 'S-s-something to say, moffie?'

Geldenhuys's chin lolls against his chest as the General stands him up with scarecrow ease then steps away. He sways but somehow doesn't fall.

'Finally standing on your own two feet!'

Here and there the soil around them begins to spot. Willem lifts his face to the sky and opens his mouth, feels a drop of rain splash on his tongue. So sweet. The heavy air lifts all around them leaving a fresh clean smell. Willem fumbles for the right word. Connor turns towards the tents but the General orders him to halt. They all stand there as the rain falls straight up and down. Petrichor, that's what it is. Petrichor.

'Now, ladies, here's what's going to happen. You,' he jabs Willem. 'Are going to fight him. And you,' he jabs Geldenhuys. 'Are going to fight back. And we'll see which one's left standing. Easy. We're going to see who the man is.'

The General raises his voice over the rain.

'And if either of you tries to walk away you both get to take on all the lads at once. Got it?'

Willem looks over at Geldenhuys and shakes his head but his friend cries, 'Y-y-yes, sir!'

Surprised, the General steps aside. He orders the other boys to form a ring. Geldenhuys staggers towards Willem who falls back. They all move in, holding formation. Somebody pushes Willem into Geldenhuys who grabs at him and they slip in the mud that was dust all summer. They land on their backs and rain washes the blood and dirt from their faces. They barely recognise each other. Hands haul them up again.

Willem stagger-slip-slides at Geldenhuys who doesn't even try to get away. The ring closes around them. Willem has no choice. Geldenhuys raises his hands and Willem clasps them both. If he does this maybe he can save them. *It'll be okay, I promise.* Willem looks into his friend's eyes and pushes palm-to-palm until Geldenhuys's hands can go back no further. And then they do. Geldenhuys faints to his knees with Willem still holding his hands. Surely that's enough. Willem turns to the General who shakes his head. Volker stands Geldenhuys up holding him under his arms and as the General shouts *FINISH IT* a car horn blasts over and over and Willem hears somebody calling his name. Gran? Then sirens. The General runs towards the gate shouting *They're here, it's time!* Volker lets Geldenhuys go and runs towards the General but the other boys just stand there blinking, coming to as the sirens get closer. Geldenhuys staggers backwards, his arms dangle uselessly, strings cut. Willem steps towards him sobbing *I'm sorry, I'm sorry.* He can hardly see through rain and tears.

Nobody spots the freshly dug pit that's not been filled in, with the big old bones at the bottom – Oupa's gentle skull with Corporal Johnson's bullet still in it, long shards of broken shin waiting with the terrible patience of calcium. And as Willem reaches for his friend, Geldenhuys sees the hand he longs to hold but for some reason his own hands aren't working and as the sirens arrive and the gate bursts open he falls.

The sun is getting tired now. Gran will be back soon. Willem resists checking his phone. He wants her to be the one to tell him it's over. There's scratching at his door and a grey-black face pushes its way in. Britney plods over — she's too old to jump up so lies down and watches. Won't let him out of her sight again.

Willem turns his pillow so it's cool. He lies back. The stars on the ceiling above his bed begin to glow and as they grow brighter he soars through the sky, comforts himself with constellations: Orion's Belt, the Pleiades and right over his head the Southern Cross and next to that a new star. It shines brighter than all the others and he reaches for it, reaches to stop it falling.

Respectfully dedicated to all
the women, children and men
who died in British concentration camps
and to all lost
during the Second Boer War, 1899–1902.

More civilians died in the camps
than soldiers on the battlefield.

And to Raymond Buys (1996–2011) who shines
bright among the stars and whose story took me to
South Africa and led me back to 1901.

A Historical Note

The Boer Wars (1880–81 and 1899–1902) are no longer taught in British or South African schools. They are now almost fondly remembered as a great Victorian adventure, the stuff of *Boy's Own* stories. Britain has waged other, bigger wars since.

By 1900 Britain had deployed 250,000 soldiers, her full imperial force, which included fighters from Canada, Australia, New Zealand and India. The two Boer states, the Orange Free State and the Transvaal, had just 17,000 men, mainly recruited from farms (*'Boer'* means 'farmer' in Afrikaans). Britain expected the Second Boer War to be over by Christmas 1900. But Boer forces were proving difficult to beat – flouting conventional military rules with their new, highly successful, 'commando' tactics.

In response Lord Kitchener changed tactics and in so doing changed the nature of war. Often called 'the last gentlemen's war', the Second Boer War introduced 'Scorched Earth': British forces torched 30,000 farms. Having created a nation of homeless 'refugees', almost entirely women and children, Britain then 'concentrated' them into ill-equipped, punitively run camps. Concentration camps. In total Britain established around forty white camps holding around 116,000 Boers. Although there were black people in the white camps, there were up to eighty-nine separate black camps. Because victors shape history, we know pitifully little about these places. The Anglo-Boer War Museum has documented 17,182 deaths, but it's likely more perished. Black people had to pay for their rations and this only bought half what white people received for free. In order to earn money, many black people were forced to work for the British in the white camps as guards. This outraged the Boers and offended their sense of the natural order. This, and the immense suffering of the camps, helped drive the National Party to victory in 1948 and provide perceived justification for Apartheid.

The camps officially closed after the Peace of Vereeniging in 1902 but many people had no choice but to stay in them for months after as they had nowhere else to go.

The true horror of the camps was revealed by Emily Hobhouse, who travelled from England to South Africa in 1901. Her courageous reporting sparked a national debate that led to her being pilloried. Hobhouse is often criticised for not visiting the black camps. She later made efforts to right this saying, 'Does not justice bid to remember today how many thousands of the dark race perished also in the concentration camps in a quarrel that was not theirs?' She was a thorn in the side of successive British governments. After she died in 1926 her ashes were taken to Bloemfontein where she was accorded a state funeral, the only non-South African to receive this honour. She now resides below the great obelisk on the site of the first concentration camp where the Anglo-Boer Museum stands.

British concentration camps were not, whatever nationalist Afrikaners claim, death camps. Their stated purpose was containment, not extermination, and there are many well-documented examples of British kindness, efficiency and humanity. But these are exceptions within a callously indifferent and consciously underfunded system designed to subjugate and defeat an entire people. During the Spanish-American War of 1898 Spanish forces interned swathes of the Cuban population. Many of these 'reconcentrados' perished. John Toland writes in *Adolf Hitler: The Definitive Biography*, 'Hitler's concept of concentration camps as well as the practicality of genocide owed much, so he claimed, to his studies of English and United States history.'

Camps like New Dawn still operate across South Africa. They are for white boys only and run by former soldiers like the General who believe that one day white South Africa will rise again and finally right the historic wrongs of the Boer Wars. Parents pay to send their sons to these places hoping they will drill in the toughness and discipline formerly instilled by National Service (which ended in 1993). They want their sons to be able to survive in an increasingly violent society. Boys like Willem and Geldenhuys and Volker – who aren't 'man enough' or who simply fall through the cracks.

Select Bibliography

Du Val, Charles, *With a Show through Southern Africa* (Tinsley Brothers, 1882)

Fairbridge, Dorothea, *Historic Farms of South Africa* (Oxford University Press, 1931)

Frances, Keith, and Gibson, William (Eds), *The Oxford Handbook of the British Sermon 1689–1901* (OUP, 2012)

Garnier, J., *England's Enemies: a Warning* (W. H. Russell & Co., 1900)

Hobhouse, C.E., *Report and Evidence of the War Commission Collated and Arranged by C.E. Hobhouse* (M.P. Bristol: J.W. Arrowsmith, 1904)

Hobhouse, C.E., *The Brunt of the War and Where It Fell* (Methuen, 1902)

Hobhouse, C.E., *War Without Glamour: Women's Experiences Written by Themselves* (Nasionale Pers, 1924)

Imperial South African Association, *The Concentration Camps. Sir Neville Chamberlain's Mistake* (London, 1900)

Malala, Justice, *We Have Begun Our Descent* (Jonathan Ball, 2015)

Malan, Rian, *The Lion Sleeps Tonight and Other Stories of South Africa* (Grove Press, 2012)

Noah, Trevor, *Born a Crime* (John Murray, 2016)

Norman, Kajsa, *Bridge Over Blood River: The Rise and Fall of the Afrikaners* (Hurst, 2016)

Reitz, Deneys, *Commando: a Boer Journal of the Boer War* (Faber & Faber, 1929)

Schoeman, Karel (Ed), *Witnesses to War: Personal Documents of the Anglo-Boer War from the Collections of the South African Library* (Human & Rousseau, 1999)

Smuts, Jan Christiaan, *Memoirs of the Boer War* (J. Ball, 1994)

South African Conciliation Committee, *Salient Facts from the Camps' Blue-books: The Official Report on the Concentration Camps* (South African Conciliation Committee, 1902)

The Times History of the War in South Africa, 1899–1902 (S. Low, Marston and Co. Ltd, 1900–9)

van Heyningen, Elizabeth, *Concentration Camps of the Anglo-Boer War: A Social History* (Jacana Media, 2013)

Warwick, Peter, *The South African War* (Longman, 1980)

Z.[pseud.], 'The War in South Africa. Women and children dying. Worse horrors than Death. Mr Kruger's "malicious lies"' (F. Longman 1901)

Acknowledgements

This book took five years to research, write and edit so I have five years of people to thank for their kindness, patience and wisdom. It has taken me to some very dark places – real and imagined – so I am very grateful all of them for always bringing their very real light.

This story began with a picture of a boy in a newspaper. That boy was Raymond Buys and he'd been killed in a camp not unlike New Dawn. He was just fifteen. This book is dedicated to him. His mother, Wilna Buys, opened her broken heart and welcomed me into her home to me when I went to South Africa and I will forever be grateful to her. Wilna introduced me to Inspector Cornell whose hard-work and bravery led to two men being found guilty for their role in her son's death. Cornell offered invaluable insight into the workings of such camps and the minds of the men who run them.

I had never been to South Africa before starting work on this book and appealed to friends for

support on the ground. Thank you to Aminatta
Forna for connecting me with Zee Cube who
started out as a fixer and who became a friend and
fellow survivor on one particularly dangerous day.
I am indebted to Tania Otto at Women and Men
Against Child Abuse in South Africa for her activism
and for connecting me locally. Gregory Nott & Liesl
Williams at Norton Rose Fulbright provided legal
help and access to vital court documents that Zirk
van den Berg translated and interpreted so intuitively.
Matthew Carkeek held base camp and collated the
footage and kept me calm. Thank you to Kirsty Lang
and Misha Glenny for introducing me to Justine
Lang and Justice Malala who took great care of me
in Johannesburg. The Anglo-Boer War Museum in
Bloemfontein is fascinating, and I am very thankful
to the staff who took time to show me around and
answer endless questions – the detail they provided
was crucial in bringing a forgotten history back to
life. My research trip was funded by an award from
the Arts Council of England whose initial investment
made this book possible. I wouldn't have thought to
apply to ACE without the encouragement of the
heroic Chris Gribble who found time to help me
with spreadsheets while magicking up the National
Centre for Writing in Norwich.

I've worked on this book at lots of different desks
and I am grateful to everyone who gave me a place
to write. Something special happens at Gladstone's

Library where you manage to forget the world outside and sink into your story – that's because of the faith and kindness of Peter Frances, the Warden, and the cleverness of Louisa Yates, Director of Collections and Research, who finds seemingly lost papers. Sarah Perry was writing *Melmoth* at Gladstone's when I was there, and our nightly sherry talks were a tonic. Thank you to Charlie Gilmour for sharing his thesis.

I finished my first draft in a fairy-tale barn behind one of the most beautiful bookshops in the world: Much Ado Books in Alfriston. It's owned and run by two true heroes of publishing: Cate Olson and Nash Robbins (and their trio of beloved hens lead by Frizzle). Lancaster University continues to educate me long after graduating so thanks to Andrew Tate and Jane Silvester. Professor Liam McIlvanney and the University of Otago awarded me the Scottish Writers Fellowship which took me to the Pah Homestead in New Zealand for three life-changing months. Thanks to Anne O'Brien and all at Auckland Writers Festival, Bridget Schaumann and the lovely folk at the Dunedin Writers & Readers Festival and the Robert Lord Cottage Trust. *Kia Ora* to Julie Hill, Jeremy Hansen and Cameron Law, Patrick Reynolds and Maria Majsa, Richard Robbins, Dudley Benson and Josh Thomas and Nigel Brown and Sue McLaughlin and all my new-found *whanau*.

Bloomsbury have nurtured me through every stage from the first few scattered pages. Thank you to

Alexandra Pringle for having faith in the idea and in me; Alexa von Hirschberg for asking the right questions and approaching each draft like it was the first; Marigold Atkey for making every detail matter and to Mary Tomlinson for the final push, line-by-line, page-by-page and thought-by-thought. David Mann is a masterful visual storyteller and he created the deceptively simple jacket perfectly linking past and present. The sales, marketing and press specialists get books into the right hands so thanks to Elise Burns, Rachel Wilkie and Ros Ellis and their teams. Linking all these people and supporting me from start to finish by elevating assisting to an art form is Rosie Chipping.

A book only comes to life, with all its flaws, when you share it with readers. The very first was my friend and agent Clare Conville who made me believe that I not only could, but should, and she has brought the same spark to this that she brings to my life. Diana Athill gave me the incredible benefit of her unsparing wit and redoubtable wisdom. David Nicholls kindly showed me where I was getting in the way of my characters. Margie Orford and Zee Cube generously provided two very different but equally critical South African perspectives. Alex Preston and Carol Biss helped me see the story. Sathnam Sanghera, Maggie O'Farrell, Garth Greenwell and Patrick Gale inspired and encouraged. Thanks to Paul McNamee, my editor at the *Big Issue*, and to all at *High Life* for smoothing deadlines.

Hosting my Literary Salon means I get to sit next to the very best writers in the world as they share their stories and I am indebted to each of them for their words on and off the page. The Salon team make it happen and have toiled to allow me time to write so thank you: Rosie, Megan, Kirsty, Daisy, Bakul, Carol, Ella, Russell and all the publishers who give us such support, most especially Georgina Moore at Tinder Press. Thanks to Emma Allam and her team at the Savoy for our storied and stunning home. And love to all the amazing Salonistas for always listening and sparkling!

My family and friends have held my hand through this and hold me together still: Mum and Dad, Tinie & Jamie, All My Yorkshire Family, Joanne Donaldson, Polly Samson and David Gilmour in Sussex and on Hydra, Jeff Melnyk, Simon Lock, Ruthe Wainman, Patrick Strudwick, Jojo Moyes, Alexandra Heminsley, Jess Ruston, Helen Chesshire, Jessica Fellowes, Natalie Haynes, David Benedict, Ann Siegel, Dotson Rader, Brian Halley and Lauren Cerand.

Not long after I first met Mike Moran – over twenty years ago now – I told him I thought I might like to write a novel one day. He encouraged me then and every day since. Every chapter starts with him.

A Note on the Author

Damian Barr is an award-winning writer and columnist. *Maggie & Me*, his memoir about coming of age and coming out in Thatcher's Britain, was a BBC Radio 4 *Book of the Week* and *Sunday Times* Memoir of the Year, and won the Paddy Power Political Books 'Satire' Award and Stonewall Writer of the Year Award. Damian writes columns for the *Big Issue* and *High Life* and often appears on BBC Radio 4. He is creator and host of his own Literary Salon which premieres work from established and emerging writers. *You Will Be Safe Here* is his debut novel. Damian Barr lives in Brighton.

@Damian_Barr

A Note on the Type

The text of this book is set in Bembo, which was first used in 1495 by the Venetian printer Aldus Manutius for Cardinal Bembo's *De Aetna*. The original types were cut for Manutius by Francesco Griffo. Bembo was one of the types used by Claude Garamond (1480–1561) as a model for his Romain de l'Université, and so it was a forerunner of what became the standard European type for the following two centuries. Its modern form follows the original types and was designed for Monotype in 1929.